CUTTING OF HARP STRINGS

Also by E.G. Kardos

Zen Master Next Door:
> Parables for Enlightened Everyday Living

THE ELIAS CHRONICLES

> The Amulet: Journey to Sirok   Book I

> The Rings: Journey Beneath Sirok   Book II

> The Elixir: Journey On   Book III – Coming Soon

Early Praise of Cutting of Harp Strings

"… a compelling and engagingly written story of friendship, the word used to describe a long, slow process of enlightenment as well as a term applicable to the process of healing and learning to make sense of life. Spanning twenty-five years, and centered around a secluded spot of inspiration, *Cutting of Harp Strings* is a strongly recommended and emotionally moving saga."
— James A. Cox, editor-in-chief, *Midwest Book Review*.

"*In Cutting of Harp Strings*, E.G. Kardos continues to show a creative imagination, a wicked sense of humor and a depth of characterization.
— Jay Strafford, retired books editor, *Richmond Times-Dispatch*.

CUTTING OF HARP STRINGS

a novel

E. G. Kardos

Pen It! Publications, LLC

First Edition 2021

CUTTING OF HARP STRINGS
by E. G. Kardos
Copyright © 2021. All rights reserved.

Published by Pen It! Publications, LLC in the U.S.A.
812-371-4128 www.penitpublications.com
Visit and connect with E.G. Kardos at www.edwardgkardos.com

ISBN: 978-1-63984-010-6
Edited by Dina Husseini
Cover Design by Donna Cook

For those who have found their courage
and for those still searching.

Author's Note

My solitary path that I journeyed to reach *Cutting of Harp Strings* began in late 1994. One word led to another and after many rewrites over many years, the story became real. I could *touch* it, *see* it, *hear* it, *smell* it, and *feel* it.

This story celebrates life and its many paradoxical but inseparable forces in our universe—some may call it the Yin and Yang. We all experience such forces both outwardly and inwardly. It's unimaginable to think of life without this duality, but life as we now know it would cease to exist.

With such duality, we learn about ourselves and attempt to find meaning. I'm not the first to say this, but we are perhaps more interested in the meaning *of our* life than the meaning *of* life. I must agree with Socrates as he said, "The unexamined life is not worth living". We are reflective by nature but we, many times, overlook or are unwilling to find meaning from our introspection. Just look at history and how we, humankind, seldom heed its message.

Also attributed to Socrates is the phrase, "know thyself". If we are willing to peel back the layers that humanity has heaped upon each of us, we may actually like—and love—who we are. It is up to us, one by one, to dig deep within our core to find a beauty we all possess. The core is always where answers live as they are seldom floating like a flower petal upon the surface of a pond. It takes reaching our hand below the murky surface to find what is truly there.

Cutting of Harp Strings celebrates, most of all, our relationships with those who matter most to us. We yearn for acceptance, affirmation, and intimacy. There is no one right path to find this in our lives. There are, however, inevitable detours along the path that impede our progress. Such detours, like denial, trick us and point us in different directions. We may have little or no clue of how we managed to be deceived—but it happens. Sometimes we are misled, urged to *fit in,* or discouraged from asking questions for any number of reasons. Some of us find the answers but continue down a misguided path. Could it be because we're humans? Just a thought.

Our existence is about the many extraordinary connections we all experience. Those connections sometimes come in the form of shared moments. Like words, moments when collected and strung together, tell the tale of our lives. Our reality is made up of more than the *big moments* but made up of those intimate, fun, quiet, scary, insightful, quirky, bizarre, and mystical moments as well. If you are like most, you have experienced such moments.

When I wrote the first sentence of this story, I had no idea what kind of journey I was on, but once in motion, there was no turning back. Eli, Aiden, and others told me who they were and where they were headed even though they were not sure themselves—such is life. I learned so much from their adventure as they invited me in. Writers don't know the answers, but they do ask the questions.

When I wrote the first pages, I was someone else. I concentrated on the "rules of the road" and what was "supposed to be" in every novel. Life isn't like that, and neither is this story. What I came to realize was that this journey is far more important to tell today than when I typed the first letter many years ago... no "spoilers" here as you will have to read it to find out.

As I wrote this story, what I learned most of all is that humanity is all about belief systems and ideologies, and because of this, humanity creates its own reality. If you will, our world is all imagined even though the sun shines, the waves of the oceans slap the shore, and the lightning strikes at will. However, life as far as I can tell is all about what goes on in our hearts. It's how we feel about and engage with each other, our world, and our creator. More importantly, we shape our life as it springs from how we feel about the one person for whom we should love first, no matter what—ourselves.

Edward G. Kardos — August 15, 2021

"Being deeply loved by someone gives you strength, while loving someone deeply gives you courage."
Lao Tzu

Contents

"The cave you fear to enter
holds the treasure you seek."

Joseph Campbell

ONE

May 1999 – Early Morning

God, the water was cold!

I must have looked stupid to the old man fishing about twenty yards downstream. Don't know where he came from, but there he stood in his tall rubber boots and fishing gear strapped all around and over him. He was a sort of rugged old warrior. On the other hand, there I stood.

Before my trudge in the river, I rolled up my pants to my knees and stuffed my wet socks, dripping and all, into my pockets. Tied my laces together and wore my shoes around my neck. Yep, out of place. I didn't have the typical look of most forty-three-year-old men on a weekend trip in the mountains. You know, boots, jeans, and gear—like the old warrior.

My wade was by chance—dipped my toe in and kept going. Extending my arms to either side of me, I attempted to maintain my balance. Teetering in the biting water, the smooth, uneven stones under my tender arches were like a warning sign as a sharp edge had to be nearby. Each step was a curiosity. No question about it, I did look stupid. It wasn't the first time, but in this moment, I did not care.

Balancing, stepping, and moving in a kind of contorted dancer's rhythm, I respected and welcomed the touch of the water on my skin treading in a river that, years before, breathed life into my soul. Though water allows for no imprints, the omens were there. They *were* there, following, with each toe, the footsteps of an old and good friend.

"Hey, you're scaring my fish away," the old man said with a scowl. His booming voice seemed to come from nowhere and startled me.

"Oh, sorry mister. It's kinda slippery—don't remember it being so slippery—and *cold*," I hollered back as my teeth clanked together.

"Yeah, yeah, I hear ya. But could you do whatever it is you're doing somewhere else? Geez."

"Oh…oh…*ah oh no!*" At that moment, I looked up, lost my balance, and plunged back into the water landing on my butt. The river swallowed every inch of me.

"What the—I give up," said the old man with a soft laugh and a broad smile. He began sloshing over to me and reached down extending his large, calloused hand. Embarrassed, I looked into his eyes, and he winked. I grabbed his hand and he pulled me to my feet nearly yanking my arm from its socket. His strength was incredible.

"Thanks—ah, yeah thanks. Oh, and about your fish, sorry. Really, sorry about…yeah, I'm sorry," I said with a loss of words and a sheepish grin.

"Ah, don't give it another thought. There's always more fish to catch," he told me. The old guy, probably in his seventies, sported two-day-old stubble and was as strong as the rapids downriver. He put his arm around my shoulder and with both a firm squeeze and a gentle tug, he steered me to shore.

"I'm Gabe by the way. My mama gave me that name cuz she always liked that angel story…I'm sure you know it."

"Hmmm, I think so."

"She said I was a gift from God—little did she know," he said with a hearty laugh. "Anyway…so what did your mama name you?"

"Huh? Oh, I'm Eli."

"Well, go on—and why did she name you Eli?"

"Ah, well, she, she—she told me she always loved that name. Not my dad. He, well, he wanted to name me something that sounded like a last name. I think he wanted Addison. But mom won in the end."

With a grin, Gabe said, "And I'm so glad she did. *Defender of man.*"

"What?"

"That's what your name means—it's a keeper, I'd say."

"Gosh, thanks. Never knew its meaning."

"You learn something every day if you're willing. So, you don't look much like you belong out here. Just look at you." He eyeballed me up and down. "Street clothes, barefoot and you're frolicking around out here in the river. Don't take it to heart, but you look a little clueless like you don't have much in the upper story."

"Frolicking? Maybe a bit clueless, but *frolicking?* You're a very funny man." My confidence appeared but faded in an instant. "Oh sorry. Didn't mean to be sarcastic."

"No problem, Eli. It takes a bit more—quite a bit more to chafe my behind."

"But I can see how you would think that. I mean being clueless." We both laughed. "I had some time to kill before things get started, and something, a feeling I guess you'd call it, just led me down here. Sounds weird I know."

"No, not really. See, I wasn't planning to fish today but just got the urge from nowhere. Sometimes that's all we need. The nudge— whatever it was, led me down here. Not weird at all. Nope, not at all, *if you ask me.*"

There was an unbelievably long pause, and I heard myself swallow. We just looked at each other and then away.

He started up again. "So, you said you were killing some time before things get started. What things?"

"I'm back for my twenty-fifth high school reunion. I went my senior year to St. Augustine's—just up the hill." I pointed one way and then another. Clearly confused.

"Uh-huh—yeah," he said, pulling off his weathered cap and scratching his balding head with his pinky. "If I'm doing the math right, you graduated in... must've been '74?"

"Yes, 1974," I said with a sigh. "Seems like a long time ago."

"I know all about St. Gus'. Yep, all about it—it's a good place. But seeing that you went just one year, why did you come back for that? Don't mean to be rude but can't imagine one year would make that much a difference," the old man smirked. "I mean to come back for a reunion?"

Hesitating for a moment, I said, "To tell you the truth, like wading, or should I say frolicking, in the river, I don't really know why. This, ah…this is the first time I've been here since the day I graduated. Just felt that nudge, you know—that nudge we were talking about?"

Gabe shook his head pushing out his bottom lip. "Okey-doke. Well, hope you find what it is you're looking for. I'm sure you'll have a grand time. Yep. I'm sure you will. But I better be getting back to my fish."

With that, Gabe nodded to me, turned, and stepped into the river.

"Thanks, and I hope your fish all come back and you catch that *big one* that always gets away," I said awkwardly punching the air. I didn't know what to say so I said that. Gabe paused and looked back at me and smiled. He just shook his head from side to side.

"Hey, I already caught me a big one today and just let him go. He's got a lot more growing to do before he's worth a hoot. Yep, lots more growing."

I wasn't listening too closely as the sun's rays caught his face and distracted me. "Gabe, you look familiar—could it be…I mean, have we met?

Gabe immediately shook his head. "Don't reckon so. You ain't from these parts and haven't been here in twenty-five years. Around the time you were going to school, I was living elsewhere for a short spell. I just have one of those faces I reckon."

"Yeah, one of those faces. Well anyway, I'll be seeing you."

"All righty, Eli."

We turned and walked in two different directions, but for the life of me, he seemed so familiar.

*****

Arriving early that day, I spent time on campus but hadn't, yet, seen anyone I knew. Wandering and wending through, around, and beyond the grounds as well, I reminisced. What I saw earlier that day, like the boys' school uniforms, was now terribly outdated and blatantly untouched by the current year. Besides the paved walkways that were once gravel, little was fresh and new. These new smooth paved paths, however, were deceptively even. I felt much happier to be back in the woods by the river looking at the peaks of the mountains and splashing in the river. Along the way, I reflected, and my thoughts fused with all around me. The sounds, smells, and colors of the moments blended with the stream of my thoughts.

Why I came back to Saint Augustine for that particular reunion wasn't truly a mystery to me as I may have let on. *Who was Gabe anyway?* He didn't need to know my reasons. Suffice it to say, I had unfinished business. I came in part, to honor my journey and that of a friend.

Twenty-five years ago, I came here my senior year and while moving toward my goal, I found more. Didn't want any more than what lay in clear sight, but more came my way. I knew all about myself—*right*. What I once thought was absolute was not as I overlooked the obvious. Unearthing all of me, however, wasn't an option. But what I was not ready for somehow took a life of its own. In a manner of speaking, my self-denial sparked new ways. Simply, I lacked courage.

Years ago, fighting my inward travel with each step, I kept looking outward and beyond. Like a recurring dream, I saw myself running a race, but the race would not end although my focus was on the finish line. I was running against no one but myself. The race was but a blur and clearly, breaking the victory tape was for naught, but only realizing later, the fuzziness of the race was everything.

As it is with time, I found what was before me only becomes smaller as my past grows with every moment. Now my past was the taste of bitter and sweet. Without one, however, I could not savor the other. But my past and my future didn't matter and still doesn't. Growth happens in the present, and the journey is always in the now. Looking back, no one could tell me this, although some tried. Sometimes I asked questions of others, and I heard them but did not listen. I did not listen! I knew everything and nothing at all. I placed the burden in the wrong place. What is worse, I denied who I was.

*****

Taking a few steps in one direction and then another, I was turned around as I searched for a path. Wet, the wind kicked up and gave me a chill. I stuck my index finger in my ear trying to rid it of a drop of river water I acquired just minutes earlier. As I shook my head and moved the thin branches out of my path, one rogue wispy twig whipped me across my face.

"HOLY CRAP! That hurt." I rubbed my cheek and wiped my weeping eyes and as I opened them, there in front of me was Gabe. He was holding my duffel bag.

"Huh? Where'd you come from?"

"Here, you might need this. I found it on the other side of the river."

"I think you're right. Thanks."

"Hey, listen, my camp is about twenty yards due west. Let's head that way, and you can find a change of clothes in that bag. You're a mess. Just look at you. You can join me by my fire for some Irish coffee."

It wasn't too long before we were sitting by a fire and Gabe was serving up some pitch-black coffee. He went light on the coffee and heavy on the *Irish*.

"Ho—ho! I think that'll do it just fine. Thanks," I said.

He handed me the mug and as he sat across from me, I began to shake my head. The water in my ear was irksome at best.

In a slow and deliberate manner, Gabe said, "You're looking a tad peculiar. What in blue blazes are you doing?"

"I've got water in my ear and can't get rid of it. Do I look stupid?"

"That's an understatement. Tell you what. If you want to look stupid but actually get the Shenandoah River out of your ear, stand up, and hop on one foot, and shake your head."

I thought, *why not?*

"Okay, okay. I can do that." I stood, hopped, and shook my head.

Apparently, I wasn't doing it right.

"No, no not like that. Let me show you." Gabe stood, hopped, and shook his head twice per hop. Being a quick learner, I began doing the same thing. We hopped together and simultaneously let out a guffaw. With our laughter, my ear became river free.

"Hey, it's out." We sat down still chuckling.

"Yeah, once the river's in you, it's hard to shake her loose."

"Pretty profound Gabe—pretty profound."

Gabe picked up my mug, topped it off, and handed it to me. He did the same with his mug and then took a gulp. His face lit up with delight as he sipped. I did all I could to down a few swigs. It was like breathing in fire. Looking at the old warrior, I just smiled, and I sipped some more. I could tell his heart was in the right place.

"So, you haven't been back to old St. Gus in twenty-five years, and you don't know why you came back?"

I wasn't sure if Gabe was asking me a question or just restating what I told him earlier. He stood and reached for a small log and tossed it on the fire. Sparks flew upward and flickered out in a swirl. We both looked into the flames and said nothing for a moment.

Gabe wasn't going to let it go. "You must have a whole lot of time on your hands."

"No, not at all. If you must know, I came back to find an old friend, but I'm not sure what I'll find."

"Well, you're not gonna find him down here, I suspect. You need to get yourself up that hill and back on campus. I'm sure if you don't recognize who you're looking for, they have nametags. Maybe they'll have the ones with the little photos, if you're lucky, as we all change— or we better. Lordy, that's for darn sure." Gabe said with a faint smile and then took another sip.

He wasn't following what I was saying, or so I thought. I told him more. "These woods and this river used to be our stomping ground and...well, I've missed it. I have lots of fond memories, and some not so fond memories of this place." I felt a knot in my throat and looked away from Gabe. "I don't know, Gabe, I just thought coming back would give me a little peace."

"You know my friend, they say no man steps in the same river twice. Believe me, I know where you're headed."

"Huh?" I said, "You sound like one of the priests I knew."

Gabe paused and seemed to smile. He took another swig and began to laugh. "Never mind about that. In your case, I'm guessing that no man *stumbles* in the same river twice."

"Very funny. Maybe you missed your calling. You are a very— funny—man."

"I've been known to come up with a good one from time to time. Tell ya what, it's just about time for a little grub. Let me fill your cup and I'll cook us up the catch of the day, and you can tell me just what went on all those years ago. I got time. That's about all we got. Time."

7

"I, I don't know…"

"What don't you know? I love a good story. See, I've spent time in other places, but I've been around these parts for most of my life and I have a few stories myself. Yeah, I know all sorts of folks who have put their big toe in or have taken the plunge as I reckon you have. Eli, now's the time to get it off your chest. Let it go." Gabe turned and looked with great thought to the river.

I looked at Gabe, the river and back at Gabe, again. All I heard was the rushing rapids and all that filled the air was the fragrance of the burning pine log in front of me.

"Well, I can't put my finger on it, but there's something about you that seems right," I said as my eyes drew to his.

With his chin jutting out, Gabe said, "I'm a good listener for sure. Who better to tell?"

"It might be the Irish coffee in me, and I am kind of hungry…"

"My unsolicited advice—just go with your gut. No pressure," he said holding out the palm of his hand.

Tilting my head and with a lopsided smile, I said, "If you really want to know?"

Leaning in, Gabe said, "And I do. Eli, it's okay. Really it is."

"Hmmm…well okay. Where should I …"

"You know where to start," he said raising his left brow giving me a wink.

"You're right…"

"Well?"

"So much happened beginning in August of 1973. As usual, Dad had to make it short and get back to D.C. He dropped me off in front of my dorm where I met with Fr. Meinrad. When Dad and I said our goodbyes, little did I know but from that first day, life would take on a new meaning."

TWO

I knocked on the door, but no one answered. I was sure that Father Meinrad told me *this* room number. Double-checking, I pulled out of my pocket a small crumpled-up piece of paper where I had written the room number.

"Yep," I said, aloud.

Turning the knob, I didn't know what to expect or whom I would find. With hesitation, I wrapped my head around the unwieldy oak door to take a look. No one was there. Creeping in, I dropped my duffel bag and knapsack on the bare tile floor and took a deep breath. Thinking I was intruding, I just then considered going down to the TV room to wait a while but, with a rare moment of certainty, I thought otherwise. After all, this was my room too.

In both oversized windows were two enormous box fans buzzing and gusting winds in different directions. I turned them down one notch and began looking around but disturbing nothing. I began to size up this guy, after all, I would be living with him in this space for the next two school terms. Tacked up on the wall behind his dresser were pictures from magazines of sports stars. I saw Jerry West and Wilt Chamberlain among the collage. Tucked partly behind his mirror was a recent news clipping of Mark Spitz highlighting his seventh Olympic gold medal. Fluttering to one side was an obscure obituary of someone named Sir Francis Chichester who at sixty-five, I found by scanning the clipping, sailed around the world alone in his ketch called Gipsy Moth IV.

"Hmmm. How odd," I mumbled to myself.

I didn't want to disturb anything, but I wanted to know everything. On his stereo was a new album. "Aerosmith—Dream On…he can't be too bad—maybe."

Mountains of books were everywhere except the bookcase in this twelve-by-something room. Zen, art history, and architectural design, you name it, he had books for all his interests. Unusual bookmarks poked out from the pages. Spoons, Popsicle sticks, and a sock accounted for a few. A tee-shirt, gym shorts, and an assortment of tennis shoes were scattered and strewn about. His knotted school necktie hung from a lamp, and his blue blazer and khaki pants draped from an ancient gray radiator under the windows—I could only wonder what he kept in his closet.

At first glance, the cell, as the monks called them, was a whirlwind of chaotic prep school life, but I sensed there was a kind of order to things. It was an order that, perhaps, only the caretaker might know the code. I wasn't going to lose sleep over it. Maybe I would care some other day.

On a stack of books on his desk, was his journal. Peeking behind me at the door and then back at the notebook, I laid my hand on its cover. Flipping it open, a sinking feeling came over me and closed it with a slap. Peering back at the door, I shook my head letting out a puff of air. Beginning to act a bit like a voyeur made me feel strange and didn't like the feeling. Even so, I was intrigued with him and speculated if we would get along. If what he collects, and what he reads, and how he keeps his space was any indication, it would seem this year would be dreadfully long.

Among the mayhem, much to my surprise, he had both beds impeccably made, so I had no clues as to which bunk was his. Feeling like a stranger heightened my anxiety. Wasn't so sure I wanted to deal with a new way of living, considering I would be spending this year working my ass off to get into Georgetown next fall. Maybe weird, but not knowing where I would lay my head tonight was bothersome. Sleeping was important. With confidence, I chose one and sat down. I slowly leaned back on my elbows just thinking about this hiccup in my life.

BAM!

Without warning, the door flew open nearly blowing off the hinges. I sprang forward. My uneasiness escalated and my heart raced faster than Spitz's Olympic record times. Like the hinges on the door, I sensed things were not going to be secure the way I was used to, like it or not. I didn't know why, but my gut told me that I had better take my steps cautiously.

He was dripping with sweat and wearing cutoff jeans and black Chuck Taylor sneakers. Without uttering a word, but with a glance, he shot past me to one of the fans to cool himself. As they were before, he cranked up both fans to their highest setting. With his side and back toward me and with his hands on his hips, I had to notice his chiseled definition. Through the skewed windowpane and the flickering fan blades, strange patterns made by the sun played on his torso. He didn't seem real. He was about my height of six feet, and that was where the similarities ended. His brown hair was thick with a luster and accents of the summer sun. Seemingly molded with a sculptor's plan, he had a natural outline of long lashes that framed his blue eyes. I later learned the girls at our sister school loved his eyes and thought he was so *adorable*. His jaw and cheekbones rolled together in absolute harmony. If there was ever a classic nose, it was his. He, of course, had an even tan. As we all have flaws, his were not visible—that's enough to piss off anyone.

Rolling his head in fluid rotation, his actions shifted from his self-focus to that of me. As he guided his neck from side to side, he said something that I could not make out.

"What did you say? The fans are too loud, *I - didn't - hear - you*," I said drawing out each word and cupping my ear with my hand.

In a single motion, he switched off one fan and turned toward me. Poking fun, he said, "*My - name - is - Aiden.* You're late. The semester started ten days ago. I thought the place was all mine until Father Meinrad stopped me five minutes ago. What a bombshell." He shook his head.

His choice of words aggravated me, and I responded the way I felt. "Oh, yeah, I'm Eli, and sorry if I'm spoiling your little plans, but are you always an ass?"

"Geez, hold on. Get a grip. I didn't mean anything by it. I figured it was just too good to be true—that's all. If you want to know the truth, I was hoping they'd move someone in here." He totally switched gears and looked at me with a smile. "I'm sorry. Really, I am. Let's start over—hey roomie. I'm Aiden."

I couldn't change my mood that fast and muttered with disinterest something like. "Yeah, yeah—hi I'm Eli, whatever."

"Okay, that's a lot better wouldn't you say?" Aiden asked.

"Yeah, I'm all for fresh starts anyway. I'm here, aren't I? So, if I *may* ask, what happened to your last roommate?" I asked with raised eyebrows.

"Absolutely, you *may* ask. Go ahead and ask," he said crossing his arms.

"All right already," I let out a sigh.

"Okay, okay, just trying to add some levity."

"Uh-huh," I said rolling my eyes.

"So, anyway, my last roommate was this guy named Brody. He's still around. He flunked a few classes, and the monks didn't like that. He went ballistic, but that didn't have anything to do with his grades because he hates me anyway. He's got issues and he made me the reason."

"Oh really—*issues?*"

"Yeah—*issues*. I'm over all that and don't care one way or another," he said with a flicker of a smile. "Hey, I hope you get good grades—and don't have *issues*. I don't want you, the monks, or your mom or dad coming after me."

Aiden began to tidy the room and nonchalantly said, "Looks like I *did* take over the place, but I just didn't figure on a new kid coming in…anyway, what's mine is yours. Yep, I know how hard it is to be thrown into strange situations."

"Don't worry about it. So, tell me more about Brody."

"Huh? Nothing more to tell." He stiffened up and looked away, so I knew he wasn't going to budge. He changed the subject. "So, Eli, what's your story? I mean, why are you just getting here now?"

"My mom, well, my mom passed away a few years back…"

"Oh man—didn't have any idea. Sorry for the crack about irate moms and dads."

"Don't worry about it. Anyway, Dad had this thought that to better prepare me for college, I needed to spend my senior year away from

12

home. Literally a week ago we, I mean *he*, settled on St. Augustine's. In the last year, he's hardly been at home, so I think that's the real reason.

"Cool. It's all good. You're here now."

"Dad says I should be away from distractions. He presumes coming here would help me, you know, with the Fathers watching out for me. He says it would give me an edge getting into college. Yep, he thinks this is my ticket to Georgetown."

"Well, it sounds like *he's* got it all figured out," Aiden said.

"Yeah, well, you don't know my whole situation."

"Oh?"

"They appointed him ambassador to Belgium, and he is going to spend a lot of time out of the country. When he is here, he's going to be pretty busy—even busier than before. He decided that it would be best if I went to a school like this one. I always wanted to be a lawyer—like him. So, if this place helps me to get into Georgetown, then this is a good place for me to be."

"Yeah, a *boarding* school," Aiden interrupted. "But old Father Meinrad may have put you in the wrong room. I mean, I'm a distraction and I know it. I look for distractions. Like, *distraction* is my middle name. To me, that's a good thing. Anyway—you're here now."

There was a long and awkward silence. I ran my fingers through my hair and felt myself tense up starting with my toes shooting upward.

"Well, I'm not planning to be around much on the weekends. We're only a couple of hours from D.C. so I plan to go home on the weekends when Dad's there."

"Hmmm. I think you'll be here most weekends…anyway," Aiden said. "There are some cool things to do around here. Lots to explore…and the Shenandoah River is pretty excellent this time of year. That's where I just came from."

"No—no. Thanks, but I'm not here for that. I'm here to get my diploma and move on."

"Yeah, yeah yeah—I hear ya. You're not some kind of a dork, are you? If we're going to live together, we may as well try to hang out and have a good time. There will be plenty of time for studying. Didn't mean to scare you with all that *distraction* talk."

I was getting aggravated, and a sigh seeped out. "Hey Aiden, I just don't need all this right now. Okay?"

13

"Yeah, man. I hear you. I gave you your first distraction," Aiden said sarcastically. "You should know, Eli, the Robes might not say it, but they want us to have some distractions. Saturdays are made for distractions. That's the way they want it. That's the way we want it too. We don't see them, and they don't see us. Today is Saturday and I'm making the most out of it."

Aiden was more interested in thinking of other things and offered his own perspective. "You may never want to go home on the weekends—or ever."

"Oh really?"

"Let me tell you…Saturdays…it's our day. Everyone needs a day off. Even the Robes."

"You keep saying Robes, what's a Robe?"

"They're a *who* not a *what*. They're the good Fathers, you know, the monks—the guys wearing black *robes* who run this place."

"Yeah, yeah, I got it. But you don't call them that to their face, do you? I mean you say, Father, right?"

"Eli, yes call them Father—for a smart dude, you may be a bit slow on the uptake. The kids here have called them Robes forever, you know, behind their backs. Sometimes they overhear us, and they really hate it. So, watch out when you use the word because some of them have a fierce backhand slap."

"Oh, okay. Thanks for the tip," I said facing my palms out his way and shaking my head.

"Anyway, what I was trying to say was that the coaches, who are not Robes, rotate to keep track of us on the weekends. It's like one coach per class and we have seventy or so in each class so it's loose, very loose. I spend time running in the woods. It's much better than on the track or on campus somewhere. It's just better."

I didn't think he would ever shut up. When he did, I wasn't sure what to do, but at least now, I knew the slang for priests. Yep, I didn't think this arrangement was going to work out.

"Well, that sounds great and all, but I think I'll pass. I've never been much for hiking or exploring, so count me out."

"Once I get you off-campus, you'll see."

"No, I don't think so. Don't think it's going to happen. Being close to the dorm is fine by me, and anyway I think I'll be spending time in the library getting ready for college."

"Sounds like your dad, *I mean you* have a plan, but I don't know… the Robes won't just let you study all the time. I'm telling you."

Aiden seemed to have an answer for everything, so I thought I should change the subject. "Well, I'm going to try out for the basketball team."

"Cool. All right. We do have something in common. Yeah, b-ball—cool."

Somehow, we managed a moment of quiet. Thank God. Aiden leaped backward onto a bed. He landed squarely in the middle of the mattress while clasping his hands behind his head. Finally, I got my answer and now knew which bed was mine. So, I began to collect my duffel and knapsack, threw them on my bed, and unzipped all the compartments. Out of the corner of my right eye, I could tell he was interested in what I was doing. Using my body to shield my belongings, not that I had anything to hide, I unpacked. Just wasn't ready to offer the same courtesy Aiden had extended to me earlier.

Seeing all I needed to see, I decided that this arrangement was awful and was ready to talk to Father Meinrad. He told me earlier in the day that if I didn't think my roommate would work out, switching rooms was not a problem. He said that several students were without a roommate. A guy named Luis, I remembered him telling me, who lived right down the hall didn't have one. Yep, Father and I needed to talk.

After a few minutes of uneasy silence, Aiden lost interest in what I was doing and blurted out, "Okay, didn't mean any harm. Sorry to intrude."

He bolted up from his bed, yanked off his worn sneakers, and peeled off his shorts. He grabbed a towel hanging from a closet doorknob, sniffed it, and he left the same way he entered. He headed down the long hall to the bathroom for a shower. Just in time, as I was ready to punch someone.

THREE

Although I was expecting to be gone soon, finding places for most of my belongings helped me to feel better about this place. Knowing my luck, I wasn't going anywhere. Anyhow, I couldn't just sit around. Order is important and so are rules. It's best to keep life straight so there's no need for guesswork. Don't have time to waste.

After a few minutes, my interest waned, and my mind wandered. Letting out a yawn, I decided that organizing my stuff would have to wait. Sitting at my new desk, I just stared out the window in front of me. Don't know why, but I did. So many random thoughts ricocheted in my head, and it bothered me. That very second, like an unexpected rescue flare was shot in the distance, I realized that my appointment with Father Meinrad was drawing close. In a flash, my eyes shot down at my watch and saw that our two o'clock meeting was fast approaching.

"Crap—I need to pick up my uniform and books. I am so behind schedule since everyone else got here weeks ago! Damn it."

We met with Father Meinrad three or four weeks earlier when Dad first talked about enrolling me here. I hoped it would never happen but that was wishful thinking on my part. Father Meinrad seemed nice enough when we met him last month, and he seemed cool when we talked in front of the dorm today so that gave me some peace of mind. Being that it was Saturday, Father was making an exception for me so I would be ready for the second full week of classes. I was happy about that. It was, however, very weird that he was the only person I had met at St. Augustine's so far. Well, now, I've met Aiden but I'm not so sure he counts.

17

Not knowing the campus, I had no idea where to go. The campus was massive and getting to the dorm was confusing enough. Maybe that was just because Dad is fairly stereotypical when it comes to asking anyone for directions when he's lost. As for me, with my meeting time looming, I was frantic and began to pull everything out of every compartment of my knapsack to find the campus map. I couldn't find it. Restless and impatient, I jogged down the hall to the bathroom to see if I could find Aiden. Walking into the steamy bathroom, I saw to one end of the room a partition with the showerhead going full tilt. Over the roar of the water, I called out to him.

"Hey, Aiden?"

"Yeah, what is it?"

"I've got to see Father Meinrad in about twenty minutes to pick up my books and uniforms and other stuff I need. He told me I can't be late and...."

"Okay. You'll like Father Meinrad. He's pretty laid back. Later."

"Yeah, yeah, we've met...you don't understand, I don't know where to go. Can you tell me how to get there?" I said with my arms folded tightly against my chest looking down to the tile floor.

"Oh, you want *my* help—I might be a *distraction* though," he said chuckling at my expense.

"Very funny. Can you just tell me?" My heart was thumping.

"Better yet, I'll be out in a second and show you."

Before I could say anything and in no time, I heard the piercing squeak of the faucet as he turned the knob. Still totally wet, and clad in a towel, he zipped right past me saying nothing and he headed to the room. It amazed me how fast he got ready—dressed and ready to go in seconds.

We left by a back door of the dorm and began to walk on a gravel path. At St. Augustine's there were four dorms, two each for the upper and underclassmen. They housed seniors and juniors on the east side of the campus while the other dorms were across campus closer to the monastery. Somewhat separated from the main campus, our dorm was down a knoll and on the border of the formal campus and the woods.

As we walked, Aiden told me in his best scary voice that just a short walk a bit farther out to the east were the graves of the monks we would never know, at least in this life. I later learned that if not for the

18

periodic pilgrimages of a few of the priests to meditate and gaze solemnly upon the tombs of their dead brothers, one would never know this hallowed ground existed. It made for good ghost stories.

Like walking on the beach, the battleship gray gravel pellets took some getting used to. As we plowed on, we approached a canopy of cedar and evergreen that allowed for a sudden change in temperature as we walked through the shade. The boughs and branches were interconnected hiding the harsh August sun as the tight winding weave of the limbs hushed any noise of the day. I felt we were anywhere else but campus. Surreal, maybe, but by the time I thought more about it, we were approaching the opening.

When we reached the clearing, we had come to the center of campus. Actually, this was the first time I looked it over since the only other time here was a complete blur when we met with Father Meinrad. There was a layer of buildings arranged in a semicircle. In front of them was a lush emerald-green lawn that was out of character for a Virginia August. It was not hard to notice they constructed all the buildings in a grayish stone with red clay tile roofs. Each structure was a miniature fortress with blocks of differing cut quarried stones. I was expecting to see drawbridges and moats. There was a sense of pageantry in how they orchestrated the buildings with the main administrative complex, complete with the cupola, in the center, and all others, in a way, saluting it and standing at attention.

Obviously, the original intent of those who built this fortress those many years ago was to keep the unwanted out, or maybe it was to keep the unwanted in. Boys came here to become men and men came here to become monks. I always thought this was a far scarier notion than the graveyard we just passed.

At the other end of the quad was an enormous pond with sheets of water lilies so dense it seemed trustworthy for walking. The church was poised directly behind the vegetation and the occasional toad. As the oldest building on the grounds, it towered in an area of campus so that the community could attend Mass and never walk on campus if they chose.

Between man's rule and God's was the semblance of education. Academic buildings surrounded the immense landscape of the quad, and that I suppose accounted for the absence of fellow students

19

roaming the plaza. To the south, the library was probably the newest building. It didn't take on the features of the other quasi-medieval Anglo world. Large glass windows with terraces and tables claimed the exterior. The auditorium and dining hall stood side by side next to the library. Like a wall, directly behind these buildings was the field house that had a breezeway to a pool. Spaced arbitrarily were a football field, a tennis facility, a track, a soccer field, and a baseball diamond. These were obvious choices for teenage boys to hang out, especially on Saturday.

"This place, you know, is full of tunnels," Aiden blurted out as we walked by a group of boys playing ultimate Frisbee. He half-heartedly waved to a few of the boys.

"Tunnels?"

"Yeah, I mean the Robes don't talk about them. They think we don't know—but we do. It's like an underground village."

I couldn't resist but I sarcastically answered him. "Hmmm, I must have missed the pictures of these tunnels in the recruitment brochure, but I did read something about the underground village."

He ignored my tone. "They're like the catacombs. I've only been through some of them. I've heard that the students who can't hack it here have ended it right there. It's a place of last resort—pretty sad that anything here could lead a kid to that."

Just then, *smack!*

A Frisbee came from behind and hit me square in the back of my head. "Ow! What the hell..."

Covering his mouth with his hand, Aiden silently chuckled and picked up the disk. A boy ran up to us. "Sorry man. I guess it got away from me."

"Yeah, right," Aiden said under his breath.

Aiden shook his head and tossed the Frisbee back to him. Rubbing my head, I told the guy that it was no big deal, but his response was strange at best.

"All right girls, I'll leave you two alone to get better acquainted." He turned and ran off.

"Who was that jerk?"

"Now you've met Brody. Nice guy, huh?"

As my anxiety grew, I peered down to my watch and saw it was about one minute before two o'clock. No way was I going to make it on time. As we rounded the courtyard, we entered the main administration building. Here, Aiden assured me that we were almost there. Creepy religious statues dotted the voluminous foyer. Larger than the others, I saw one white angular depiction of St. Augustine. Picking up our pace, we took a turn at the end of a long marble corridor. Obnoxious and ornate molding encased the door of the bookstore, and I thought it looked as inviting as a mausoleum. We entered and to my surprise, the room was bright with windows, had thick colorful Persian rugs and powder blue walls—not the tomb I had expected.

Father Meinrad was folding cuffed wool pants. Just the sight of it made me itch. Like a sheep startled by a wolf, Father's face went from serene to shock as we entered the room. He quickly regained composure and approached us with a smile. His smile, I would find out, was his signature.

"Looks like you two are out and about. I hope you are both hitting it off."

Aiden began meandering through the hanging uniform pants and blazers paying little attention to what Father and I were doing or saying.

"I'll get you set up in a jiffy. I know you and Aiden probably want to do some exploring this afternoon before supper. He likes that river. You will too."

As he had done probably thousands of times, he began pulling together the basics of the St. Augustine uniform. Three pairs of khaki pants, five white oxford cloth shirts, a blue blazer, and two black watch plaid neckties. Aiden appeared to get bored, mumbled something, and left the room. As I began to sort through the clothes on the counter, Father walked down another aisle and began to pull books off the shelf and pile each one on top of the other next to my newly acquired apparel. He carried each edition as if it were fine crystal and placed them gently on top of the other. With delicate precision, he lightly laid the literature book just topping off the tower that he so adeptly constructed.

"I'm not sure, but I believe you are in many of Aiden's classes. Mr. McKilty teaches senior Lit, and he is a real treat. He's one of our graduates. We don't usually hire our own, but he is as good as they come, and I was glad he made the headmaster's cut. You know we don't have too many of us *Robes* left."

He caught me off guard with his use of the student's slang but looking into his eyes at that moment sent a feeling of reassurance through me. He let out an unexpected burp and raised his fingers to his lips. I couldn't hold back, and Father and I laughed so much that I, too, let out a burp. As we regained our composure, he said, "What? Didn't you think priests could burp? That was a good one too, Eli."

"Gosh…thinking about it, you might be right. I now have a new way of thinking." I said with a lilt in my voice.

"I'm happy to oblige Eli. Hope it doesn't stop there," Father said and then he quickly turned the conversation. "You know, Aiden's a good boy. I think you are both quite lucky to have each other as roommates this year. You will learn from each other if you keep an open heart."

"Father, I appreciate your wanting me to feel comfortable here, especially in a new place and all, but I'm here just for one measly year. My eyes are already set on graduation…that's about it. I'm keeping my sites on college, and then toward law school."

Father picked up his pipe from the counter and began to pack the bowl with cold tobacco shavings. Like an Arctic blast, it felt cold, and the moment grew stale. He said nothing and all I could hear was the tick of the wall clock. Perhaps another burp would ease the tension, but I knew I couldn't muster one up and figured he was done. He then gave me a grin that I could not decipher. He leaned toward me, and I stood like one of the creepy statues out in the hall.

"Let me tell you something—promise not to tell?"

"Yeah—I mean, yes Father."

"Eli, I need a favor from you. I assigned you to his room because I am worried about my boy Aiden. You see, he had a rough go of it last year. Oh, he's not going to tell you that, but trust me, he did. He has a bit too much pride, that boy, but he needs you. Do you understand?"

"Huh? He needs *me*?"

"Of course, my son. You have a good head on your shoulders, and truthfully, he could benefit from someone like you this year. I think it is an important year for the both of you. See, Aiden has no mother, and his father left before he was born. You can see why I have some worries, don't you?"

"Well, ah, ah, I guess so."

He gave me a wink. Many things raced through my head. *What was I getting myself into? I didn't have time to take on a project—what was I going to do?* Father Meinrad just looked at me and I felt trapped.

"Well, I probably don't need to be in the library every day," I grumbled.

Father Meinrad glowed brighter than the ash in his pipe. "That a boy! Remember, Eli, don't overlook what you have today by always reaching for something else. Use this year to learn more about yourself. You will gain so much—trust me."

I hate to say it, but I wasn't listening to him at that point. I was in a stupor. What I really wanted to talk to him about was the possibility of changing rooms, but he beamed as he spoke of Aiden. I couldn't find the nerve. It was way too late for that anyway—not now. The door opened and in walked Aiden. Confounded, I looked at Father. He winked back at me. My response to him was more of a smirk than a smile. Looking away, I stood there like a lump of butter while Father hastened to put everything into a couple of canvas tote bags. I said nothing else but nodded to Father. Saying little else, Aiden and I left.

When we got back to the room, Aiden was eager to show me what lay beyond the boundaries of St. Gus'. Kind of annoyed by the whole day so far, I was not interested in taking another tour, but I was ready to do what I wanted to do. For some reason, I could not be mad at Father although he knew it would be almost impossible for me to refuse his request. Perhaps, I thought, that maybe his hope had more to do with me than he let on. Anyway, knowing my *deal* with Father, however, I thought Aiden could wait a day or two.

"How about a rain check?"

"Cool…yeah, we can wait. I'll catch up with you at dinner."

He left to do only God knows what. Dinner, I understood, began promptly at six o'clock, so I finished unpacking, arranging, and rearranging my desk and dresser. Hanging up a few of my shirts I couldn't help but to notice the closet was small and musty, but so was the room—so was my life right about now. I decided to arrange my desk with the supplies I brought from home. Only a minute after I was done, I rearranged it again. This was something I did frequently—it was just how I was.

Sitting back, scanning the room, and seeing my personal belongings where they should be, at least for now, I felt much better. This was my place and wanted my things to be where I wanted them to be.

As I tended to my needs, I heard a faint knock on the door. There, standing about six-four or six-five, was a skeleton of a figure poking his head through the doorway. He said nothing and waved so I motioned him to come in.

"Come on—come…yeah you can come in," again nodding, I gestured to him to join me. As he did, we introduced ourselves.

"You can call me Vandy, everyone does. My real name is Melvin Vanders, but only my parents call me Melvin. Hate that name. HATE IT! I'm going to make the freshmen call me Sir Vandy. It's a good b-ball nickname. One day there'll be the Sir Vandy basketball shoe. Just wait."

Vandy made himself at home by plopping on my bed, and with his jetliner-sized feet, he unwittingly zeroed in on my clean clothes. He pulled a Baby Ruth out of one pocket and offered me the first bite. I grabbed it, took a bite, and handed it back with a big grin. He brightened up too.

"You can do that? I mean, so we can make the freshman call us something other than our name? Why? Why is that a thing?" I asked pulling my clothes from under his feet.

"Can we? Hell ya, my man. Of course, we can. In fact, in theory, we can haze you," Vandy said nodding and pointing his skinny index finger my way.

"What? Noooo."

"Don't worry. We have a kind of unwritten agreement to leave new senior students alone."

"Glad to hear that," I said shrugging my shoulders with a tight grin.

"But we could."

"Okay, okay, I hear you." I continued unpacking.

"As far as *why?* Because we can. Yeah, that's it. Because we can. When we were frosh, the seniors did that stuff—and worse—to us. Yeah, the freshmen are ours until Thanksgiving break."

"It's like a rite of passage—becoming a man, kind of thing? Gosh,

I should've asked a lot more questions about this place a month ago."

"Sure, it's that kind of thing—you want to be a man, right?" he asked with a chuckle.

"Well, yeah."

"So, is Aiden out somewhere?" He looked side to side as if he thought he'd magically appear.

"He said something about the river, I think, but I wanted to do anything but go. I wanted to get settled in."

Vandy quickly sat up. "Settled in? What are you an old geezer or something? Aiden doesn't offer the tour to just anyone. In fact—*no one*. You don't understand. I'd lighten up if I were you. I mean we're talking about my man Aiden."

Vandy pursed his lips blowing upward. He jumped up and looked at himself in the mirror and patted his closely cropped Afro. He grabbed a basketball that was under the desk chair, laid back on the bed, and began tossing the ball toward the ceiling.

"What's all this about Aiden? Geez, that's all I'm hearing today."

"You'll like him. Everyone does, well except for Brody. But that's another story for another time… So, do you play hoops?"

I decided to put down my stuff. Pulling up my desk chair, I folded my arms and sat leaning back on its rear legs. Perhaps I was being a bit cocky, but I didn't care and bragged about my basketball prowess. Much to my wonderment, though, we spent the next forty-five minutes talking about nothing in particular, but we had a great time. I don't know why, but we did. One minute he told me I had no jump shot, although he had never laid eyes on me before, and the next moment he told me that I was going to have a great time on the team.

Vandy was one of those guys you meet who is immediately likable. He's the kind of guy who goes through life as if tomorrow were too far away to give it a thought but is really the opposite. Vandy made me comfortable, even though he called me a *geezer*. In conversation, he was engaged but demanded little from me. It was the kind of conversation I needed at that very moment. Thinking that was the way he wanted it as well, I really couldn't blame him as he stood out on campus. If I were to place a bet, his focus was to make the grade on and off the court and no one would bother him. Vandy was a good guy with his penchant for hoops and his unpretentious bearing.

I had quite a bit for one afternoon, but then, dinner was coming up.

FOUR

Etched in my mind, the events at dinner that first evening was disturbing for many reasons. First off, the food was beyond gross. Students many years earlier and since have suffered the same experience in our cafeteria. I'm sure of this. Decades before my arrival, the boys who are now men and probably some of the school's biggest donors, nicknamed our dining hall. Instead of Hurley Hall for which the good monks named it after Father Kiernan Hurley about a century ago, the students called it *Hurl Hall or The Hurl* or some variation thereof. With great affection, the name stuck. In the late afternoon, we would frequently ask a friend or a hallmate, 'are you going to Hurl tonight?' when any of us wanted a companion on the walk to dinner. The Robes never caught on to this or, maybe, they just didn't pay much attention. They probably just didn't care. We still ate three squares there every day and we never went to bed with empty stomachs.

That night the place was full of boys of all ages, so it seemed. Visions of the movie *Oliver* played out in my head. Seeing no one with any authority, an invisible power herded us to a trough of food—presumably. What we found in front of us was anything but recognizable much less appetizing. Looking from side to side to determine what to do next, I couldn't help but notice that my fellow schoolmates, though, from diverse ethnic and cultural backgrounds all shared a common language when it came to our behavior at mealtime. Looking back, we were pigs, no matter our G.P.A. our zip code, or shoe size.

*****

St. Augustine's was the oldest Catholic college preparatory school in the country. The price tag was anything but the traditional inner-city parochial types, but the flavor of the institution was diverse. The monks painstakingly sought to include all. This kept us not so private of the private schools that we knew of and usually learned about on the playing field.

Money, in fact, did help make diversity a standard. The good Fathers were the benefactors of a thirty-million-dollar bequest sometime in the late 1950s. Scholarship endowments among other endowed funds were now quite abundant. St. Augustine's was attainable for many who wanted to attend.

A middle-aged widow, without an apparent heir to her name, left the mother lode to the monastery. Episcopal by faith she was independent by nature and rumor had it that she had a deep desire to be the school's ultimate benefactor. She imagined that by being a philanthropist her ticket for redemption would be waiting for her at the pearly gates. After all, she had nothing to do with the school.

Technically, the campus automatically expanded fivefold as her home in the middle of her own acreage now lay to one end of the property the monks owned. Rarely visited by anyone, her old mansion, and the land it sat on, was beyond the monk's cemetery below a hill and up another.

Legends, tales but mostly rumors arose about the *old lady*. They said she was once married to a wealthy Brazilian Catholic who brewed his fortune as a mogul in the coffee trade. He left her a widow due to a bitter business deal. Distressed, beset, and plagued with a paralyzing heartache she followed him in death only a few short years after. Kind of romantic it seemed, but who knows if that was the real story or not.

Other rumors had it that she knew, quite intimately, a Robe after the suicide of her racketeering husband. When one of the novices discovered them, she died soon after of anguish and guilt. It was as if she had two hearts to give and her very different lovers pulverized them both.

Another version insists that when she took her own life, she left the monks more than money and land, whatever that means. The monks found her strung up, as the tale goes, in one of the tunnels leading from the monastery to the cemetery. The *old lady's* house, again as rumor would have it, was the location of their frequent rendezvous. I saw all this as gossip, but Lord knows, boys and men don't do that.

*****

The dress code was lax on Saturday at dinner. Most of the boys wore cutoffs and tee-shirts, the universal dress code of the day and our generation. Sounds of clanking plates and flatware blended with the murmur of banter and friendly laughter. Acoustically this abyss of a building was atrocious. High ceilings with massive wooden beams served to rebound the clamor of the activity twenty-five feet below. It was as if all below was set in motion by this same invisible force that I felt when I walked through the door.

Nothing was elegant or formal about Hurl Hall. However, a stone fireplace at the end of the narrow structure was unique, and thought it was beautiful but I, of course, didn't want others to know I thought so. I didn't want to be *that guy* that pointed out such things. Anyway, it had an inlay of Chinese symbols and figures. It was stunning. This structure came from the *old lady*'s house, but it looked out of place and unappreciated. Perhaps I was projecting somewhat as I felt, and probably looked out of place just like that old carved-up slab of mahogany and stone.

Hanging from the rafters were gigantic chains holding Gothic-looking lamps. Some were brightly illuminating while others painfully shed the equivalent of candlelight. Twelfth-century Vikings, I always thought, would be mirthful in these digs. Huge portraits of old white men, mostly priests, underscored with plaques adorned the walls. *Who reads these plaques?* No one here, I presumed. Someone took time to preserve their images but their substance if they had any, was missing. Their moment was long gone, but their roving eyes followed me no matter where I was in The Hurl.

I was merely going through the motions that night. Going to The Hurl to eat was what we did. I wanted to fit in, so I did what the others did. Although the food was conspicuously ordinary, it did the trick by keeping me upright and functioning.

Since Vandy and I arrived late, we ate with freshmen. Normally being late was an infraction, but Saturdays were altogether different

29

here. Thinking about it, every day was unlike anything I had ever known. It was as if we were in a parallel universe.

Swimming in an ocean of freshmen, I couldn't help to notice them as they stood out. I had forgotten that they were so tiny and boyish. In the past few years, it was evident, I conveniently forgot about my own physical evolution. Then again, a new lens was now in front of me. While thinking of that, I became somewhat mesmerized and engaged in *freshmen watching* out of the corner of my eye. They were acting very bizarre. It was weird. Bizarre might not be the best way to describe their behaviors. Anxious, troubled, or overly stressed-out might be more like it.

It was easy to understand why they were this way as hazing hung over their heads. They didn't know what to expect; at a moment's notice, things could change. It was as if they were all waiting for something. I just sensed this and can't say why. Scared, intimidated, self-aware they sat gulping their feed awaiting a slaughter. Noticing the air getting thicker, I was uncomfortable just thinking what was going through their thirteen-year-old heads.

Vandy, seemed detached as he, gobbled, nonstop his plate of meatloaf and lumpy mashed potatoes. I found, however, the whole exploit odd and unnecessary. It affected my appetite. Maybe the summation of the day so far made me feel altogether full of empty calories. Funny, I found myself looking for Aiden. He said he'd catch up with me at dinner.

"Vandy, have you seen Aiden come in?"

Like a harpoon, Vandy was spearing his green beans as he answered. "Aiden rarely shows up for eats on Saturday. He obeys mealtime rules when he has to. That's Aiden."

CRASH!

At that moment, a freshman dropped his dinner tray in front of the senior section. As uneasy as I felt, I was glad not to be the underling standing a bad breath away from the stony-faced seniors. They were even unnerving to me. This moment seemed like months—nagging, Jupiter winter months. The visibly distraught ninth grader stood frozen like a store mannequin—the kind that someone twisted the head around when no one was looking.

There he sat, an oversized fiery and curly-haired senior leering at the little freshman. He looked like he was ready to blow a gasket. Was this guy playing around? Apparently, he was not. What little hair I had that grew on the back of my neck sprung outward. I later learned this was Luis.

What was the big deal?

Luis, the one and the same who lived in a room down my hall, was an upperclassman on a mission. Seniors, however, didn't take him seriously anyway—mission or not. He intended to show the new students that he was boss, at least in his own mind. Luis was so peculiar from top to bottom. Always disheveled, he had tiny eyes and a noticeable tick as if he was giving you a high sign when he talked. Unfortunately, teenage boys judge and can be very mean-spirited, but Luis didn't help himself by putting up a tough guy veneer.

Emerging from an obscured point of origin was the humming of a tune completely unfamiliar to me. They all knew it—as if the whole student body had rehearsed it many times. Soon the hum boomed like a locomotive roaring closer. The roar became a chant and it increased in volume. I saw Luis fidget and he seemed like a popped beach ball that was about to be kicked around a few more times before someone would end up trashing it.

A full verse of a homespun campus hit was coming from almost all in the building—well, except the freshman. The coaches overlooked the full assault on Luis' person, and I suspected this was usual. It didn't take a savant to detect this ditty was not one of Luis' favorite tunes although it seemed to be his theme song.

> *"Orca, Orca you are fat and silly.*
> *Orca, Orca pockmarks you have plenty!*
> *Orca, Orca . . ."*

It also didn't take much to detect that this attention hurt him, but I could see he stood tall. Hell, was it just me who could see this? Apparently, my new school chums were heartless. Empathy or compassion was not in their dictionary.

Only after the second verse did the coaches begin to stand and walk around the room to restore order. Interestingly, I saw one coach mouthing the words with a smile. Peace didn't come easy as bursts and jabs of delirious laughter stabbed the tension from one upperclassman in particular. It came from Brody, the jerk who beamed me with the Frisbee. The wiry-haired, pale face and nameless freshman who started the chain reaction scurried to redeem his lowly stature with his classmates. The ruckus now quelled, and all was back as before.

"Vandy, what the hell was all that?"

Vandy leaned toward me with his fork poised for another helping and mumbled, "Brother, you ain't seen nothing yet."

"You mean it gets rowdy like this and no one gets in trouble? Poor guy."

"Yeah, that's what I'm saying. During the week, the Robes spend time in here and guys kiss up to them. But the coaches let things go. The Robes allow other stupid things. You know, like the whole hazing thing—and that's okay with them, so you never know. I try to fly under the radar if I can."

"Oh, I see. The Robes are okay with seniors making freshmen do things in the name of hazing?" I asked knowing the answer.

"Yeah, you've got it. The alumni expect it," Vandy said waving his fork.

"What kind of things?"

"We make them sing the fight song, do push-ups—things like that at a moment's notice."

"Yeah, I see how that makes you into a man—whew," I said shaking my head.

"It gets out of hand when the Robes are not around, that's for sure."

"You think?"

"I know, I know," said Vandy. "But I told you before, seniors can make *you* do things too. They don't because of what I told you. *The unwritten...*

"*... unwritten agreement.* Yeah, I know."

"Yeah, but old Luis or Brody might go by their own rule. Who knows?" he whispered looking from side to side. "Yeah, now come to think about it, maybe the unwritten agreement is bogus. I could when you least expect it..."

"WHAT!"

"I knew that would flip your switch. Not to worry," he chuckled.

"Like I said, seniors leave new upperclassmen like you alone, but Luis is different. I mean you're the only new upperclassmen this year so, to be on the safe side, I'd avoid him at all costs."

"Okay…I think I'm over this conversation," I said looking to the ceiling."

"Even if he can't physically push you around, he can make you do stuff, and if you don't do what he tells you to do he can turn you over to Hazing Court."

"What? Hazing Court?" I said perking up.

"It's really called Orientation Court. But, even if he turned you in, I wouldn't worry. They probably wouldn't take him too seriously. You know he's Orca. No one takes *Orca* seriously."

Luis despised the nickname. I was not surprised. At that time, I didn't know Luis, but my first impressions of him and all the remnants in front of me were anything but flattering—not in the least. However, I didn't like the way the students treated him. No one should have to put up with that.

I didn't bother asking Vandy to elaborate any more on the St. Augustine ritual; I didn't feel like learning about barbaric hazing customs. Here, as evidenced by this event, was the resounding notion that it was up to older students to, somehow, break down to build up the St. Augustine man. Like it or not, this was part of the culture. Just think, if only all the inhabitants of the world knew it only took a measly four years at a prep school to realize the wonders and riches of humanity, all would be enrolled at St. Augustine's or one of the many prep schools that were littered throughout the country.

Conservative in my upbringing, I perhaps, should have seen some intrinsic value in the ordeal. These folks like my dad, after all, prize the strict game plan that swelled from these kinds of schools but perhaps, I was beginning to understand another way of doing things. At that moment, I saw the fright and humiliation in the eyes of that freshman for absolutely no reason. It triggered a conviction within me. It began with caring less about ritualistic events that were ancient and rooted in the name of tradition. I didn't expect it, but it hit me hard. What was I here for anyway? I was preparing for college and high school was a way of preparation and not the culmination of the mind and soul. It was not an end. I yearned for more, and perhaps here I was alone in this ultimate aim. I felt different from the other boys. So much was reverberating through my mind.

In his unassuming manner, Vandy asked me if I wanted to shoot some pool and hang out with other seniors that night. They were all meeting later at *The Cave* in the Commons. Saturday night was the night upperclassmen could stay out of the dorm as late as eleven o'clock. I declined. Pool was not my thing, but I didn't want Vandy to know this. There would be other Saturday nights anyway. After spending only twenty-five minutes feasting with my new schoolmates, I was ready to cruise back to the dorm. I remember that most of my first night, I spent alone in my room. The first dining experience, after all, was disquieting and depleting. This was all too much, too soon.

Many of us left The Hurl at the same time but most went to the Commons and others disappeared on unfamiliar spokes of the path. Heading back on my own was just fine by me. I saw Luis talking with Father Meinrad and Father Tobias, the headmaster. I kept my head down, and I was pleased that they took another direction. Just didn't want to deal with all that.

The evening sky was darker than usual as gray clouds moved in while we ate. A large full moon was emerging and taking over as the sun was losing its command of the sky. The puffy, dense billows that rolled in kept the sun from full view, but the mellowing orange ball was clearly there as beams of color escaped around the edges of the invading clouds. Though, on the surface, my experience seemed black and white, I knew better. Taking in the fresh cool mountain air was heady and felt uplifting. All was different from the feeling and smells that lingered earlier that day.

A few priests were traveling down another path. Thinking before I acted, like the moment before, I decided to behave as if they didn't exist. With their hands folded under their garb and heads slightly bowed, my existence to them didn't seem to register anyway. Maybe, too, they saw me and declined to acknowledge my presence. They were reflective, I supposed, after evening prayers. This was good, but I wanted nothing of their confining religious world. Their walks were frequent reminders they were there, along with their set of rules and traditions.

FIVE

Although getting back to the dorm took me a few extra maneuvers, I managed without a problem. A couple of times I veered from the path but always found my way back. Entering the dorm, it had a certain smell. It reminded me of my Aunt Lucy's home for some reason. Everything was stinking old. The floor, the molding, and even the paint seemed to be closer to 1943 than 1973.

Climbing the staircase, I took two steps at a time and bounded to the second floor. The place was empty. Even though the building was a couple of stories with about fifteen rooms per floor, most of my dormmates were probably in *The Cave* playing pool with Vandy. As I walked down the hall, a few doors were ajar. Curious, I wanted to know who lived in each room. *Were they like me? Was my neighbor Orca? What would I do?* Worn out from the day, I decided not to worry about him right now.

My hand entered my room first as I felt for the light switch. I was funny that way. I liked the lights on before I entered a room. I flicked the switch and closed the door with my foot. I pulled my shirt from my pants and let out a yawn. Not knowing exactly what to do, I looked around and scratched my chest. As usual, my next thought was to use this time wisely.

Settling on rearranging my belongings, again, I found new homes for some. Shoes went neatly into my closet, while underwear and tee-shirts went into my top drawer. Shirts were placed into the second drawer and in the bottom drawer were my jeans and some sweatshirts. Dad told me I would be wearing uniforms most of the time and that I would not need much. Thinking of this as I was rearranging, I wondered whether coming here was a good thing or a bad thing. In a moment, I decided I shouldn't care.

As the night grew, I played with the lighting to help contrive a serene mood wanting to taint the glare of the day. Even the delicate shadows made by the desk lamp were welcoming and as the hours rushed forward, I no longer wanted much detail.

The last thing I pulled from my duffle bag that night was my favorite photo of Mom. Grace and peace portrayed my affections as I stared at her portrait. My eyes welled up, but it was okay by me because I was alone. Dad was always *there* for me so to speak, but Mom was always *here*, for me—right in the middle of my chest. She was always with me, behind me all the way and, I suppose, still a part of me. Her face was now behind glass in a scratched-up frame I found with some of her keepsakes.

Mom may be with me in spirit, I thought, but I wasn't sure what that meant. This whole spirituality thing—how did it work? Could she see me or hear me? Did it mean she lives in my imagination or in some cosmic space? Did she know what I was doing? Could she still help me and guide me? Was she in some better place, say, talking with other dead people like the saints or movie stars? Did she still care about me? Did I matter to her anymore? Could she be in a new place where she didn't know these things or care about worldly events? Was she absorbed with all things God? Did she know God firsthand? After all, I was just a person. Yet for me, right now, she lived in black and white and was two-dimensional. Her absence at times was insufferable.

Answers, I thought, may make death more meaningful or bearable for me. I did not want to experience death anytime soon of anyone else I loved. As a saline tear meandered down my face, I placed the image of her on my dresser. Using the heel of my hand, I stopped the likelihood of a flood. So many questions rolled around in my head. Dad always told me I thought about things too much. This time he was wrong. What? Should I just shut things off like a radio?

I laid down on my bed, opened a book, and read. About halfway through the third chapter, I began to drift and read the same paragraph several times. This was summer reading and since I arrived late, I had much ground to cover. Salinger's *The Catcher in the Rye* was riveting, but the ending, no matter how gripping, would have to wait for another day. Wow! Holden Caufield—what a mess.

Today was unusual. Father Meinrad, Aiden, and even Vandy were friendly and likable, so I couldn't blame them for my feelings, but I wanted to. This was all new—boarding school, roommates, and being away from home. Burying these thoughts in the back of my mind was the best thing to do for me to move forward.

A shower—that's what I needed. Like a baptism, showers were sometimes more than just a way to get clean, but a way to feel untainted and whole, and I needed that. Knowing I was the only one in the room, I yanked my shirt off in a quick tug and unsnapped my shorts with an abrupt pull. For some reason, I took off my socks last and ran each finger between each toe. Naked, I wrapped a towel around my waist and walked straight down the hall. It was wide with hardwood floors and with each step I took, it felt like I was walking on duct tape. You know, making a ripping noise with each step. No one was around so I jerked the towel from my waist and held it to one side as I walked— for all of two seconds. This episode was my limit of outright boldness. Daring, maybe it was a little bit—for a whooping blink of the eye even though no one was around.

I approached the door to the bathroom at the end of the corridor. My room was on the corner on the opposite side of the building, so it was a long haul. The bathroom was dark. I couldn't see anything to include the light switch, so I ran my hand on the wall while clutching onto my soap with the other. The walls felt slimy. I widened my eyelids thinking I'd bring in more light. Finally, I found the switch and flipped it on. Only a few bulbs took the hint and lit up. Naturally, I began walking on the outer sides of my feet. Looking around, I decided to inspect the room more closely. In such a rush earlier in the day, I hadn't taken a good look around.

First, I examined the sinks and commodes. Water was running in two of the sinks, so I turned the handles only realizing that my actions did nothing. The toilet begged for a flush, so I put it out of its misery. It was one of those toilets that make you sweat. I mean when flushed, water filled the bowl precariously high and swirled the contents around a couple of extra times before sucking it away. One ounce more and it would have gushed over the lip, and I would be wading ankle-deep in crap. This all helped to double my heart rate. Something I *really* needed right now, but with this flush, I was lucky.

Two large windows were wide open. At home, I would pull down a shade, but I wasn't in the mood to be conventional. Good thing because there were no shades. I pulled the towel from my waist and hung it on a tiny hook. I stood completely vulnerable in the dim light. Reaching out to find the nozzle and stall that suited me, I turned the knobs below. In no time, I was under the spray of the water. It pulsated on my face. As I moved my neck and chest, it felt like tinges of needles as they, one by one, kneaded my fatigued muscles and overburdened spirit.

Eyes shut; the combination of mildew mixed with the mugginess of the room hung in the air as the tepid water gushed on my trunk. Lathering in slow motion, I wanted to spend time with the water, its sound, its sensation, and its steam. Thoughts in no order bounced through my mind as I kept my eyes to the world closed and my gaze inward open. Whatever it was, I began to feel calm. The solitude, the warmth, and the mixture of senses came together to clear my mind and refresh my spirit. Cleansing my body was assuredly a secondary purpose to the sensuality of the experience. Tasting the drops on my tongue fulfilled all my senses, but there was more. It was a high, or a rush. Like I was knocking on a door to a new way to sense and see.

The shampoo bubbled and lathered so much that, as I looked down at my feet, the puffs of suds rolled off my head as I scrubbed my scalp. My hair, my arms, and my thoughts lay limp in the fog of the space that I filled. It was amazing that a bar of soap and shampoo could be a part of this whole affair.

As easy as it was to begin my binge, I ended it with a turn of the squeaky knob. The absence was a welcomed hush for the moment. Shaking my head to help dry my hair, I thought this was perfect for me, at least tonight. A breeze whipped through a window and treated me to a chill. Giving me a stir, it helped me to move on.

Somewhat still dripping, and at a good clip, I got down the hall and back to my room in no time. Yanking up my shorts, I was ready to call it a night. One fan on the low setting sent a steady flow my way. The quiet rumbling sound was soothing. I jumped into bed pulling the sheet up over my chest. My bed created a refuge. I never thought huddling on a plastic-covered institutional mattress could be so comfortable.

The desk lamp was the only obstacle between me and the black and white of the dream world. I reached over to turn off the light. It must have been eleven o'clock when my eyes began waning, so I put my left hand under my head and my eyes slowly closed. Not knowing what tomorrow would bring, I wanted to sleep.

The white noise of the fan continued to lull me to sleep as the lunar lights flowed through the panes. I remember that my thoughts were sketchy, random, and made no sense—this meant I would be asleep within seconds. This, however, was to be short-lived. Somewhere between reality and dreamland, the door sprang open. Laying there and moving little, I rubbed my eyes and all I could see was this figure hovering above me. Was it Luis looming over me? Every muscle in my body tensed. Was I his new target? As my eyes cleared, I realized it was Aiden. He turned on the overhead light.

"Hey, are you asleep?"

Calming down, I slowly sat up. "No…no, I was just laying here in bed with my eyes closed with the light out—what's up?"

"I haven't seen you since this afternoon and thought we could talk awhile," he said as he turned away and began to kick off his shoes.

I was in anything but a talking mood but gave in because I didn't think I had a choice. Aiden then realized that I was just about asleep when he bounded in, so he turned off the overhead light and switched on a small light he had next to his bed. It did little more than keep us out of total darkness.

"Oops…sorry."

"No problem, Aiden. Really, no big deal."

Aiden then turned to the fan and shut it off without consultation. The sharp moonbeams seemed to pierce through the panes and create more light as my eyes began to adjust to the change. Aiden asked about my afternoon as he pulled off his tee-shirt and shorts. He wrenched his arm around his neck to scratch as much of his back as he could. Rummaging through his drawers, he found some gym shorts and pulled them on.

Only knowing him a day, I wondered about his unorthodox ways in his actions and assertions. He was a puzzle to me. Because I was his roommate, or perhaps because he liked me, he wanted to talk— something like that. I don't know, but he wanted to know about me, and that felt good. Something in my head changed at that moment. Settled in and my anxieties at bay, I decided to look at Aiden differently. What Vandy told me and what Father Meinrad requested of me, looped in my mind. Learning more and more about Brody and Luis shifted my thinking too. It was much too soon to pass judgment, and I needed an ally so why not the most charismatic guy at the school?

As we talked, I remember looking over his way and seeing his face in shadows, his hands behind his head, and the sheet around his navel. He was content, uninhibited, and natural. He genuinely wanted to hear about the rest of my afternoon and evening. I told him that Vandy and I spent time together. By his expression, I could tell Aiden liked Vandy, as he lit up when we talked about him. Because things were going so well with our conversation, bringing up anything about my gut reaction to the incident at dinner didn't seem wise. I resisted bringing up any emotional thoughts or personal hullabaloos about the day or the school—not ready to go that way. Now was not the time.

"You know, I'm not going to forget about your rain check?"

"I'm not either. You better honor it," I answered.

Aiden began to tell me that he knew of places near campus that he wanted me to see that he promised I would think were *totally bitchin'* to use his words. He said he thought that most of the boys looked for planned campus activities. Aiden went on to say that there was so much more than kicking or throwing a ball. Not sure what he was talking about, I sat and listened and now wide-awake.

"I'm game and ready for the ride."

"Cool. We'll do it. But first, you know we've got to go to Mass in the morning?"

"What?"

"Dude…it's Sunday and you go to a Catholic school."

"Ah…yeah, I was just…just…"

"No problem Eli. You've had a long day. I'll make sure your up and ready to go."

As abrupt as his entrance was that morning, he said nothing more and rolled over. He faced the window with the moonlight streaming through. Just as the sunlight danced on his torso when I first met him, the moonbeams were quieting and motionless on his skin. Energy was now inertia in an instant. As I took my last few glimpses of him, I wondered if I too looked content before I slept—or any other time for that matter.

SIX

H e kept his word. Aiden whipped the top sheet off me that next morning jolting me out of the deepest sleep that I could remember.

"Can't sleep in today. Gotta head to church in a few," he said.

"Okay, okay. I hear you."

Anxiously, I found my bearings and dressed in the traditional navy blazer and school tie. By the time a comb was through my cowlick and a toothbrush over my molars, Aiden led me to the enormous doors of the church. He choreographed my placement. Like Moses, he separated a sea of boys and led me to where he wanted us to be. Only Aiden could get away with cutting in line with no repercussion.

It was hot for so early in the morning. The haze overhead was thick, but the sun's relentless rays began burning their way through. The gargantuan doors that we faced had baked every day and every year by the sun and had the scars of old age to show it. Cracks and greenish-black flakes of countless coats of paint looked ready to pop from its surface. Looking beyond the blemishes that come over time, the doors were as beautiful, I assumed, as the day some artisan added their final touch. The entire facade of the church held a sense of majesty, which I am sure did not register with the likes of most of my classmates.

As we waited in virtual silence, barring an occasional burp or some other kind of bodily noise emanating from the zigzag line, I wondered if this were commonplace every Sunday. Not the teenage antics, but the preparation for Mass as it was intense. There was an order to doing this. Everyone knew his place. In their finest regalia, the Robes to our backs were contemplative and pensive. The altar boys in front of them were adjusting their cassocks while a couple hundred of us were anything but prayerful.

Oh, and there was Brody. He was at the rear of the line flicking earlobes of unsuspecting boys. Maybe others did similar things, but this turd stood out.

*****

Tradition was pivotal at St. Augustine's because the Robes consciously embedded fragments of the past into all they did. Now, when I think about it, everything is so sketchy. With every passing year, I lose more of these vestiges or, perhaps, I have misplaced them. That's fine by me, as it is now clutter causing me to stumble occasionally.

What was clear to me, however, was that those conventions passed on to the next generation of the St. Augustine *man* were significant to the Robes and countless self-respecting alumni. Meaningless to me, this was just the way it was.

Alumni told students during every Homecoming weekend how wonderful the place was because of tradition. Their proclamation always came with a caveat, and that was that the school was at its pinnacle when *they* wore the navy and khaki no matter if they graduated in 1930, 1947, 1962, or any other year. How could that be? There's no good answer for that, but I was sure it was the fodder for good old rallying cries during Homecoming. They all swore that St. Augustine's was *what it is* because of our traditions. These traditions, I gleaned, were like a drug that they all inhaled...and no one seemed to want to define *what it is* that made St. Augustine stand out.

The Robes required all students to attend Mass although many were not Catholic. I grew up Catholic but never paid attention to it. We rarely went to church. Here at St. Gus' what generations of monks and students did in the church, whether you knew what was going on or not, were morsels of an ancient tradition that they acted out solemnly. Knowing this, I figured, it was going to be a long year. They venerated the fear of God, so to speak. That was the Robes' number one concern in those days to a fault. It didn't matter so much about any anxieties or problems we might be experiencing.

Catholic prep schools did not hold the position in society enjoyed by other similar Protestant schools, and I suspect that was so because those other schools were drenched in money. Although the coffers were full, the Robes took a vow of poverty which means whatever they possessed they shared among their brotherhood. Could that be socialism? That was a different message than some other schools articulated, as they focused on acquiring—not sharing. Could that be capitalism? Whatever the label was, it was meaningless in the greater scheme of things.

The good monks did without but lived based on their values and not on their purses. In a way, Catholic schools boasted only what they were—nothing more but sometimes less. Prestige and social placement were unimportant, so they touted. Catholic Schools, like St. Gus' painstakingly went beyond sensible limits to inform others of its *Catholicness*. Here, going to Mass, prayers before class, and other observances were the way.

To be fair, despite the rigid exterior, the environment at the school was warm and inviting—if you were Catholic or not, it didn't matter. The Robes aspired to treat everyone the same—for the most part, they tried to steer away from having favorites, but they were human too. The environment was full of contradictions.

*****

"So does this all happen every Sunday?"

"Well, yeah. This is how we do it. What do you expect?" Aiden answered, shrugging his shoulders.

The Church portal finally opened. Seniors led two lines of students through the proscenium. The sunlight transformed into chilly drafts as we crossed the threshold, and the place smelled like the Byzantine exhibit at the Metropolitan Museum of Art. As we paraded in, I heard one voice coming from many singing Beethoven's 9th Symphony, Ode to Joy.

> Joyful, joyful, we adore Thee,
> God of glory, Lord of love;
> Hearts unfold like flow'rs before Thee,
> Op'ning to the sun above.
> Melt the clouds of sin and sadness;

> Drive the dark of doubt away;
> Giver of immortal gladness,
> Fill us with the light of day! ...

The beauty of the sound was like none other I had ever heard. The pipes blended with an array of masculine tones both old but mostly young. A clarity and consonance engulfed the structure as oneness emanated from the loft overhead and to the rear. I, of course, have kept this to myself, as boys aren't supposed to think this way.

> ...Field and forest, vale and mountain,
> Flow'ry meadow, flashing sea,
> Singing bird and flowing fountain
> Call us to rejoice in Thee....

We walked, slowly, toward the sanctuary. I wanted to look at who was singing, but I dared not. Robes frowned upon heads turning. As we filed in, I sensed the stagnant breath of the congregation on my neck. The temperature raised a degree with each step we took. Having good peripheral vision, I glanced slightly from side to side and saw throngs of townsfolk gazing at us. So early but the place was so full, I thought. With an immediate panic attack, I hoped my fly was up and nothing was hanging out of my nose. Didn't they have anything better to do than gawk at us as we paraded in?

> ... Thou our Father, Christ our Brother,
> All who live in love are Thine;
> Teach us how to love each other,
> Lift us to the joy divine...

The music merely underscored the magnificence of the Church. Like many thousands before me, the leather soles of our shoes polished the gleaming and uneven tiles below. On the other end, the eaves of the roof were nearly undetectable. The radiance from below dissipated as it climbed to the apex of the church's nearly invisible rafters.

To the walls to each side were scores of windows, one after the other, and all reaching to the ceiling. Sapphire, rich purples, and reds stained the asymmetrical panes that, together, begot biblical spectacles. We slowed our snail pace even more and peeled off into our pews. We always sat in the pews upfront, and the community sat behind us.

> ... Mortals, join the happy chorus,
> Which the morning stars began;
> Father love is reigning o'er us,
> Brother love binds man to man...

The immensity of the church was unbelievable, and its splendor amazed me. The altar was pure and white. The candles and all the lighting were simple. Real in many ways, a plaster molded six-foot Christ, was hanging from a cross. Eerie, but thought wrenching, this display captured my attention. I didn't like it at first but dismissed this from my thinking as quickly as I could. Who knows what the consequences might be of such thinking? As I stared at what was before me, I pulled down the kneeler with an unexpected thud noticed only by my classmates. As my face turned red, we kneeled, made the sign of the cross, and prayed.

> ...Ever singing, march we onward,
> Victors in the midst of strife,
> Joyful music leads us Sunward
> In the triumph song of life.

"This—this whole thing is what they live for," Aiden whispered with a grin. "I, for one, dig Beethoven's 9th."

Without punctuation, a different, unknown, and nondescript hymn began as the monks shuffled up the aisle. They adorned themselves in white drapes with colorful stoles bearing symbols from one end to the other. Most monks had silky white hair, if they had any at all, and peered down their noses to their hymnals lip-synching the words. The real singers were in the choir loft.

Directly behind the troupe were the altar boys and the Abbot. He was tall and walked with the ancestral staff. He looked like a high rolling shepherd. He gazed out upon the flock with the faintest smile.

Like he was right out of central casting, he would make a good Pope for a movie—these were my youthful thoughts at the time.

With a torturous pace, the monks gathered around the altar while Abbot Edgar took center stage. Soon everyone was in place and Mass began. Not coming from an especially religious home, I thought that this must be a High Mass. Today, incense and chanting throughout were the norms. They seemed to carry it a bit too far as the sweet vapor got to me in a hurry. I decided I could do without it. Nevertheless, they pulled out all the stops as this was the official opening Mass for the school year.

When it was time for the homily, Abbot Edgar approached the stairs to the ominous pulpit and looked to its summit. Unhurried, he climbed each step—one, two, three... Once there, he began to fumble with papers. It was quiet except for a cough here and there. He looked out to the congregation, and then up to the choir loft. He then looked down to us directly in front of him. He began to speak soberly of St. Augustine as he did every year on this particular Sunday.

"Everything is good. Everything is pure and chaste—EVERYTHING. How can this be true, you may ask yourself when we see carnage and destruction on the six o'clock news. When we collect coins for starving children...when we feel betrayal from someone, we thought was different? St. Augustine's inspired words tell us that we should aspire to believe that the reason and origin of all we know and do not know is the work of our Creator—the only true God. Therefore, we must trust in God.

Furthermore, we all come from our triune God and, therefore, MUST be good, pure, and chaste. Simple as that! Now, being created good does not mean created the same. St. Augustine called this a universe of admirable beauty. Beauty is found in everyone and in every particle and fiber in us. Although we are good, it is not so easy to stay that way. IT IS the *deprivation* of good that allows evil into our lives. We have choices to make.

Think of disease...it may contaminate you or me, but sickness isn't you and it isn't me. When we are cured, the disease and its evil are vanquished. Evil is happenstance, it is misadventure and sometimes out of our control. Evil is ALWAYS lurking by, but it is not you, my boys. We must remember, though, it is in our choices that we make that enable us to stay healthy and be resilient to what is evil. Good can only come from good and every being in a diseased state retains the essence of their origin—they are *always* good.

As a word of caution, just as the same good soil may produce the fleeting beauty of a flower, it may also be the foundation for the misplaced beauty of a poisonous plant. So, you must know what is inside of you—listen to what is in your heart. Do it now. Now's the time. If not this moment—when?"

What happened next took me by surprise. To this day, I do not know what it was. Within the recesses of my brain, something aroused an untouched connection. I felt the leap of a synapse or something. At the time, I didn't think it through, but I knew the sensation was honest. What the Abbot said has always stuck with me. His words attached themselves to me, and I don't know why. His oratory style was awakening and would never have imagined this coming from him. Perhaps, being close enough to see into his eyes at his heart or soul… or something. It was a strange but good vibe.

Although he mesmerized me, I could not help noticing that only a few boys listened to his message. They were staring into space, nodding off, or rolling their eyes. Maybe, I was just weird. Thinking more, so much came together. Could it have been the newness of the experience? Maybe it was how the Abbot talked to us—as if I was the only one there. I felt alone although I sat with hundreds of people.

During my senior year, I was taking baby steps that led me to places that only began that year. So much was colliding within me in a brief space of time. It was not until years later that I understood the nuances of his sermon, but my interpretation stuck. Suffice it to say, I liked what I felt and heard that day, and that was, *I am good.*

SEVEN

Sunday Dinner, as the Robes called it, *always* concluded no later than one o'clock. Finished or not, we had to sit there until the final blessing. Afterward, the Robes would then cloister themselves in the monastery to pray—just to pray. Most of us decided that they would retreat to play cards, watch TV, or nap. If this were the case, more power to them. But *Hope and Prayer* was the motto of the Order, so they had to do their share of hoping and praying, I assume, to live up to why they exist. Reading the newspaper or watching television must have given them enough material for which to pray because they rarely left the grounds to see what was beyond the confines of St. Gus'. I was not so sure they had to go too far anyway. We gave them much to work with, as well. Hope, they would tell us, was the power behind each and every prayer. Hope, I'd have to agree, is a good place to start.

As for the students, little happened on campus on Sunday by design, and the Robes expected us to keep the day holy—whatever that meant. It was also the day that many boys enjoyed guests, mostly parents, who brought them goodies. Aiden and I were similar in one respect as neither of us ever expected visitors. Dad was always traveling and Aiden, well Aiden was on his own.

Not wanting to stay cooped up any longer, Aiden coaxed me to slip out of The Hurl before the final blessing. On a rare whim, I gave in, and we vanished without a trace. Having escaped before the others was as prized as a blue ribbon according to most. Once outside we bolted until we were well out of sight. As we slowed our pace, the sounds of our penny loafers on the gravel path created a cadence with each crunching step. It's funny what I remember.

About halfway back Aiden had already stripped his tie clear of his collar and held his blazer with his index finger as it floated over his right shoulder. He unbuttoned his sleeve cuffs, and they were flapping in the warm breezes. I, of course, looked about the same as I did when I walked through the church doors several hours earlier. This was typical of me when I was seventeen.

"It's time to redeem your rain check. Get some shorts on and let's head on down to the river. We'll go to the part that's off-limits. Few dare to go there, but that adds to its mystique," Aiden confessed as he wiggled his fingers in the air.

"No—can't. Got things to do. Plus, we need to keep the day holy."

"Right. You and me both. That's a joke."

"Well, I haven't been to one class yet so I'm so behind. Gotta paper due tomorrow from what I was told."

"Blah-blah-blah...Look, it's hot as Hell right now and you've got tonight to write that paper. Anyway, you're the new kid and they'll cut you some slack. Besides, you told me yesterday that you'd take a rain check, well?"

"Hmmm. What's there? I mean, why go there? If no one's supposed to go, it sounds, well dangerous."

"Wimp...I knew I shouldn't have told you that it's off-limits. Look, it's just a hunk of rock, say about two stories high, and below the water is a cool fifteen feet deep. It's not *really* dangerous. The part of the river I'm talking about is calm with no current, but it's like no other place I've been."

"Why go there? There's a pool on campus."

"Oh my God! Did you just hear me? How about we hoof it down there, and you can see for yourself? You can make up your own mind."

Worried he would label me a wimp forever, and as the piercing rays beamed on my forehead, it did not take too much persuasion for me to concede. Undertaking the unfamiliar was atypical for me, but then again, I told him less than twenty-four hours ago that I'd go. Now I could check this off my list—doesn't mean I have to go back.

"All right. What the hell." I was ready. My decision, with no warning, *did* make me feel rebellious. I kind of liked it. First, our vanishing act moments earlier at Sunday Dinner and now this. It was like an out-of-body experience. Was this, in fact, me?

"Excellent!"

"Yeah, like Abbot Edgar said, if not this moment, when?" I didn't know where that came from, but I guess there was no backing out now.

"Right! The moment is now. Totally Zen. That's what I'm talking about—let's get down there," Aiden said as his eyes brightened and gave me a grin.

We picked up our pace to the room, pulled off our Sunday uniform, and quickly replaced it with shorts and tee-shirts. We left our room within seconds of our arrival. Out the back door, we walked in the opposite direction of the main campus. I didn't know what came over me. A rush of excitement and a gush of elation emerged from somewhere inside and then burst upwards to the muscles of my face. I liked the fact that no one knew our plans. Welcoming what lay ahead was new and different for me. This wasn't the first time someone asked me to stray from my better judgment but, perhaps, the first time I actually did. The temptation of adventure gave me a high.

During our hike down some godforsaken path, I remember we conveyed much to each other without uttering words. We did not even have to look at each other as the energy was there and it was a creation of our own doing. Feeling this way was new. Was this part of being *totally Zen* like Aiden said? I was ready, now, to see what was out there. I, however, didn't want to get lost. Just then, Aiden looked at me and sped off. I chased him and caught up with him.

"What are you trying to do? I mean I don't know where the hell I'm going," I said slightly winded.

"Lighten up…that's all I got to say."

As we traveled further into the woods, I would tell myself that Aiden knew where he was going. He had been this way countless times. But to me, all was fresh and raw. Before I knew it, we were on a different but well-trod path. The route turned out to be rockier as we went along and led us uphill, but I immediately readjusted. As we climbed, the path narrowed and to one side was a slippery edge. We turned sideways and I pressed my body against the rocky cliff wall.

"Here, take, my hand. It's okay," he offered.

Catching me off guard, I looked him in the eye and said, "I'm fine—keep walking."

"Eli, it's okay to grab my hand. You don't look sure-footed," Aiden said in a low tone.

So, I did. He smiled at me, and I felt my shakiness melt.

"Eli, don't worry—you're gonna be okay."

The thicker the woods grew around me the dangers seemed real, but the more I trusted him. I had to. The path, then, led us away from that terrifying edge and opened up. Aiden's advance slowed, and he turned to me.

"Shhh. It's right over there," Aiden squatted and pointed to the green blur of the woods.

"What? Why are you shushing me?" My heart raced.

"Keep it down."

"Okay," I whispered and crouched down beside him. I looked at him as he peered into the woods. Then I looked at the woods—and back at him. I mentally shook my head as I saw nothing. I've seen trees before, and these trees were like any others I've seen. One tree was identical to the next, but they all blurred and appeared endless. Sure, communing with nature on an August afternoon was cool and new to me, but for the life of me, I didn't know why he *shushed* me. It wasn't as if I talked over the most important line in *The Godfather*. Then, Aiden stopped in his footprints, and it startled me. Not paying attention, I bumped into him. Tense, I backed off to one side and spun my head around like an owl. My pupils enlarged tenfold to take in as much as I could.

"What…what?" I asked with shortened breaths.

Aiden with a bold whisper spoke. "Keep it down."

"Okay, okay. What am I missing?"

"Did you see that?" Aiden asked as his eyes widened.

"What? Is someone following us?" Like a cat, I froze and then looked from side to side.

"No, no. Right there," he pointed.

"What…what?"

"A bald eagle just flew over that hill. He was beyond cool. Shame they are endangered. We don't even take care of our symbol of freedom." He said sighing.

"Is that what you were looking at? I didn't see him."

"He was a big one—huge wingspan," Aiden said stretching out his arms.

We continued our trek down a meandering path. All was quiet

except for the rustling of the formidable evergreens, the faint murmur of the distant river, and other indiscernible sounds of the wood. Leaves gracefully flipped to show their muted underside as a gust of wind whipped through higher elevations of the trees. Cicadas chattered and tittered intermittently only to remind me that summer pests were closing in on us. Walking farther along, Aiden grabbed my shirt below the ring of my neck. I can't say I appreciated this sudden disturbance.

"Stay still. Look right over there past the dogwood tree and you'll see something pretty amazing."

Aiden leaned forward with a kind of bow and aimed his index finger. I looked and saw nothing—again. First off, I didn't know what a Dogwood tree looked like, but replied nevertheless, with a lie. I was pissed that I didn't see anything and then lied about it. There's something about me that tries to please and avoid being judged at the same time. That was me—always fearful of what others might think of me even if it was about a moment like this. I just gawked ahead, bug-eyed, and hoped he would yield me a clue of some kind so I wouldn't, again, look like an idiot. A second later, he spelled it out for me.

"That's a mama cardinal and right beneath her are two babies. To her right, you'll see the third coming out of its shell. The daddy is the one that is blazing red on the branch above. His bright color is a way to keep the focus of predators away from the future."

"Oh yeah…I was just going to say that…pretty cool, huh?

"Uh-huh," he looked at me with a half-smile.

It was then that colors formed shapes and the shapes created definition. I missed it moments earlier though my eyes were pointed in the right direction. I said I saw it, though it didn't register with me at all. But when all in front began to take form, I understood just what was clearly there. They *were* beautiful.

I've seen birds before, some far prettier, but this moment was unique. They were singing to each other as if to celebrate new life. They spoke to each other in a way that we will never understand. There's so much we don't understand, and that *is* clear. All around us stood still as we savored a moment that nature has repeated since the beginning of time but becomes more significant with each new generation. Nature, in a short time, would separate these five fragile lives for their inevitable and singular passage through life. I don't know what mystified me more, catching a glimpse of these fragile lives or capturing Aiden in this new light.

In retrospect, it had nothing to do with the birds but all to do with Aiden—and me. Aiden unfolded to me a part of himself that caused me to unfold a part of myself. His passion was so unexpected. Like an artist's palette that's full of colors, they remain uncelebrated until the brush strays from one hue to another creating something new. My joy was that *something new*. Fleeting as it was, it was a discovery that is tattooed on my soul.

Aiden spoke up. "I'm sorry, man. I don't know what came over me but seeing what we did is so rare. I mean to see what we saw at that moment—eggs in a nest are one thing, or some baby birds feeding is another, but when babies take their first breath and become part of the world, that's it. It's a defining moment. Life will never be the same and somehow we are better for it—I'm not exactly sure why, but we are."

"I know what you mean, it was awesome," I said meaning every word, but somehow it came out with a bit less intensity than Aiden.

Only a moment later we hoofed farther into the dense brush. The meandering and narrow footpaths brought us to jagged limestone cliffs high over our heads. Using my hand to shade my eyes, I looked to its summit. The cliffs were daunting, to say the least. Aiden beamed as he began to climb to the pinnacle of this wall of irregular stone. Feet planted, I was stunned as I didn't bargain for a rock climb today, but I watched as he scaled the bastion.

When he reached the peak, he called down to me. With sudden audacity as if possessed, I began my climb. Steadfast, I concentrated on each foothold. With streams of sweat running down my face, I grasped each cranny as if it was my last. I was driven by some internal force—had to be. Fatigued, about two-thirds of the way up, I was slowing down. I managed to crook my neck around and looked up to him. He was perched on a knob with his shirt and shoes already off, cheering me on as I struggled.

"I'm waiting for you, and we can dive together. You're doing great. You'll see; the climb will be worth it. I mean the view is spectacular and the dive is surreal."

I knew I was not going to do any diving from a bunch of rocks today, but I just nodded and worked myself up the barrier. I hoped

Aiden would forget that thought as he watched me wrestle with the protruding rock. When I finally reached Aiden, I doubled over. I don't know which hurt more, my hands or my lungs as I tried to catch my breath.

"Look, here's what I was talking about. This is it, the river. Next to it is *the spot*," he said pointing.

I pulled myself together and stood up. The splendor of everything between the horizon and me slapped me squarely in the face. Rising from the glimmering water below, the sculpted stones emerged like a shrine. The mountain range framed the scene, and it all just blew me away. My mouth hung open; I was speechless. I've seen trees, birds, water, and mountains before. I've been hot, sweaty, and dirty with bugs dining on my skin before, but this was different. This was all so different from what I expected. Why I cannot say. This was a time when an experience was indescribable and better left that way. Aiden said little more as I know he reveled in this moment as did I.

Gone in a heartbeat, the moment ended as he looked at me and asked if I were ready to dive. I was on the diving team a summer ago, but this was not my water. Pretty and sparkling, it was, but clear and chlorine-filled, it was not. This was not what I had in mind. Anything but embarrassed this time, I was ready to stand my ground if pressed.

"What do you mean? Come on, let's stick it."

Now I was growing self-conscious and couldn't focus. Because of my own discomfort, I began to stammer and stutter.

"I, I've never done this before... I'll pass this time, but you go ahead."

Immediately he sensed my trepidation and wanted to make me feel comfortable.

"I'll tell ya what. Let's climb down, say, about twenty feet and do it. It's a different story from there," Aiden said as he pointed to another landing. "C'mon...like *Butch Cassidy and the Sundance Kid*. You know we'll do it together. You saw the flick, right? We won't dive. We'll jump. We'll make believe we have no choice and it's the only way out. You still have an imagination, don't you? What do you say?"

"Okay. If you want to, let's go," I said with a great deal of reluctance. Yeah, I stood my ground.

We climbed down to the other landing and before I could give it another second of thought, he grabbed my hand.

"S-H-I-T," we said in unison as we launched ourselves.

Airborne, I saw colors and light. Euphoria filled my mind for what seemed like ten times longer than the two seconds it took us to disturb the face of the river. We plunged about fifteen feet below into crisp, cold water. Invading feet first in the water, my skin suddenly tingled, and it was exhilarating. Getting below the skin, this abrupt submersion cleansed a part of me that I didn't know needed cleaning. Upon entering, not touching anything but dark bubbly water, a soothing hush engulfed me.

Tranquility.

We sprang from the water, one after the other with our faces only inches apart. Like I learned the secret of life, a huge smile overtook my face as the endless circles we made in the water drifted away. Looking from side to side, I noticed that this part of the river was more like a cove or inlet and many tributaries branched out taking bits of this mojo somewhere else. Checking out the hunk of rock we jumped from, it seemed a mile high from where we were now treading water. Aiden began to motion and swim to one side of the cove. I followed and up ahead I saw a tower of rock covered with moss, vines, and branches that lent an air of secrecy. I thought that this must *the spot*. It was an entrance to a cave.

"Hey, over here. Let me show you a place that most have only heard about, but few have been."

"Cool, yeah I'm right behind you," I shouted. "Hope it lives up to your hype.

Passing through the large oval threshold, the sounds of the river and all outside were instantly muffled. The sun showed through the portal just enough allowing for our eyes to adjust to the sudden change but giving us plenty of light to navigate with ease. A coolness surrounded us, and goosebumps took over my wet arms and legs. Couldn't help but notice a certain smell to the place that was like no other. Maybe it was a faint mix of honeysuckle and mud, but whatever it was, it was new and pleasing. Avoiding a few embedded stones along the short narrow passage, we made our way to a room larger than my new home at the dorm.

"Well? What do you think?"

"I've got to hand it to you Aiden—I'm blown away."

"See, I thought you'd like it down here," Aiden said sitting on a slab of limestone. I joined him and laid back on the smooth surface just catching my breath and chilling out. A time or two, we'd glance at each other and just chuckle. A waft of air would occasionally rush by from an undetected direction giving us a shiver, but what a welcome relief from the heat outside. Looking over to Aiden, he looked like a vampire as his bangs came to a point on his forehead.

"Hey, I like your hairdo, Count Dracula. So, is this cave your usual *hang* out?" I chuckled.

"Yeah. Glad you like it—my *do*. Thinking about keeping it," he said plastering down the sides of his hair to match the look.

We were both dripping and cold. Hearing my teeth clank together, he turned to grab a towel that had been drying over a rock and threw it my way. Stiff as it was, I wrapped it around my shoulders. Not clean, but dry, it did the trick. He grabbed another towel and he wrapped it around his waist.

"You mind if I take a look around?"

"Please do."

Aiden had a few belongings ornamenting the cave. Wooden placards inscribed with old Coca-Cola ads and other signs with unintelligible words and faded colors made up some. He had one stiff leather hat, some brown bottles, and the jagged triangular-shaped piece of the bow of a dinghy. Polishing off the place were other items that he collected from the area. Commanding my attention, though, was a ledge that precariously balanced five radiantly colored canvases—all of which were of distinct scenes.

Folding my arms in front of me, I began to speak as if I were admiring his Manhattan loft.

"You know, I like your stuff. This is an awesome place."

"Yeah, it is. I love coming here to just veg out. Yep, this is *the spot*. Hey, you want a beer. I've got some Rolling Rocks right here in this cooler."

"What? Ah…sure, I'd love one. Drink them all the time…so this is *the spot*?" I blurted out before I knew what I was saying.

"I keep a stash here. It stays cool, not cold, but cool."

We sat in our towels, beer in hand as if we were at a spa at a hot springs resort. He was quite generous with his stow and we downed a few before I knew it. It wasn't long before the effects of the beers made themselves known—I was buzzed. The feeling, though, didn't just come from the beer. The whole adventure placed me in another state of mind. The sun, the climb, and the plunge added to my intoxication.

"Is this your first time?"

"My first time? What do you mean?"

"The beer…it's your first—and second, isn't it?"

"No way…Nope…"

"Eli…it's me you're talking to."

"Well, yeah—um, it is."

"Thought so. I bet you've never been with a girl."

"What! It's none of your business." I shook my head, stood up, paced in the small confines, and ended up right where I originally sat.

"Yep, you just answered my question," Aiden said with a smile.

He reached out with his beer bottle in hand, clanked mine, and laughed. I couldn't help but join in.

"I know you like the back of my hand," Aiden added.

"Yeah, right. You don't know me at all."

Dismissing what I said he continued, "So—did the good padre put you up to this, Eli?"

"What? No way. What are you talking about?"

"C'mon Eli, you can let me in on your little secret. Father and I go way back. I know his intentions are good as gold."

"Well, yeah he did, but he didn't really sell me on the idea. I wanted to see what you've been babbling about anyway. *The Spot,* the river, the woods, the mountains…wanted to see for myself."

Aiden shook his head, rolled his eyes, and said, "You're a good man Eli, I can tell. It doesn't matter how you got here. It matters that you're here."

"Well, I'm here," I said with little thought.

"Okay then, let's down these suckers. I've got another one with your name on it."

Idle time gave way as we lazed on the rocks. Not too coherent, I noticed my eyelids become heavy and they closed. Anecdotal remarks from both of us dotted our time. Sometimes what we said made little sense but we both seemed to know the meanings that lay beyond the words. Out of the blue, our words, gestures, and expressions began to connect. Aiden pulled his thoughts together first.

"Yeah, this is *the spot.* You know what I mean. All is exactly right—right now. No one needs to define this feeling—this moment. This point in time is a moment of…well, truth—of awareness. It seems so apparent, but unexplainable."

"Have you been smoking weed?"

"No doobies for me—not into that scene. Anyway, what was I saying before I was so rudely interrupted? Oh yeah…awareness. Awareness. It's as if I know exactly, what's going on and what I'm thinking and feeling. It's all mixing together. When it's time to begin talking about it, though, the moment is gone so I can't share the feeling. It stays personal. It's mine and only mine forever."

Aiden paused and reached for a beer and offered me one. I declined. Just when I thought he was finished orating, he continued.

"You know all the great men *and* women of history had these moments, but they knew how to do something about them. When the apple conked Newton on the head or when Marie Curie isolated radium… when Jesus knew it was time to make wine in Canaan, it was one of those moments of no going back. Just think of the moment that Sojourner Truth decided it was time to speak out risking her safety, or Anne Frank, brave as she was, she wrote to all of us and became the face of millions. Hell, when da Vinci took his last brushstroke on the Mona Lisa, it was one of those moments that live forever. Those moments made the difference."

"Yeah, it took da Vinci something like fifteen years to finish the Mona Lisa. I don't think he quite ever finished it," I said.

"Ah, yeah, maybe. I'm not so sure you're getting what I mean…and whether he finished it or not, there was one brushstroke that was his last."

"Oh, yeah…yeah. Yes, that's right."

"Inspiration is not a thing, and you cannot touch it. It's invisible but they just knew they had it. How about when Edison finally burned the first light bulb? He went through something like a thousand different filaments. The thousand and one was it. The time was right for light, so to speak."

"Funny…very funny Aiden."

"Never before or never after was the time right to do what they ended up doing. Their past helped them to get to a certain point, and the future didn't matter. The moment they nabbed in the present made the difference for the future."

Whether he was finished or not I jumped into the conversation. "Come on. So, you're trying to tell me that flinging ourselves into a river, hanging out in a cave—*the spot*—with a beer is some kind of moment of awareness, of, *of enlightenment?*"

"Yeah, I would say so."

"What?"

"Whatever it takes. But Eli, you don't get it. See you just described the scene—it's not the scene it's the subtext."

"Subtext?"

"Yeah. Let me put it to you this way. Humans are doers, but it is why we *do* things, beyond a doubt, that counts. It's not the deed, it's why the deed. Taking action is meaningless unless there's something behind it." Aiden stood up and walked over to me, squatted down, and looked directly into my eyes. I squirmed some.

"Our past got us to this point in time—our future doesn't matter—maybe even non-existent. Right now, this moment will lead us to our future. We can't get there without this step. And I think it should be a good one. No, a GREAT one."

I shrugged my shoulders and gave him a lopsided smile. Aiden stood and walked back to where he was sitting.

"Don't be so cerebral. We're just a couple of guys hanging out."

"Whatever man. I can see you're not ready for this," he said as he examined his dirty fingernails.

We sat in uncomfortable silence for a few minutes while we both took swigs of beer. I walked over to his paintings and picked one up off the ledge.

"Tell me about these…what's this all about? I mean these paintings?"

"Good one. I know you just want to change the subject."

"Well, yeah. Can you blame me?" He laughed and I joined him.

"Okay, okay. I write, so I keep a journal. I paint too. This, with music and other things, make me—us human. At least that's what I think. I'm inspired when I come here. Sorry—hope I'm not being too *cerebral* again."

"Okay, okay. I got it now. So…tell me about your music."

"No, no. I was just telling you what made us human. You would think I was a liar if you heard me sing or play an instrument."

"Yeah, me too. So Aiden, what do you mean when you say this place *inspires* you?"

Aiden walked over to me and took the painting out of my hands, looked at it up and down, and gave me a half-smile.

"I tell you what literally gives me an awesome high is when I take that jump or if I'm really into it, that dive. In that split second from when I launch myself to when I touch the water, a hundred things go through my mind—at least a hundred. They are my thoughts and mine only. Then, I hit the water and I get such a rush. When I come up for air, all the thoughts bend into one single thought." Aiden said and turned to me with such intensity in his eyes and he continued. "Just like today, I caught a glimpse of what my next painting might be—it's just a good feeling."

"Wow, man, you sound like you're on some good drugs— kidding—kidding," I said playfully.

"Yeah, yeah, yeah. You know you're a really funny guy. Some might even say you're a comedian. I guess most lawyer wannabes are funny dudes."

Was it me saying what I just heard? Suddenly I felt flush. What was coming out of my mouth? I could not believe my words. I was beginning to understand what Aiden was getting at and knew what he was saying, but my mind seemed to detach from my vocal cords.

I wanted to say so much more but could not figure out how to do it and do it well. My famed self-control was more like self-paralysis. He confided in me. After all, he had never shared *the spot*, or anything out here with anyone and my silly-ass response was lifeless and narrow. I wanted to tell him that I agreed with him. I wanted to tell him that this moment brought a feeling that all was right—*just right*. It was intense and real and maybe it was what others look for—those moments of meaning. I can articulate this now, but at seventeen, I floundered. So, I had to refocus.

"When you take that dive, do you usually dive from the top?"

"Nope. Always about where you and I jumped from today. I've never dived or jumped from the top."

My back stiffened and my eyebrows almost touched. "Wait a minute! You wanted me to take that leap and it's my first time here? I mean you've been coming here a long time and you expected me to do what you haven't done yourself?"

Aiden stayed very calm.

"Just a minute. I wasn't going to make you do anything you didn't want to do. Hey, I thought if you said yes, well then, I'd get enough courage to do it too. Hey, no one's perfect. I just look for the perfect moment, not the perfect person, and that includes when I'm looking at myself."

This was a rare time Aiden's vulnerability showed through to me. As for me, mine are on constant display. More than that, I was surprised that he looked at me as a trailblazer as I was only looking to follow.

"One day I'll go for it, and I'll make that dive and see if it is any different higher up. Maybe it won't be, and I won't feel that spark that day, but I'll stick it. I'll nail the landing and that's all I'll need."

"Aiden, man I'll tell you. You're like that Bald Eagle we—*you* saw earlier today."

"Oh?"

"You're a frickin' endangered species."

EIGHT

Ahandwritten sign thumbtacked on the door of Mr. McKilty's English Lit class read:

UNDER NEW MANAGEMENT. SIT IN A DIFFERENT SEAT—IT'S A NEW DAY.

Gathering around the sign, my puzzled classmates and I just looked at each other as some shrugged their shoulders. It must have been a month or so into the semester, but this hour stood out. Walking in as others followed, we were in for a surprise. Aiden and Vandy took this class with me but so did the likes of Luis and Brody, so I never knew what to expect even on a good day.

Typically, Mr. McKilty arranged the desks in his room in a semicircle of fifteen desks knowing very well his classroom had many windows with vivid and magnificent views of the mountain range. He wanted to prevent us from gazing to the horizon and daydreaming. This arrangement was Mr. McKilty's attempt to focus our attention away from outward muses to those inward and to the lesson he planned for the period. Today, however, started out with another twist. The desks were now in three neat rows of five like every other classroom in the building.

*****

Obviously, no benefactor gave funds to refurbish classrooms at St. Gus'. To offset the battered walls, McKilty covered them with colorful posters. Some were classic renditions of known artists, but many were wild and abstract bordering on psychedelic art by little-known 1960s painters and photographers.

Painfully new was the huge bookcase that was teeming with volumes. On some *special* days, he would select a thick tome with brittle yellowed pages for us to read a section aloud and pass it along. Seemingly written in English centuries ago, it was difficult for us to interpret but it did provide some levity during the hour, and that he cheerfully allowed.

When we entered Mr. McKilty's classroom it was commonplace for unfamiliar music to bellow from his stereo. At times, the window shades were completely pulled down, and already in progress, a foreign film beamed against one of the cracked walls. He would stop the film at some curious point and ask us to write, always in fifty words but no more, what we thought could or should follow the scene in question. He would chat, nonstop, to us while we attempted our stint as screenwriters. His energy was amazing and contagious whether we were open to it or not.

*****

Despite all we knew, today would be different. I wasn't the only one, but we all felt a sense of ambush. I could tell this by the sighs and moans that hit the stagnant air from my many classmates as they scurried to find a *different* seat. The sentiment running through our minds of knowing what was once good was now gone, was troubling. Mr. McKilty's room was now like every other classroom. Like it or not we had grown accustomed to where we were sitting, but now we were aimless. What did he mean—*under new management?*

For some unknown reason, I followed the lead of the likes of Luis and others. Everyone viewed the seats in the rear of the classroom as primo seating and rushed to them nearly knocking each other over. Aiden watched everyone scurrying to place and decided to take one of the last seats available, which were upfront. With a goofy grin, he rolled his eyes and shook his head before he sat.

After a minute or two and to our surprise, Father Meinrad then entered from a second door that was in the rear of the classroom. The buzz in the room abruptly died. The good Father began to give us a half chuckle as he strode up the middle aisle. His robe seemed to flow like a superhero's cape as he made his way to the front of the room. He spun around and scanned the classroom.

"Let me tell you what I saw. Twelve of you filed through the door, looked around, and answered the situation given you with no thought to guide you. You reacted like hyenas, and you moved in the direction of seemingly fewest obstacles. Perceived at what you thought was the desired place in the pack all scampered to find your rightful place. The alpha dog led the pack," Father then looked at Luis.

Half of us heard what he was saying as the other half looked around in a stupor. *What was going on?* This question, for sure, was rocketing through everyone's mind.

"Oh, I bet you're wondering about Mr. McKilty."

Everyone looked to Father and nodded in silence.

"I will be taking over his Senior Lit class—well all of his classes for that matter."

Brody placed his hands on either side of his cheeks with his mouth wide open not even trying to hide his insincerity. "Uh-oh. Is he okay?"

"Yes Brody. He is fine but has taken a leave of absence to care for his ill mother," Father said dismissing his antics.

It was now morbidly quiet, and Father walked to the side of the room and in front of one of the large open windows. He folded his arms and surveyed the landscape.

"But enough from me—what was *your* perception when you entered the room?" Father asked as he pivoted on his heel with ease and looked in the eyes of a few of the boys. No hands went up. The moment lingered. We were going to sit there until someone raised their hand. Luis' hand slowly pointed up.

"Ah, Luis—the alpha dog himself. What do you have to say?"

Luis grinned. "I kinda like that—me the alpha dog."

Everyone, except for Father, burst into uproarious laughter. Not the kind of good-hearted laughter one would hope for, but a condescending one that Luis overlooked.

"Don't get used to the alpha dog thing, Luis—you're still Orca to us," said Brody, which ignited even more cackling laughter.

Taking a deep breath, Father Meinrad then chimed in and said, "Boys, boys—that's quite enough." Automatically the room fell silent. "Let's hear what Luis has to say. Go ahead…go ahead, Luis."

"It's like this—whoever strikes first gets the prize. You know you snooze, you lose. Sitting in the back is prime seating. *It's as easy as that*...ah, no offense Father."

By this time Father had meandered to where Luis was sitting and with a friendly smile, he patted him on the shoulder.

"No offense taken—I appreciate your bold honesty. I think what Luis is saying is that to the victor go the spoils. Isn't that about right Luis?"

"Ah yeah, Father, I mean *yes* Father, that's what I am saying. I couldn't have said it better."

The room exploded with more laughter. I shook my head and kept from joining in. I kept my head down and looked at my notebook hoping to be invisible.

"QUIET," Father said raising his volume only slightly as if he was singing. He was never loud. "Let's remember to be respectful...let me hear from others. Ah, Eli. You should know by now that looking down at your desk acts as a magnet from teacher to student. Give it to me. What do you think?"

Gathering inspiration, I cleared my throat and suddenly genius struck me like Hank Aaron's Louisville Slugger pounding a low inside pitch.

"Well—okay. Man is...well, man is, most times like an animal. Winning at any cost, he overpowers a weaker foe—to survive. See, the way I look at it, they don't reason or make decisions based on what's going on in their brains, but make decisions based only on instincts. We did the same thing—we acted on impulse."

I felt pretty good about my contribution to the discussion. Most of the guys were nodding with approval. But then Father Meinrad swooped in.

"Well said, my boy. I believe you are referring to the herd mentality. Luis looked at the situation as a chance to be victorious and to strike first to gain status. Luis raced to what was most perceived to be the best seat in the house."

"Yes, I did Father." More laughter filled the room until Father raised his index finger as if to determine the direction of the nonexistent wind.

"Eli, however, took us to a different level of thinking. He brought us more to the core of who we are as humans and, I might add, humans are very much a part of the animal kingdom. Wouldn't you say Eli?"

"Well, yes Father that sounds about right."

"Eli, please say so if I am not characterizing you correctly, but you said that we are like animals most times. This must mean that during brief times, man is something else. But what?"

I shook my head as I drew a blank.

"This other place gives us a choice to respond to stimuli in different ways. We decide either to control it or have it control us. Options for us surface as they always do—but we have choices. Eli has said that it is our intellect that should decide our next move. Others? Please jump in."

Perhaps I was stretching it a bit, but I had more to say so I raised my hand.

"I think man uses his instincts far more than his intellect. If man used his brain, we would prevent a lot of death and destruction that we see every night on TV. You know the whole Vietnam War."

Father paused. "Okay, Eli. Don't you think it is more than our intellect that will save us? Our intellect may have even gotten us into that mess. We must, I believe, see life from many perspectives and not only from an intellectual perspective—saying that, but we must also see it from more than just instinctual one too. We must dig deeper in ourselves, and we will find more. We should *be* more."

I now felt like crawling in the desk. Father released me from his stare and began to walk to the rear of the classroom and as he did everyone's head turned to him in unison. He, again, looked out the large window. It was unusually quiet. All I could hear was the air I inhaled.

Brody broke the silence. "I want to know why you felt it was okay to watch us in secret."

No one moved. Father continued his gaze to the mountains.

"Your conscience watches you in secret as well. Hmmm. Have you ever heard of karma? Don't answer—let's leave it at that," Father said in almost a whisper.

Brody said nothing. Father just stared at the mountain ridge, took a breath, and turned to pan the classroom. Still, with a whisper, he said, "Everyone—close your eyes."

A collective sigh filled the room.

"Just do it. Close them. You too Brody—see if you can keep them closed without me *watching* you."

Most of us chuckled as did Father. Brody sulked.

"Good. Now keep them closed. Whatever is going on in your head is a different landscape than what we see with our eyes. They, of course, overlap. The slant has changed, and we begin, for example, to see not only the Renoir still life but also what's behind the fruit in the painting. Are you following me?"

I could hear Father's leather soles shuffle up the aisle in an uneven cadence. He continued.

"When we see from this vantage point, we are seeing with something that separates us from the beasts. We see life through our souls...ah, ah, Vandy keep them shut... Okay now, see boys, our souls always sing the beautiful songs and write the most provocative poetry. Souls paint the glorious sites and embrace what is right and pure. Our souls, most times, attempt to evade torment and the agony of worldly reality. When we feel this, we are in touch with something else. This very part, if you will, separates us from the beasts. I'm not talking about instincts. I'm not talking intellect. It is our evasive soul. It is unique. It endures. It is who we are."

"I thought this was literature class, not religion class," Brody blurted out.

"You are absolutely right, Brody. Thank you. I, however, am not talking about religion. I am talking specifically about literature. You are just not following me."

"Father, you were going to tell us something more about our soul—I think," said Luis.

"Thank you, Luis. Now, where was I? Oh yes...our soul is a gift that makes us human. Fortunate are those who experience their souls in this lifetime as it beckons us, but many seldom hear it. When we hear it, many seldom act. When we act, *others* seldom hear it in our words and actions. When this happens, we frequently retreat. How very sad. We become motionless and are stagnant, and our soul lies dormant."

"I'm not getting it," said Luis.

"Think of it this way, we don't care about Babe Ruth's strikeout stats but care about the number of balls he sent over the fence. If he withered with every whiff, Aaron would be chasing Roger Maris' record not the Babe's. Our challenge is to listen to our soul and to act even though no one may hear. Open your eyes. Thoughts?"

Without hesitation, Aiden abruptly called out.

"Now, I'm not trying to be disrespectful like some people," he said, taking a quick look at Brody. "But I think I know where you're going with all of this."

"Oh, you do, do you?"

"Sure. So, Robert Frost scribbled poetry about taking the road less traveled, and Tennessee Williams wrote about fragile lives in the Glass Menagerie. Well, and Mozart composed music never heard of before or since and Picasso's blue period captured his delusions—that kind of thing."

"Yes Aiden, you must have a point in there somewhere…"

"Exactly. They all followed what was in them. They knew themselves. Yeah, we can react *and live*, but *to live*, we need to do more and to be more."

"What *the* … Aiden, no one gets you man. What are you saying anyway?" Brody interrupted.

"Let him finish, Brody. Geez," Luis spoke up.

"Ouch," Vandy added as our classmates reacted with a chuckle.

Over the laughter, Aiden continued. "Father M. is right. If we dig deep, we can hear what our soul is saying, but if we want to react to the world, we can rely on instincts or even our superior intellect to carry us. But that's never enough. There are a lot of very smart crazies out in the world, and they all have a soul that they can't find, don't want to find, or don't even know they have one to begin with," Aiden said and turned and looked directly at Brody.

"Very funny Aiden," Brody sneered.

The room grew so quiet that I could hear a fly erratically zip by. In just above a whisper, Vandy spoke up, "Instinct—intellect—all that doesn't matter if the soul we all have is buried by me or someone buries

71

my soul for me. It's more than listening to it, it's freeing it. It's hard to do it alone. Sometimes we need to step up with others to free it and then, support it. That's what I'm talking about."

Father began to clap and the whole class joined in. "Well said Vandy—you carried it a bit farther than I had planned and glad you did." Father took a moment and then continued, "Boys, you have the capacity in you to learn, to reason, and to dream. You can look at life in ways no other creature has or ever will. In literature, we have only touched the veneer of our being which is full of passion, love, pain, and suffering. Literature, and all the arts, evoke the spark that begins our journey to be more human. What I mean is... our existence should be about stretching ourselves to reach our true selves."

Father walked to the back of the classroom to the window once more.

"Boys, join me around this window."

"Aw, do we have to?" seemed to bellow from most of the boys.

"Come on, get up and join me."

Everyone hopped up and gathered around Father. There was the usual amount of pushing and shoving. Brody purposely swaggered over and stood somewhat apart from us. Aiden squeezed through the crowd and somehow planted himself right next to me.

"From a jail cell for the insane, a man peered out between the bars of his cell. Stirred with emotion from the pit of his soul he created a beautiful work of art. Can anyone tell me who I am talking about?"

I looked from side to side and saw my classmates shrug their shoulders. Many turned and looked at Aiden, but Vandy spoke up.

"I think it was the guy who cut off his ear."

"Yes, Vandy. He was Vincent Van Gogh, and his work of art is called The Starry Night. Physically limited, he has captured the hearts and souls of millions for nearly a century."

In a moment of genius, Luis whispered so all could hear, "Gosh, being in jail and everything, do you think he may have been secretly watched?"

With that, the boys laughed as Brody rolled his eyes and stoically looked on. He actually cracked a smile.

Father began talking over the laughter. "You, my dear boys, are more than a few ounces of testosterone coursing through your body.

Competition, power, and winning at all costs are definitely part of the animal kingdom as well as ours. Particularly in males. But the conveyance of passion, the reflection of our soul, and the uniqueness of our spirit are ours if we want it and don't bury it. Again, in particular in males. Be more...be *more*.

"How? I mean, it seems like all we ever hear is the importance of winning," Brody said in an unfamiliarly hushed tone.

Father Meinrad paused and looked at Brody. "Yes, you are exactly right...and that is the reason we must stay vigilant and work harder. You ask the most important question we all face—how? Let me try to answer it this way. War has been an unfortunate constant in our humanity but most of us do not glorify the countless atrocities it brings about. Winning in this case merely means we have overpowered our enemy—and we do this by every desperate means possible. Should we aspire to this and glorify any of it?"

"No!" Luis shouted.

Father continued, "Likewise, humans have elevated and enshrined works of art to pass from generation to generation. Both war and art are very human behaviors. Actually, both are the same."

"Huh? War and art...how?" Brody interjected.

"Both activities are our expression of self. My question to you is, what do you think is more important in the long walk of our ancestors and our descendants? Which expression of humanity do you want to express?" Father asked waiting for no response and went on. "On this planet, the way we behave, both rationally and irrationally, toward each other is owned by man. We *own* it. But we must *be more*. Brody, we have a choice. You, my boy, have choices. Be *more*. That's how."

He finished his lecture at that moment, and then took a path with his thoughts to the mundane.

"Now, before we return to our seats and turn our attention to today's lesson, I want everyone to listen to these instructions."

Almost all moaned at Father's pronouncement. Some of the boys began talking and shoving each other disregarding all that Father was saying.

"Here it goes. I have fifteen desks arranged in three rows of five. So, I want everyone who is seated in the first and third rows to turn your desks to face the center of the room and spread them out. I want those seated in the second row to push your desks in the gaps and fill the space."

We got to work and arranged the desks just as Father instructed. In just a moment, the desks were back in a semi-circle just like before. Everyone was now in the front row, so to speak, and no longer in the back *primo* seating.

"Gosh, just like that, all can change," Luis said.

What was new was old, but what was old was now new. Aiden's position was essentially the same and Luis, who used to sit on the sides of the semi-circle, was in dead center. Brody was on the opposite side of Aiden, and I sat next to Vandy.

NINE

I don't know how he did it, but he did. Before the sun had a chance to show its first ray over the Blue Ridge and Allegheny Mountains, Aiden awoke and he promptly convinced me against my better judgment to get up, get dressed, and follow him. I suspect the Pied Piper wasn't as gifted.

I remembered it was right around the time the leaves were beginning to change. It was a time when many things began to change that year. For early autumn, Mother Nature disguised the day as summer taking the chill out of the air as it was already warm for so early. There was still that autumn fragrance that you only encounter in the mountains of Virginia—a kind of century-old scent of dying leaves on a swatch of a musty breeze.

I had never seen this shade of morning. The clouds that hid the sun turned the sky into something altogether different. Colors blended and, at the same time, separated themselves creating a sense of mystery and magic. The purples and blues hidden in the ribbons of clouds, only moments before, floated high in the altitude. The gold glow of the morning sun was just hinting to take hold and move the last moments of darkness into light.

It was just too early. As it was grueling for me to get going in the morning, how Aiden held sway over me was a feat. He navigated me away from my commonplace thoughts of going to class and led me half asleep down a path that became all too familiar. He told me that we were going to a branch of the river that would be mystical and foreboding. He put it exactly that way—*mystical and foreboding*. Still in la-la land, I freely gave in to his charismatic way.

It had to be early, around dawn, to sneak to the river without detection. In silence, we took the narrow, uneven stairs off the side of the main stairwell. They led us to a level below the basement of our dorm and to one of the openings to the tunnels. Aiden thought this was the best way to go incognito. I knew my eventual introduction to the tunnels was inevitable, so this was it.

The tunnels were dark and sketchy arteries running under our lives and, I felt my heart race just thinking about entering one. My day would begin in such acute contrasts, and I was intrigued with our adventure. We walked maybe seventy-five feet in the dark and damp tube. Steam spewed from rusty pipes that formed a maze throughout. Seeing Aiden's outline, at least, was reassuring. I have no trouble saying that it was a bit creepy especially considering all the bizarre and horrific occurrences I heard about these tunnels. My hope was never to return.

Like bears emerging from hibernation, the new and soft glow of the day made us squint. Surfacing near the cemetery, we were not completely out of sight of the dorms but safe from any unsuspecting human eyes. From there, we ventured past *the spot* and beyond a quarry further east and down a path where I had never been before that day— or since. Now, with the addition of the tunnel and going deeper into the woods, I was a veteran explorer. Beyond the humdrum of acceptable limits, we had the world to ourselves.

Getting used to trudging through the thickets and the briars to places unaccustomed to me, I was now more accepting of Aiden's detours going from place to place. His innate need to inhale his surroundings would never change. Most did not appreciate his unhurried ways. However, being an indoor sort, the more I went on these expeditions the more I, too, liked inhaling.

Never before, I thought as we walked mostly in silence, had I cut class in my thirteen years in school. Like the reddest of apples, today was ripe for the occasion as the morning was falling into place. What could the Robes do about it anyway? Sure, academic life at St. Augustine's was intense and rigorous at times, but I did not anticipate any trouble earning Valedictorian. At least this was what I was telling myself as I was trying to shift the position of a pebble in my sneaker without removing my shoe.

Preoccupied with this whole train of thought, I was certain that Aiden must have cut many a class during his time here. Skipping school was just part of him like his freckles. Reassuring this notion in my mind a couple of times, I was in good hands. He *must* know the rules and how they bend. He had been going to school here for three years and spent so much time away from campus, surely, he must have cut class before. Anyway, I sensed it was a special day—*mystical and foreboding*. Moments like this happen on a whim. Overlooking the spontaneity of the day, unfortunately, was the norm for me. Not today.

That morning Aiden, in a manner of speaking, shook me from the serenity of my sleep and charmed me from my comfort zone. It was always that way with Aiden. But that was me, trying to concoct as opposed to experiencing what was around me. Aiden was good this way; he was the luckiest guy I knew. His plans always seemed to come together, no matter what. Good fortune and intuition were just a part of him, and some of this might just rub off on me.

Like some sort of dreadful switch, during our hike that morning, I woke up—completely. My joy evaporated and began worrying about the day. Apprehension took over. Like worrying my hair would catch fire in a swimming pool, down deep I knew I was being ridiculous. Anxiety has its ways. As we worked our way through the woods, my mind wandered. I no longer lived in the moment but in a nonexistent future. Aiden easily read my thoughts by merely looking at me. This time he ignored my apparent unease. He knew, however, I had complete trust in him.

*****

In a matter of two months, I went from a jaded and distrustful perception of life with Aiden and St. Gus' to one that went farther than I thought I'd ever allow. A speck of some unknown particle somewhere inside me was now larger and taking up room. That speck, concealed deep inside, made the difference between one-sided and shallow days and those filled with surprise and change. Without a doubt, this level of awareness was the outgrowth of our friendship.

Inherently honest and a good guy, he exuded confidence. I liked this and I now implicitly trusted him. Should I be skipping out? Why did I feel compelled to do so? Questions about our friendship frequently resounded in the recesses of my mind. Aiden was hardly perfect, but he *was* magnetic. He was a charmer. Aiden was like no one

I had ever met. Judging no one and nothing, he sucked in what was living but when he finished, he replaced it with something sweet and satisfying. He was giving of himself, and this only strengthened him. The beauty was that it was his natural way. More than once, I asked myself if I was as true to myself in that same way.

We walked down what are now paths blazoned in my memory. As we journeyed, Aiden told me that we were following a trail that he cleared himself. He relished telling me such tales, and I was always on the verge of believing him. Now, however, I could pick up the signs—like how he'd smile afterward or the same quirky laugh that punctuated his lore. Today he claimed that he was the first human to lay eyes on the soil upon which we stood. I could only envision that it must have been God and then Aiden—not Adam—at least that was my musing.

*****

We reached a clearing and there, tied securely to a tree was a neglected, banged-up green canoe. Most noticeably were the two enormous patches on one side of its crinkled flanks. After just a moment to process what was in front of me, my eyes flashed to Aiden eager to see if this canoe was as much a surprise to him as it was to me. In a split second, and without a sound, I had my answer. This was no surprise. Aiden's smile was a dead giveaway as my eyes lunged out of their sockets. I wasn't ready for what I was imagining.

Soon after our banter began, I caved, and it was then I began to brood. At that point, I decided not to negotiate anymore knowing that I would eventually submit to his logic. I thought, right then, that just maybe Valedictorian candidates need to remember to ask pivotal questions at crucial moments. Perhaps the crucial moment was when I was laying half-naked in a cozy and toasty bed. Trusting Aiden was one thing but depending on a flimsy aluminum boat with mended cracks was another. Aiden was a good decision maker but maybe today the trend would change.

With a big old grin and slapping my shoulder, Aiden motioned to me to help pull it to the river only about twenty feet away. Aiden caught me off guard as he flung the lone life jacket my way. I put my left arm through one hole but yanked it back and threw the jacket to the bottom of the canoe's wet floor. Inexperienced though I was, I had pride. *One life jacket and he threw it my way!* Why does he think I should claim ownership? Wimp—not me! Why did he think I needed it? Was my life more important than his?

As Aiden untied the bruised and dented canoe from the tree, I stewed with my arms hugging my mid-section. Unsure of my next move, I watched Aiden as he studied the patches and tightened knots or some such thing. Obviously paying no attention to my silent but peaceful protest, he motioned to me to help untangle a rope by pulling one end. I was pissed and the air from my lungs sputtered out with a sigh. Tugging the rope from him, I motioned to him to stand back so I could take care of this web of rope that I felt obliged to unscramble.

Trying to gauge his reaction without directly looking at him, I spotted one side of Aiden's mouth pointing skyward. His tongue was sticking out all while making his eyes bulge. The look was classic, and he knew it would defuse my mood. He reached out as if to hug me but grabbed my shoulders instead and gently shook me. I would've preferred the hug. The one-sided tension now had all but dissipated. The moment was amazing.

"What's the deal with the canoe?"

"I found it only a week earlier caught in an eddy. No sign of ownership so I took it."

No telling how Aiden negotiated the boat in its precarious state, and I didn't ask. At that point, I didn't really care. Enterprising as Aiden was, I noticed the oars were makeshift but later found out they were more than adequate.

"Hey, I didn't want to tell you until we got here, or I would have never gotten you to skip school."

"Uh-huh."

"I know you like the back of my hand," Aiden reminded me with a wink and scrunched up face. Never liked when he said that.

"Next time I'll keep my hands in my pocket." I couldn't think of a better reply to his declaration. "I still have time to get to class you know?"

"Nooooo way. Nothing doing. You're here so let's do this."

My feet and my brain were frozen. Something in me wanted to stay and that something kept nudging its way to my lips.

"We're making memories for a lifetime—just you and me. What do you say?" he asked.

"Okay, okay…okay. Let's do this," I said, feeling a shocking sense of gratification. Aiden smiled and immediately began to bark out instructions preparing for the launch. By now, I knew my place as the first mate as the ship was his. I waited for him to tell me just about everything at that point. I looked for no responsibility, and I was feeling like nothing else mattered.

We pulled the pathetic, second-rate boat to the banks for our maiden voyage. Once we were river bound all was effortless—much to my surprise. The lack of rain over the last month was evident as the river was calm. The sun warmed our skin as we drifted downstream as Aiden sat upright with an oar in each hand like he was sculling a boat on the River Thames.

"Just relax and sit back, Eli, and enjoy the ride."

"Aye, aye Captain!"

I took advantage of his order. In little time I learned how to shift my weight to keep an even keel, and finally felt at ease. My hands behind my head and looking at the wispy streams of clouds, I closed my eyes only to see vivid red as the sun ignored my eyelids. We had little reason to disturb the water with the oars as we rode the current.

"So, Eli, you should know a thing or two as we go through uncharted waters," he said shading his eyes from the sun with his hand as he glanced in one direction and then another.

"Huh? What are you talking about?" I felt my muscles tighten.

"Never go against the current, go into it. Kind of like a skidding car —turn into the force. Not against it," he said focusing his eyes downstream.

"I have no idea what you're blabbing about."

Looking directly at me, he said, "Let me put it this way—we're not going to row upstream. We're going to *ride* the current downstream. If we go sideways or something, just don't fight the current."

"Oh yeah—of course. I get it."

"It's like an old Zen saying."

"Oh, and what may that be, asks your humble student?" I followed with a slight bow from my seated position.

80

"We're looking for harmony on this voyage. So, to create peace or harmony in all matters, instead of *pushing* the river, *flow* with it."

"Got it…seems obvious, though." I turned away and smiled to myself.

Aiden acted as if he didn't hear me as he looked past me and cast his eyes downstream. He occasionally dipped the paddle under the water's surface. He surprised me with what he said next.

"Ah, this is excellent. Yeah…you know if you weren't so neurotic about studying and getting into college, you'd be pretty cool—you might even have some friends."

I just laughed to myself and rolled my eyes under my eyelids. I wondered if he could tell. Then I spoke.

"Who are you? Sigmund Freud? I'm here aren't I—and, by the way, I *do* have friends. I was actually wondering about you. Lots of people like you, but are they really friends? Huh? Huh?"

Aiden shook his head and said nothing. God, he could be aggravating at times. A moment passed and he sat back. I hung my arm out and touched the water and dipped my fingertips beneath the surface. It felt good. It was peaceful. Looking to either side of the river, the mountains seemed to be so close and so ominous. Feeling protected by their immense size, I felt calm and soothed.

A hawk overhead let out a squawk catching my attention. Billowy clouds overcame the lacy variety that floated above only moments before. They seemed to trail our every move. To each side, the forest was like a green jewel with flecks of fall color as it sparkled in the rays of the sun. Huge boulders lined the shore. Every rock formed captivating and unique shapes. No one was around. It was ours.

"Don't those rocks over there look like breasts?" Aiden blurted.

"Where?" I asked with my neck stretched looking from side to side.

"Right there Einstein—they're right in your face," Aiden said as if to present them with both open palms.

We laughed.

"And over there—looks kind of like … ah, never mind," Aiden said tapering off and pointed his shoulders upward.

"What?"

"Nothing," he said looking at me and placing his hands behind his head and closing his eyes.

"Hey, and right over there…hips and a butt. A big one at that," I replied thrusting out my arm to point and nearly tipping us over.

More laughter.

"That's classic—very good, very good indeed," Aiden said with a scholarly tone.

"How can something so big and hard make us think of sex…?" I asked innocently.

"Think again," Aiden answered. "Life is at its best when *engorged* and *gratified*." Aiden took a satisfying nod.

"…think you're right. Kind of fell into that one," I said as my cheeks suddenly felt warm.

We weren't the first to partake in this sophomoric practice, I was sure. After all, we were seventeen. We laughed as we wondered how the rocks could possibly look so soft, supple, and sexual. Laughter spawned laughter with more creative interpretations. We decided nature, not us, must be obsessed with sex. Gosh, it was all around us.

"So—have you ever been with a girl?" Aiden asked.

"Why are you asking me that again? I mean, at *the spot* you said my reactions and my actions answered your nosy question."

"Yep, I must be right. Just wanted to see if you could be straight with me but I guess not."

Aiden began to whistle, and I just looked off to one side. Along with his whistle, all I heard was the sound of Aiden's oars as they occasionally stroked the calm water.

"Well, my man, neither have I—I'll leave it at that."

I just shook my head as we looked at each other and just howled. But this was quite a bombshell for me. The sixties still fresh in the minds of popular America and sex being open, carefree, and unabashed, I thought Aiden would have been right there when the opportunity knocked. Surprised, I expected Aiden would have drunk from that well long before I had a sip. He was teeming with knowledge, with experiences, with smarts, but no sex.

*****

He revealed something to me that I was sure he had not divulged to anyone else. These were the things high school boys lied about and did so with delight. In the scheme of things and amongst ourselves, it was natural and expected that we do so. Lying about such things was more comfortable and easier than telling the truth. We were, for heaven's sake, still boys even though we thought we were men—ha! We had lots of questions and most of us never dared to ask our parents or some other adult. We sought our answers elsewhere. Not such a good way to be, but society has so many hang-ups and holds a power over every speck of our lives, and this subtle pounding drones on. It seems to have no origin and it is difficult to destroy as it is part of the muscle of society. Thus, it is another *unwritten agreement* so to speak. So, it's best to be resourceful—and secretive. If our questions weren't deemed *normal*, whatever that was, we could be in big trouble. Answers had to come from somewhere. Diligent in our search, we were probably not so selective as to the source.

*****

At that moment, our parallel lives intersected. Aiden and I were at the same point. We heard so much about sex, saw our share of dirty magazines, but neither of us knew what it was all about—really. He and I were similar, and I liked it. We laughed to the point our stomachs could take no more.

"I'm having a good time Aiden. Just wanted to tell you that."

"Me too. I knew you would."

A few moments slipped by without a word. A breeze kicked up. Drawn in by the moment, I decided to take a good look around. As I scanned our surroundings, the landscape appeared unfamiliar. The mountain range looked higher and the river wider. Not sure about it, but just knew that they all together looked different than earlier that morning.

"Aiden, we've been out here for a while—how do we get back?"

"Beats me," Aiden said as he jockeyed to find a more comfortable position.

"What!"

"I've never been down this way before. Hell, I'll let you in on another secret," Aiden said in a monotone.

"What?" My back sprang straight up.

"I've never been in a canoe before either," Aiden said leaning over and reaching his hand into the water.

"What?"

"Don't keep saying—*what*. Okay?" Aiden said furrowing his brow.

"I'll say it again—WHAT?"

"Kidding—kidding. Don't get your panties in a wad. I'VE BEEN IN A CANOE." Aiden shouted sending an echo throughout the gorge.

"What a liar...gosh you piss me off sometimes! So, do you or do you not know where the heck we're headed? It's like you try to ruin the moment." I added. My nostrils probably flared—unfortunately.

Aiden sat up and leaned my way and blurted, "Wow! Sorry for ruining the moment. Maybe you need to cool out—does it really matter how we're going to get back right now? Geez. Besides, if I told you that we didn't have a plan, you would've bailed on me this morning. Right now, you're freaking out. It's not a good look for you."

I leaned toward Aiden and said, "No. No, you've got it all wrong, I'm not freaking out. I just think knowing where you are, is important."

"Okay, we're in a canoe. We're on a river. And," he paused and looked to the sun and continued, "we're going east. This is the same river we've been riding all along. What else do you want to know?"

I felt deflated as he was right. "Sorry, Aiden. I guess I did kinda freak out," I said looking away from him.

"No worries. So, we'll just follow the river in the opposite direction. We'll ditch the canoe when we're done, and we'll hoof it back. We'll just follow the shoreline—easy as that. We'll figure that out when the time comes."

"Cool...cool," I said nodding like a bobblehead.

"Right now, let's just have a good time. Are you cool with that? Because if you aren't cool with that, I can dump you out here, and you can walk back on your own."

"No, NO. I'm cool. I would've liked for you to tell me all this before we became virginal sailors together," I mumbled fidgeting and looking at my hands.

"Well, you didn't ask. If you would've asked, I might have had to lie to you. You wouldn't want me to lie, would you?" Aiden said with a grin.

True, he did know me well. I would have never gone if I had known everything. Putting our words behind us, he marked his expression with a contagious laugh. He was contagious. I calmed down pretty fast.

"Guess you're right, I mean that seems easy enough. It's just going to be a long walk," I said.

Aiden began to direct the canoe to the shore where there were several enormous boulders. A massive tree was growing right on the riverbank with a large branch sprouting out leaning over the water.

"Grab ahold of that branch as I move us closer to that slab of rock. This looks like a good place to rest for a few."

I grabbed the branch and we drifted over by the rock and docked. Aiden pulled off his shirt and stood up. The canoe rocked back and forth, and I grabbed the sides with a firm grip. He pulled himself up onto the huge boulder and as he did, I steadied the boat. Before I knew it, he dove in the river creating a wave giving the old rickety canoe a bit of a sway.

I threw the rope around the branch to keep us from drifting downstream as Aiden swam around. With my arms folded, I lounged on my side watching him. He swam under the boat so I contorted my neck over the side seeing if I could see him underwater. He popped up gasping for air not far from me.

"Hey, give me a hand. I want to get back in."

"What? Just climb back on the rock and get back in that way. You'll tip me over if you try to get in this way. I even know that."

"Just give me your hand. I'm weak from all this swimming."

"Hmmm. Okay, okay…"

I crouched making sure I was in balance and reached out my hand. He looked me in the eyes and his face turned into one gigantic grin. I knew what was going to happen next. In fact, I knew all along that this was what he had in mind. He grabbed my hand and pulled me in as the boat capsized. My mood lightened the moment our eyes met right before he yanked me overboard. The water washed away a mood for which I was happy to let go. I needed the plunge.

After a few minutes of swimming, Aiden followed my lead as I pulled myself up the boulder and laid back to take a breather. Out of breath, we were cold, and our teeth clinked together. I felt goosebumps all over. Aiden sat with his arms and legs comfortably stretching in different directions leaving me little room. The sun felt good. No, it felt great.

*****

It wasn't long when we were back in the canoe heading just thirty more yards or so downstream. With no warning, the rapids became testy as the shore on either side grew farther apart. No longer was this a joy ride. Placid, still waters were now history as the waves below us created sporadic thumping on the paper-thin sides of the canoe. *Bang, bang, bang!* As the force of the water battered on the flanks of the canoe, Aiden didn't appear worried, so I took my cue from him. By this time, we positioned our oars on either side to help manage some stability and direction.

The once serene clouds overhead rolled inside out to show an unexpected gray underbelly covering much of the sun's rays. Shadows cast on the rocks to either side were chilling. No longer did visions of our libido well up when faced with these masses of limestone. As our pace picked up fourfold, we were flying as we careened over the callous and ugly waters. Behind me, I heard Aiden's frenetic laughter, but I kept my eyes fixed on every boulder in front of me. He sounded like a rodeo cowboy knowing he's broken a stallion. It was so infectious— so contagious. The rougher it got, the more a burst of ridiculous laughter came from me too. My eyes still glued forward, I noticed Aiden's booming laughter was now silent. I whipped my head around to see what he was doing, and he was gone.

I was no longer controlling or even guiding the canoe—I never was. The river splashed on me and on the rocks anchored only a few feet away. The river, now, roared at me as I was going into its throat. The canoe spun sideward and turned like the arms of a clock as the river's claws kept dragging me downstream. I tried to guide the boat into the rapids remembering what Aiden said earlier. Don't fight it, go with it. *Go with it!*

Gaining an ounce of order I felt, all at once, my pores emit sweat drops covering my entire body that felt like pricks of straight pins. Bobbing up and down and from side to side, like a ping-pong ball, I regained enough coordination to spot Aiden on a boulder about fifteen

86

yards to one side and up ahead of me. Apparently, he had run alongside the uneven rock-lined riverbank to catch up with me. He was standing tall flailing his arms and hands and screaming something. What he was saying was a true mystery as the moment disappeared.

The next thing I knew, only twenty-five feet ahead, I was closing in on an enormous waterfall. What he was screaming was now evident. To hell with the canoe, I jumped overboard and swam like a torpedo over to Aiden's haven. Exhausted from the ordeal, he extended me the lone makeshift oar. Gripping it with both hands, he pulled me up. With the adventure over, I collapsed and fell to my knees.

*****

What began as a glum return hike through the woods and on the river's edge, turned into talk about our flirt with the river. Aiden went from an exuberant description of the day to a serene attempt to search for answers to my endless questioning.

"So, you got thrown out?

"Yeah, it was crazy. I could've gotten killed, but you, my man, handled it. Shows you can handle anything. Good thing you jumped before the fall," Aiden said.

Saying nothing, we walked for some time in silence before I asked one last question. His answer took me by surprise.

"Aiden, don't you think we were fools today? I mean we challenged a force of nature like idiots."

"Eli, maybe we were *idiots*, but we challenged nothing today when you think about it. We badgered nature, we aggravated it, and we traveled with it but never challenged it. The way I see it, anytime man tries to challenge nature he will always lose. *Always*.

"Sounds about right, Aiden. The river won."

"The river will always persevere. But if you look at it in black and white, yeah, the river is here forever, and it won and it always will. We journeyed with it as far as we could take it. Yeah, it whooped our butts today—nature has its way. Don't go against nature is all I have to say."

It was time to get on with the rest of our day—whatever that would be.

87

TEN

Maybe, that morning, the river won—or not, but winning changes things. Winners gain and losers walk away with less. Just as a winner must have a loser only time would tell me if, on that day, we walked away with less.

As we sloshed next to the riverbank, we looked for no more answers. But I realized that humans have little control over anything especially when it comes to the forces that could emerge from nowhere. Nature is definitely one of those powers with its formidable energy. It is a force always to consider but one that we have absolutely no authority over. Nothing can alter a power thundering forward. You cannot slow shear momentum with any success, but sometimes it doesn't matter as our fate may already be sealed. Then again, maybe fate doesn't exist.

During our journey back to St. Augustine's that afternoon I remember spotting a house clearly out of place.

"Aiden, that house up there on the hill, is it the *old lady's*? You know, the lady who I heard about at Hurl Hall?"

"In The Hurl? How'd that come up? You never told me that."

"Oh, I thought I had. Anyway, the first day I was here some of the guys at dinner told me of some widow who had millions and lived near the school. When she died, the monks got everything. There are tons of rumors about her and the monks. You know, hidden dirty secrets. I'm sure you know all about it."

Aiden in his casual manner said, "Yeah, that's her house all right. It's a big momma, isn't it? As for the rumors, the one I like the best is that she haunts our campus during midterms and freaks out some of the students. It's the only time of the year we've had suicides."

"Suicides?"

"Yeah, the year before I got here, some guy killed himself in the tunnel...and someone, about ten years ago, hanged himself right up there," Aiden said, slowly raising his arm and then pointing to the house in his best grim reaper pose.

"Really?"

"It happened all right. She wanders through the dorms and tunnels and whispers hypnotic thoughts of death in the ear of a student who can't hang, so to speak, with what's going on. What can I say? We've got our very own ghost on campus. Who could be next? Spooky, huh?" Aiden paused and smiled. "Hey, listen, you can't always believe what everyone says. Take all that gossip, cut it in half, and then cut that in half. Then you might have something that resembles the truth. Tell ya what, let's take a detour and I'll show you around."

"What? Go up there? To the house?"

"Scared?"

"Uh...no?"

"Trust me. It's not what you think. Look, this way you can see firsthand what some of the featherweights have been too scared to see during their four years here."

Mystified, I nodded in silence and agreed to take a quick look. What was the harm in doing that? Every step we took, as we neared the house, the water squished out of the spongy foam of our sneakers. I thought that I'd rather get back to dry clothes than creeping around some old house, but my curiosity got the best of me.

Aiden and I strayed off our course by the river and up a hill to get to the *old lady*'s house. The trails leading to her home were worn and clear of growth. Others have made their way here from time to time, but Aiden seemed to think that only a few made the trip with any regularity. One thing I knew was that they did not allow students to trespass on this part of campus. They did not permit us to walk this far to the eastern grounds though it was technically part of the campus. Anyway, we must have walked a good football field to get there from our path.

The path we were taking by the river was pretty much off-limits as well. No real surprise there, as that day we followed no rules. Aiden had a basic respect for the rules but that was only now and again. He thought they wrote the rules for someone else. It wasn't so much that he was arrogant or cavalier, but he was willing to take chances. He wanted to know what was beyond the walls. He felt rules were walls and walls only kept out the truth. He didn't want to miss anything, so he would glean the brightest spark from the mundane and wiggle his way to places most teenagers didn't go or care to venture. I didn't think of it that way at the time.

I thought it odd that this house was in shambles even though it sat on the school's property. She had left bags of cash for the Robes to use as they pleased, but they didn't even keep the only physical representation of her in better shape. I couldn't believe it. Maybe I was wrong and something else represented her legacy—like her name on a building or bench or something. Could there be a plaque somewhere? This, I would eventually learn.

As we approached the front gates, I could tell that, in its day, this mansion rivaled any other estate. Today was another story. Broken shutters precariously hung on by rusty hinges and banged against the brick walls. Roof tiles were missing in chunks and the shrubs had grown out of control. They had grown in contorted and weird ways that gave the façade an unsettling feel. The same went for the lawn, or what little was left of one. Only weeds, hip-high, and other volunteer growth were prominent throughout. Running the images through my head, I'd have to say this was a typical haunted house, and yes, I would call it spooky.

Aiden took me around to the side where he eased open a window. We entered what must have been the parlor. Houses like this one always had a *parlor*. The only objects in the room were two big filthy wingback chairs that faced a huge fireplace. It looked more like a hole in the wall. The hearth in Hurley Hall must have come from that very opening. For some reason, I found myself on tiptoes as we looked around and approached the fireplace.

"Hey, you can walk regular Eli."

"Oh yeah...not sure what I was thinking."

Under closer inspection, the big black hole glowed. The embers were fresh. I didn't like the frightful feeling that had just come over me.

"Who, who do you think was in here? I mean it still feels like summer and *they* built a fire. What goes on here?" I stammered.

"Devil worship—I think there's an evil spirit or two still here," Aiden said shooting his eyes from side to side. "Hey, this isn't an Alfred Hitchcock movie. Just relax. I've been here a million times and I'm sure others have been here too. I think some of the Robes come up here as a kind of retreat. They pray, or reflect, or do whatever monks do."

"But why a fire? I mean it's not winter."

"It doesn't matter the time of year, this place is drafty and cold, so it makes sense to build a fire not only for warmth but for light too. If you haven't noticed, it's kind of dark in here. With no electricity, what can you do? It's a great place to come and veg out."

"Do you ever see them when you're up here?"

"Are you talking about evil spirits or Robes?" he said at my expense.

"Funny Aiden," I shook my head.

"Nope. Neither and never—well almost never. I've seen one here a few times."

"Father Meinrad?" I guessed.

"That's who I'm talking about."

I did notice a few kerosene lamps and some other furniture as I took time to look around. The house was amazingly clean but stark. Aiden showed me around and he had evidently been here quite often as he alluded to earlier. I didn't even try to guess why he had been here. He told me that other students stay away because of the rumor mill that had been churning since she died in 1956. All I could think was that she must have been an extraordinary person if so many people were interested in her so long after she died.

An elaborate staircase was certainly a main fixture in the hall that extended from the front door to the back terrace. We climbed the stairs and as we reached the top step, Aiden warned me of a loose plank.

"I learned the hard way when I was first exploring the place. Unaware of this board," he said pointing to it with his toe, "it tripped me up, and I went flying until I caught a banister and flipped over the side that softened my fall. That, Eli, could have ended in disaster—you and I would have never met. Maybe you'd be Brody's roommate."

"Yeah, if I was lucky."

"Very funny—like I said before, you are a very funny guy."

To the rear of the house, at what must have been the master suites, were French doors that opened onto an immense balcony. Because the house was perched high on a bluff, the view was spectacular. Almost in the clouds, it reminded me of the cliff we climbed—where Aiden tried to get me to take that leap. In fact, as we scanned the panorama, he pointed out to me the exact location of the cliff and *the spot* although it was still obscure to me. Like many things, I found I took him at his word. This, I feared, could surface as a frequent problem.

We sat on rusty wrought iron chairs and kicked up our heels on the railing. We relaxed and said nothing. All we could hear was the breeze filtering through the trees below us. The sun was hot, and our wet clothes were drying. I broke the solitude with another one of my questions.

"Aiden, so tell me, what's Orca's story?"

"Oh, you mean Luis? One thing I know, you are very persistent."

"Yeah, I can be. But, for some reason, it seems like I'm putting a puzzle together and it keeps coming back to a few of the same guys. Anyway, just wanted to know why he thinks he's such a badass."

"Well, I wouldn't call him Orca to his face. Freshman year we were roommates. Just like us. No one knew each other so our class, so to speak, started with a clean slate. But they tagged him right away. He's not so bad, but he likes the reputation that he's been given over the last three or so years. He's used the negative attention to create an image—at least for him."

"Hmmm. He and a few others, the way I see it are the faces of hazing so they pop to mind more than they should…I'm not sure I get it—hazing. Do you get into it?"

"As freshmen, the seniors hazed us. Now we get to do the same thing, that is if we want to. The Robes like to call it the St. Augustine Orientation Program. We call it SOAP."

"What? That doesn't work."

"Nope, but you know how things get pegged by our fellow students?"

"Yeah, I guess so."

"Anyway, the program *inculcates*, that's the monks' word, the spirit of the school—and anything else that they want. Somehow it helps us to become tight as a class, like a surrogate family. In adversity comes a bond, you know, that kind of stuff."

"It is a bunch of older kids picking on the little or powerless ones. How's that going to bring people together? I mean it is so negative. Does positive action come from negative ones?"

"Well, you heard that opposites attract, right? How about, for every action there is an equal and opposite reaction?" Aiden paused and looked away to the mountains, "Hell, I don't know. I think it's pretty crappy, too."

"Why do parents pay thousands of dollars to have their son trampled by other kids? Do they even know it happens?"

"First, most of it is in good fun. We learn the school's fight song—we do projects together and our big brother, a senior, usually keeps things in check. I will tell you one thing, we got to know each other really well and pretty fast. We got to know the seniors too."

"From what Vandy tells me I'm a target for the same crap as freshmen. I don't have a big brother to keep things in check for me."

"Has anything happened so far?"

"Well, no."

"I wouldn't worry about it. You're part of our class and although the rules say we can harass you, we just don't do it. Lots of new upperclassmen have come in here and I've never seen them get hazed. Anyway, it's just until Thanksgiving," he said looking directly into my eyes with a fiendish grin.

"Hey, it isn't funny. That's why I asked about Luis. Vandy told me to stay clear of him because he was wielding his power this year."

"Maybe so, but don't worry about it so much. You've gone nearly two months without hearing from him—or anyone else. It's likely there's nothing he'll do. Boy, the things you fill your head with—*sheesh!*"

Our conversation shifted as Aiden brought up something I hoped he wouldn't bring up again.

"Eli, when are you going to start doing what you want? When are you going to start being you? I mean this lawyer thing doesn't fit you. Can you tell me that it's, for sure, your dream?"

"Aiden, what are you talking about? Yeah, that's what I want to do. Are you saying I wouldn't make a good one?

"I'm not saying that at all. You'd make an excellent one. You'd make an excellent banker or an excellent archeologist, or an excellent whatever you want. You've got the brains and the drive, but I think something's missing. Something that comes from you. You know, something that comes from deep inside you."

"You're full of yourself. You've known me a few months and you think you know all about me. Well, you need to know something. I've got what it takes. From top to bottom and inside and out."

"Eli, you're missing my point. Don't get so riled up, geez. By getting so defensive, you are playing right into my hand. Don't you see that?"

"What are you talking about?"

"Look, your dad's this hot-shot lawyer who is now this big-time ambassador. I don't know him, but he probably wants the best for you, but he probably influences your future too. Did your dad go to Georgetown?"

"Well, yeah, he did."

"So, did he ever ask you what you wanted to do with your life?"

"Ah, ah...well, no."

"There you go."

I couldn't help but think that he had a point. One that I kept buried inside. I settled back in my chair and said nothing but gave myself a moment to collect my thoughts.

"Did he encourage you to consider following any of your other talents?" Aiden asked.

He pressed me to a point that a rush of unexpected memories spurted up, and I finally answered him.

"Well, no. He didn't have to, my mom used to do that. I mean, my dad wasn't around so much—still isn't, but she showed me other things. She had an endless imagination, and I remember we played when I was little. It didn't matter what, but we had fun."

"Yeah, she sounded like a really great mom...go on."

"She was warm. I felt good when her hand held mine when I was small. She wrote poetry, and she painted too. So, yeah, I know what it's all about. I know there's more out there than law."

My diatribe instantly made me feel used up and empty. Picking up on my mood swing, Aiden altered his course.

"Hey, man, she was wonderful. You're a lucky dude. You know, I never knew mine and don't even have pictures. The same goes for my dad. I never knew him. All I know is that she died, and my dad deserted me, but a really cool lady about fifty miles from here took care of me—for a while. I called her Sissy. She was more of a sister than a mom...she died five years ago, and I was sent here. God, I loved her. During that time, she allowed me to do just about anything, so I spent a lot of time in the woods—a lot of time in my own thoughts. She was a big reader and that spilled over to me. Most of those books in our room were hers. And her pancakes were *awesome*. I miss her."

A loss for words, I gave Aiden a reassuring look, but he didn't look at me long. It was hard for him. It was tough to hear him talk this way.

"I became the monk's project since then," he paused, turned his head, looked back at me, and continued. "Don't get me wrong, they've been great, but I've never had parents, so I haven't had all the good, and bad, from adults. Hell, the Robes keep hinting I would make a good priest. Can you believe that?"

That cut the tension and he let out a fake laugh that turned real and I joined in.

"I didn't know any of that—I haven't asked because I never wanted to pry."

"Pry? Are you an idiot?" he asked in a manner familiar to me. "Just ask when you want to know something. You *are* going to be a lawyer one day, right?"

"Damn right and a great one at that."

"Then don't be afraid to ask questions. You got to ask them of yourself too. You know, to be truthful in the court of law, you should start with being truthful with yourself. You could be a great one if it were your idea. That's all I'm saying. I mean if the passion was definitely yours and not pop's. Mom had some good ideas. I bet she tried to get you to think on your own."

"She never said much, well, not much when Dad was at home."

Getting pissed at the resurgence of his unsolicited advice, I couldn't believe he just wouldn't give it up. That's when it hit me, and I stomped my feet on the floor and leaned to the railing. My sigh sounded like wind through a tunnel.

"Aiden, you're a pompous asshole. Forget it. You don't know the first thing about the law. You don't know why we even have laws because you think you're too good for anything other than *Aiden's law*. I don't want to talk to you about this anymore."

"I'm sorry. I didn't realize I hit a nerve. Sorry. Yep, maybe I don't know much about law. Let's leave it at that. We don't have to talk about it anymore."

"By the way, I know you *meant* to hit a nerve, because I know *you* too...like the back of my hand."

"Touché."

"Yeah—touché."

Only seconds passed and it was as if I was underwater gasping for my next breath. I had to find a pocket of air. Don't know why, but I was the one who extended the conversation.

"I'll tell you why I don't want to talk about it anymore."

Looking surprised, Aiden responded, "Ah, okay since you don't want to talk about it, let me hear what you have to say."

Frazzled I continued, "The law is special—this country is special. The great men that first explored this country were men looking for freedom. Our Founding Fathers were searching for justice and escaping tyranny. I think we should preserve that and fight for it. That means searching for truth in all we do and protecting it. The Constitution helps all of us as we try to find the answers to help *everyone*. I know what's important, and I know the truth."

"You sound good. You really do. Sounds like you rehearsed it pretty well. C'mon, Eli, being a lawyer isn't about finding the truth. It's finding something that *sounds* like the truth. Something that people will buy into if it helps them in some way. It's about money and competition. It's about outsmarting your opponent. It's a game of negotiation and getting what you want whether it's good for all or for one."

"You done?" I asked.

"Hell no. It's a big game. Most of the old white men lawyers in D.C. are nothing like our Founding Fathers, especially how we've fictionalized them. They sit in Washington making decisions and sending guys, a little older than us, to kill people half a world away. I guess the *leaders* today have found justice—they found the truth. It just takes a lot of death for it to be visible."

Calm and relaxed, Aiden made himself clear. I wasn't so sure he was wrong. But I droned on.

"You don't know what you're talking about. Nixon is getting rid of the draft and that's a great move not only for our generation but also for what it says for war and peacetime. It's over. The Vietnam War is over. They are evacuating as we speak." I spoke as if I was well versed in current world affairs, but I knew little. Like most others my age, I wanted to think that my grasp of world affairs was real. At the very least, I wanted to come out ahead in an argument with my pain-in-the-ass friend.

"Eli, listen to yourself. The war isn't over, not for all those Vietnamese stuck in the middle of all that killing. It's still going on for them."

"Yeah, but, but…"

"By the way, over something like fifty or sixty thousand U.S. men are dead. No one seems to care about the thousands of other men and innocent kids and moms—all slaughtered! Christ, the war is in their backyard. These are the people who would stand out in a crowd here at St. Gus'. None of our grandmas, mothers, or children were in harm's way in this war."

"Yeah, but…"

"It was nothing but destruction. You know Eli, all of us and especially those who lost someone, on both sides, will ultimately be the ones who suffer for this decision. You watch. All because of what? Does the average twenty-year-old soldier know why they were fighting?"

"To… to keep communism from coming to our shores, gosh you don't let me get a word in edgewise," I hollered.

"Please, Eli. Someone tells them who the bad guys are, gives them a gun, and tells them to blow them away to preserve our corner of the world. Do those mammas and their children know why they live among minefields? The sixty-thousand men dead translate to many, many more family members that must go on with big holes in their hearts. Did we really fight for democracy or for the truth?"

"Ah, yeah. We need to keep the enemy from changing our way of life."

"Do you absolutely think the enemy is on its way over here? The enemy is already here. The enemy walks unnoticed."

I decided just to nod and sputter to an unspectacular finish. No longer looking at each other, we sat in nothingness. Fuming, I could not believe he was so calm and matter of fact about everything. Didn't he realize he just offended the hell out of me?

Aiden went inside and with sober eyes, I stared at a knotted tree that was directly in front of me. I examined the crooked lines of the bark and the dead branches interspersed with the living. I could not believe him. I wasn't sure I liked him anymore. No, I hated him at that moment.

Minutes later, he came back outside with a cigarette in his mouth. He motioned to me asking if I wanted one. My immediate reaction was to push him away, but it seemed as if he was offering me a peace pipe of sorts so, with a nod I took one.

He lit it with a lighter he kept with the cigs somewhere in the house and, we continued to sit in silence. Coughing a few times, I decided to hold the cigarette just bringing it to my lips without inhaling it. I watched the red glow burn the white paper and turn the tobacco into dead burnt ash. A coal-black buzzard circled close overhead. All I could think was that he was waiting for one more blow to my ego, and he would swarm down for my lifeless remains. Maybe pick at it first and then, move on to something tastier.

Apart from the breezes, the solitude accentuated the prattling of the river that claimed victory a few hours before. Now being on the river's edge my perspective became clear. That morning the river's erupting power sprang from nowhere leaving me raw and exposed by its romp. Now I saw another kind of energy radiate forward. This time it came from Aiden. One for which I wasn't ready. One that would capsize my boat leaving me thrashing about without an oar or hope to which to cling.

Looking slightly his way, I noticed him blowing smoke rings to the clouds. Deep down I knew he was only being himself and meant absolutely nothing of our verbal sparring. He tilted back in his chair, kicked up his feet, and crossed them at the ankle on the railing. He blew more smoke rings. On the other hand, I took one last puff of what was now a mere glowing nub between my dirty fingers and held in the urge to cough. This time I was successful.

Mulling over what just happened, I cooled down, way down and real fast. Thinking about it more, I didn't hate Aiden.

I hated myself.

ELEVEN

May 1999 – About Noon

"What a day that was! Hate to interrupt you, but I'll say it again, what an *incredible* day," Gabe said as he threw four fish fillets he had just caught and cleaned on a hot iron frying pan. No sooner than I heard the sizzle, came an alluring aroma.

"It *was* incredible. Lots of highs and lows," I added. "So, what's on that fish? I mean it smells fantastic."

"You've heard of the Colonel's seven herbs and spices? Well, I've got *Gabe's five fabulous flavors*. I'll give you two of the five: garlic and ginger, but the other three will remain with me forever. Maybe one day...maybe one day." He said with a toothy grin.

"Whatever it is, it smells delicious."

Without a hint, Gabe grabbed my cup, filled it with more coffee, and topped it off with another splash of whisky. He looked at me as his many forehead lines pointing up as to ask if I wanted more, but I waved him off.

"Gabe, I think what you have already poured will be just right."

"Okey-doke. Compared to what other poor souls experience in a month...no a *year,* you guys had in a day...if you know what I mean."

"That's for sure. I mean, our friendship shifted then and it's one day that has stuck with me—there were many others. Believe me, that was just one of many revelations that year." With that, I stared off to the mountains for what seemed to be a while.

*****

Coming back this weekend and riding a roller coaster of memories, has added symmetry to my life. Sitting on this stump I am well aware that this moment is the only real time that exists. It doesn't matter if I want it to be so or not. But by leaving the ordinary behind, for no more than a short while, gives me a look at who I am that led me to this very point. It gives me clues as to how to welcome the next moment...and the next. Otherwise, some of the best parts of me could and would stay hidden.

Yep, I would love to have a conversation with my seventeen-year-old self, right about now. I only began thinking of my time on this planet when half my life was well behind me—well, almost half. I had lived for *the now*, so I thought, but in daily life, my thoughts have taken me to places that have robbed me of my *now*. Sometimes this isn't easy to see at the time, but it surfaces later. The whole notion of time is anything but clear.

For starters, time evades every sense we have—can't hear it, touch it, see it, smell it, or taste it but it is always present...or is it? No matter what, time cannot hurry. Can't be lost or changed. It's the same for everyone and because of this, it should be inconsequential or something that doesn't take up more of our, well—time.

The reason we pay homage to the whole suggestion of time, I suppose, is that for eons we have drilled into each other the *value* of time. Humans have a habit of defining *everything* and then they force a value on what they define. Why? It's unclear to me, and tiresome at best.

We think of time and our place in it as something special—too special. We count it, think about it and lament over it our whole lives. We say we don't have enough of it, or it goes by too quickly or not fast enough. I bet this has something to do with our lost moments and why living in them becomes difficult.

Time, some say, heals all wounds. That one, I think I must believe.

Time, I figure, is just *nothing* but it's what we fill that *nothing* with, that makes this *nothing* worth remembering. That's why that day—the day of highs and lows stood out.

I now see some moments, as my youthful thinking captured them, as magical. Even if my memory does not serve me so well, I have a certain fondness for that year—that time. Just as I can't pinpoint that very last drop in a cup that creates the overflow, the moments that take me elsewhere most times go undetected. It's hard to say what one moment made the difference in me that year. Perhaps it was the merging of insignificance with what was truly important but mostly hidden, that made all the difference. An ethereal thread by which I strung these moments together gives me *my* meaning. It's my reality and only mine.

Since I don't truly possess time, there's no way to hold on to it and it slips away. It has disappeared, one grain at a time, through my own hourglass that has always been in sight but out of reach. How I had wished to turn it over again and again. Any hourglass has only so much sand, and I frittered much of it away. Time, however, may not stop for us but remembering moments, no matter how minuscule, helps in a weird way to recapture what still lives but is tucked away. What we think, after all, *is* real. Time *is not*. That's how I see it. These pauses along the path define my life and give it a heartbeat.

In those late teen years, I could only think that I would never cut class again—was that important or what? Oh, there was more, but what occupied my thoughts was like week-old bread as its freshness was gone. It was much later when I figured out that moments dangling precariously on fragile filaments may be woven together to create meaning—*my meaning.*

*****

"Hey there Eli! Hey," Gabe said, snapping his fingers a few times. "Huh?"

"Yeah, you zoned out for about twenty seconds, and I gave you another five before I thought you should come back. You know…to this moment in time. Heck, I like your company and you've got more to the story—I'm sure. What happened next?"

TWELVE

With a bruised ego and tattered emotions, I buried my feelings deep inside of me that day and got over it. But this was my way. Aiden unwittingly opened doors I just assumed stayed shut. That was his way. Too much was at stake this year, so I trudged ahead.

My grades were important. Classes were important. College was *important.* Not so important was some kid dissecting the very being I was becoming. How does he know what's best for me? He doesn't know what's best for him.

Only a day after we skipped school, I began to think that what we did was no cause for celebration. Justice most assuredly prevailed as we paid for our unexcused absence that day. First, we came face to face with nature's powers, and then we came face to face with the headmaster. I'm not sure which I feared more.

Come to find out, Aiden had never cut class before that day. I assumed when I followed his lead that morning that he was a pro at playing hooky, but I was wrong. Father Tobias, our school head, called us into his office and he said little but looked right through us as he, so articulately, tore into us with razor precision. My insides were rattled, and my jaw hurt afterward as I bolted it closed from the inside ensuring that I would say nothing other than to apologize.

Before we received word to stand before him in judgment, some of my dormmates warned us to say nothing other than a short and sweet apology—no smiles, just affirming nods at everything he says. This was my plan and I stuck to it. Aiden, however, was a bit casual about it all. I mean he apologized to Father Tobias, but I sensed a smirk under his steadfast appearance. I, on the other hand, expected full well that my remorseful apology with downward cast eyes would be sufficient, and I would then be on my way. After all, I assumed that I enjoyed a certain immunity being first in my class. What was taught and assigned that day I, undoubtedly, could make up without a problem. Certainly, Father Tobias would know that. My assessment was that I would be back in the dorm studying within the hour. There are times, though, that the unforeseen happens.

*****

Together, the monks and the school owned five cars—enormous cars, swollen at the fenders and bloated hoods. Energy Crisis of the seventies or not, the monks were riding high. Rounding out the fleet was two buses, and, of course, gigantic at that. The next Saturday, while the rest of the boys were kicking back or playing sports and enjoying the diminishing and uneventful weekend in October, Aiden and I washed five cars and two buses. We only had to wax one car because the students in detention were to take care of the others. It was hard work but at least we were outside. Some of the inside punishments dealt with cleaning commodes and showers among other sickening chores. By the end of the ordeal, our hands were unrecognizable and ghostly white with wrinkles on wrinkles reminding me of the face of my new *favorite* monk, Father Tobias.

Aiden and I stayed silent during the first half of our *sentence* mostly due to the fact I would not answer him when he asked me questions. Most were stupid anyway. Ignoring him for as long as possible, I eventually gave in just to get him off my back.

We spoke.

"I'm never, ever going to let you talk me into something as ridiculous as skipping school again. Geez. This is degrading. It feels like I have soap up my nose. Guys just walk by with footballs and basketballs laughing at our expense. It's as if we're on display. *The two school idiots who got caught*," I said, ending with jazz hands for emphasis.

"What's a little soap up your nose—all those guys have been here before. All of them. You just don't know. Besides, we had a great time getting here and you know it. We both experienced new stuff, and what a great way to take it all in. Taking a gamble and through the eyes of a friend…you can't ask for more—*can't ask for anything more*," he said playfully imitating me with his version of jazz hands. "I think there's a song like that."

That's how Aiden approached life. He, at times, was in denial of the facts—not me. He thought that by overlooking them, all was okay. I responded to him in a practical manner that I thought he should hear.

"I know what I learned. Never cut classes and never go out on the river with an inexperienced captain. You know, you're no Sir Chichester, or whatever his name is, and that canoe was no *Gipsy Moth.*"

"Ouch!"

"Oh yeah, I learned to never sit on the balcony of a dead lady's house and talk about the world and my future with the likes of you," I said in the cadence only found in a Neil Simon play. Aiden seemed to be tuning me out. He turned his back to me as he reached over the hood of the car with a huge soapy sponge. Then, he fired back.

"Ah, come on. Look at it this way. Cutting classes gave you a day off and the bonus of spending an extra day with me washing buses for some old men who can't do it for themselves anyway. As far as the river, we had an awesome time, and you know it. You need to experience these things. Life is all about risk. It makes it worthwhile and makes it fun and makes you happy. Like your idol, David Cassidy says, 'C'mon get happy'. That's why the chicks dig him so much; it looks like he knows how to have a good time," he said with a rumble of laughter.

"Hey, he's not my idol! He's yours!" I bellowed. I hated it when he tried to aggravate me like that, especially using humor.

"It will give us something to talk about when we come back for our class reunions."

"What? Do you think I really want to come back and see you?"

"Besides," he persisted overlooking my agitation, "when you're an old man, are you going to be sitting around telling your grandkids about all the time you spent in the library? Are you going to tell them of all the time you obeyed every rule, even the stupid ones? No, you're going to tell them about the cool things you discovered in your life and the risks you took. What you championed and won or lost. Times you

107

carved out that were uniquely yours that made a difference for you and, maybe, no one else. We all have the same time, but the difference is how it's spent."

Fuming, I winged my sponge and hit him squarely on the back of his neck.

"Bullseye," he exclaimed and started to laugh. I just shook my head.

"Everything's a joke or a philosophy to you...you know Aiden, you're not always right. You know you bother me. I mean, what the hell do you think I'm doing? I'm working toward a goal and once I get there, I'll have plenty of great experiences to tell everyone. I've got the discipline to work toward a dream. What do you have?"

"Okay, okay. I don't want to piss you off like last time. I get carried away. Yeah, I must admit it, you make a lot of good sense. Should've told you that before. Uh—I'm sorry."

"What?"

"Yeah, I mean it—I'm sorry. I don't want this to become a wedge. You're right—I know I'm not always right. Believe it or not, I don't mind being wrong. Now c'mon over here so I can give you a big hug and kiss."

Leaving me utterly speechless, his timing was flawless. He disarmed me, I couldn't help but smile, and he flashed one back at me. After all, he said he was sorry, and he admitted he's not always right—can't ask for more. We continued to scrub the cars and in no time, we began to share some good-hearted banter. It no longer seemed like hard work.

At about five cars and one bus down, along came Luis. He was sporting a camera he hung from his neck. Aiden stopped what he was doing and greeted him with a pat on the back. Luis looked my way as if he expected something from me that was more than the nod I delivered. Suddenly a sinking feeling dropped in the pit of my stomach as I looked at him through the corner of my left eye. I kept washing as Luis deliberately strolled around the vehicles kicking dust and pebbles as he bumbled around. Aiden saw all this and decided to engage him in idle chit-chat.

"So, Luis, what's up?"

"I thought I'd stop by for a photo of you two losers for the school annual."

"Good idea, old Luis. Hey Eli, get over here for this photo opp."

I tuned out Aiden's plea, so he came to where I stood. He put his arm around my shoulder, looked at me, and whispered.

"Smile for the camera Eli and let's get this over with, huh?"

Luis held up the camera. "Now on the count of three, say sleaze. One, two, three."

"SLEAZE."

At that, Aiden expected Luis to be on his way, but he just stood there. Aiden then said, "Hey Luis, you called us losers? You wouldn't call us that if you knew how we earned this project. I mean this is a *trophy*!"

"Don't give me that, you guys got busted. You don't see me washing buses or cleaning crap from toilets."

"You're too good for us," I said under my breath.

"Did you say something to me, *loser*?"

Aiden spoke up, "Luis, no worries. My friend likes to mumble to himself. He's got kind of a problem that way. Don't ask," Aiden said pointing to his head.

I rolled my eyes.

"I know what you're trying to do," Luis said.

"We're not trying to do anything, are we Aiden?" I asked wanting to play along.

"Sometimes a little adventure is worth a Saturday like this," Aiden said.

"C'mon Aiden. He doesn't want to know so let's forget it."

"Yeah, I think you're right Eli. He probably can't handle it."

Luis couldn't take it anymore and said, "Okay guys, I want in."

I wished I hadn't gotten myself into this little taunt as I was doing fine Windexing the windshields. Too late, though, I began to enjoy where this was heading. Wasn't sure if my participation would shine a spotlight on me or not, but now I didn't care and started making it up as we rolled along.

"Well, we were down to the *old lady*'s house. You know there are a lot of rumors about her and the house. Ghosts, suicides, and broken hearts you know—all that," I said and finished with a frown showing my clenched teeth.

"Yeah, yeah…everyone knows all that," Luis said grumbling.

"Well, hold on, I'm getting there," I said. "Anyway, we heard from a good source that she left a treasure somewhere in there. Don't know what kind of treasure, maybe gold bars, maybe bags of cash, or maybe something altogether different, but she was loaded. We were trying to find it. You know whoever finds it can keep it."

Aiden turned and picked up the water hose and began rinsing off the car. I knelt and scrubbed the hubcaps.

"No fooling?" asked Luis.

By this time, like the sponge in my hand, Luis was soaking up all that we could slosh his way. But within a sliver of a second, Luis was now trying to show disinterest and toned down his excitement. He began to spout off knowing I was in a vulnerable position.

"Huh, well I don't believe you two clowns. I especially don't trust the new guy. What kind of name is Eli? Sounds prissy to me."

"And, what's your name again. Is it Loogie? Or is it, Lois? Oh yeah, it's Luis. Knew it started with an L like *loser*." Maybe I shouldn't have, but I was tired of his tough-guy drama.

"Smartass—I'd like to…"

"Hey brother Luis, just leave Eli alone. He's never seen you in action," Aiden said and winked at me. Luis slithered away like a snake shedding his skin and leaving a kind of curse on me.

"Talking about losers, so what's Luis' deal? I mean for real. No more bits and pieces. Is he really the jerk he appears to be? I mean, he just doesn't know how to ease up."

Aiden finally gave me more than I wanted to know about Luis. His father beat him one last day and left for good. His mother had recently died of cancer, and the pastor of his parish arranged for Luis to attend St. Augustine's on a scholarship. Luis' kept this all a secret.

Hearing what Aiden told me, I regretted concocting the treasure story and felt awful about what I said to him. I only wanted to believe what I wanted to believe about the kid. Gosh, I felt bad for him a while back. Now I turned into one of those jerks who harassed and taunted him at The Hurl that first night. Truthfully, I obviously didn't know him, but that was no excuse.

"You know Aiden, if I knew all that, I wouldn't have egged him on."

"Hell, I knew it. No problem. Don't treat him differently now. I mean, he wants to fit in. Don't pity him. Listen, bullying the guy is one thing—playing with him like the way he plays with us—no big deal. I don't stand for bullying."

*****

Before we turned in for the night, I was laying on my bed and Aiden on his. We were both reading. All was quiet and still. It was the kind of solitude that we only found around here late at night. As I was adjusting the lamp on my bedside table, to my surprise, my bogus treasure story popped into my head. Wondering where that whole idea came from in the recesses of my brain, made me giggle. Yeah, I giggled. Aiden's head popped up and he glared at me with a puzzled look that melted to a warm grin. As if he could read my mind, Aiden spoke up.

"Never heard you giggle…where in the world did you come up with the treasure shtick anyway?"

"You read my mind."

"Not really. Just reading the same sentence over and over again thinking about the day. So…why a treasure?"

"Well, everyone likes to think they can find a treasure, you know, something special in their lives—don't they?"

"Yeah."

"Maybe there's not a pot of gold or briefcases stuffed with cash somewhere, but there are treasures all over the place. You've shared in some and so have I. I'll leave it at that," I said using a little Aiden philosophy on him. Proud of myself, I said it as if I knew something—and maybe I did.

"Nice, nice," Aiden said. "You *do* have an imagination after all. That's good, real good."

Aiden went back to his book, and I put mine down, closed my eyes, and smiled.

THIRTEEN

At one end of the long rectangular floor, eighteen to twenty of us lined up three deep. It couldn't be so bad one would think, but it was. For many of us, the game was already over. Three hours of the first day of basketball tryouts and we had yet to play basketball or anything that resembled a game.

Sure, we held a basketball, dribbled it, passed it, dove for it, but never shot it. For a team sport, we were all alone with our own hustle, skills, talent, or lack thereof. This was November 2, a Wednesday as I recall which many affectionately christened *The Holiday*. Hundreds of students over the years who were basketball player wannabes likened the experience to something larger than life, thus the nickname.

The second day of November marked the day of the year schools could officially begin basketball practices. On this date, as well, the Catholic Church celebrates the *Feast of All Souls* or what Catholics commonly call *All Souls Day*—a day to revere the dead.

The day being a holy one, the Robes held no classes, but we *could* play basketball. The day was not too hallowed a day to stop a game, but learning had to cease, no question about that. No complaint from me, but perhaps it says something about what's important.

Aiden was right. He told me that the Robes expected us to try to play sports. To *try* was the operative word. Many boys didn't make the basketball or baseball teams, but we had to try some sport. Everyone, though, could play football or run track, but that wouldn't do it for me. *No way!* I was enamored with the game of basketball ever since my dad took me to see the Celtics many years earlier. I remember watching number seventeen John 'Hondo' Havlicek hustle for every loose ball or make a steal just at the right time.

Although we had to play, or at least try to play a sport, the inflated number of boys sparring for a coveted spot on the basketball team somehow made playing basketball some sort of privilege. It was like an invitation to an elite club. The basketball squad was by far the most desired team to be on at St. Gus' and the one that students and alumni revered, more so than the Pope in Rome.

Practice began promptly at ten immediately after Mass. This annual holy day ritual was always the precursor for tryouts. Coach Kidder had to be patient, but moments after Father Tobias blessed us and told us to *go in peace to love and serve the Lord*, Coach expected us to be ready for an aggressive, winner takes all practice.

All Souls Day and The Holiday fit hand in glove. All sixty or sixty-five of us during those first three days were definitely souls worth praying for, but no number of prayers could help any of us. I know this firsthand. I spoke to God begging for practice to end with what felt like the one-thousandth lap around the court and the one hundredth groin tearing drill. God may have heard the prayers of other kids somewhere else, but not mine as He declined my offer to be a better Catholic if He helped me out. The day just got worse.

This feast day on the first day of tryouts, without a doubt, was more or less a celebration for Coach Kidder to *feast* on us. His sadistic and cowardly ways made his job easier. We ran for most of practice those first few days. The running was relentless, it was nauseating, and it was painful. He told us that to be good basketball players we had to be in top physical shape and more so than our competitors. His thinking was that, if need be, we could rely on our endurance to win games. Get us in overtime, he would say, and we'll be certain victors. We would outlast the best of them. Yeah, I get that, but I still thought he and his ways were barbarous and cold-blooded at best.

Unlike the coach, with our first game being five weeks away, we weren't worried just yet about overtime games. All we wanted was to be one of the lucky dozen or so to make the squad. No, what Coach Kidder really wanted us to do was to eliminate ourselves. It worked too. Each day fewer and fewer boys showed up. This natural selection process was humiliating to teenage boys. Worst of all, some jerks who thought they were *God's gift* teased the boys who didn't return when they saw them on campus. They called them losers or wimps among other choice names.

Most high school boys aren't very compassionate, and in those days, you could say anything and get away with it. Even the coach gave them the cold shoulder when he ran into them on campus. He only remembered the names of his players and all others he called *sonny*. It makes me sick looking back.

The drills were thorough and by themselves stressed fundamentals. If we didn't do them the way Coach liked, he made the drills even more of an excruciating experience. We ran five laps around the court after each one. Calmly, crossed armed, Coach looked on with his whistle securely lodged between his lips.

He knew who was cutting corners. He had a gifted memory for such things. He allowed a swig of water only when he said it was okay. This dictate usually came with two short bursts of his whistle and his four rigid fingers pointing to the hall, like a referee signaling a timeout to the bench. Antiquated water fountains that dispensed a weak stream were about all we had. If, however, a boy was sneaking water at some other point during practice, Coach always caught the guilty party somehow. He wouldn't catch him in the usual sense of nabbing him right away but would make mental notes on everything. *We* paid for it in one way or another.

Luis was the team manager, and now a veteran in his fourth year doing this thankless duty. This I did not know until the first day of tryouts. The boys thought of him as a spy. They presumed this because Coach always seemed to know more than a coach should know. He knew what players did over the weekend. He knew the goings-on at dances, in study halls, and, often, in the privacy of our dorm rooms. Looking back, the whole thing was just weird.

Despite all this, Coach was a legend at the school. He had been varsity coach for twenty years and won thirteen championships with his teams. Like a field general, he was a strategist. His smaller seemingly less talented teams would pull off amazing victories. Larger public schools fell as easily as our peer Catholic ones. Coach likened us to David, as in the one who slew Goliath. Nothing gave him more pure delight than to see his team walk into a large boisterous public school gym with a few thousand spectators in the bleachers and leave them silent at the end. A grueling thirty-game schedule was the result of playing local public schools and non-league Catholic school games against the likes of Dematha and St. John's in D.C.

Although we were good, very good, we never received the recognition Coach Kidder always wanted. We were in the mountains. Other schools up and down the Mid-Atlantic merely traveled across town to meet their rivals. We sometimes traveled one hundred fifty miles to play a game. Once we left D.C. or Northern Virginia after a game, they essentially forgot us. Dozens of Catholic schools playing basketball in those suburbs and cities made it impossible for us to stand out. Nowhere in the city newspapers would we get much attention, and we were known for winning. We were forgotten even before they turned off the scoreboards.

Sportswriters overlooked Coach's savvy and keen abilities to assemble excellent teams, year in and year out. He, however, brought more notoriety than fame to the school because of his antics on and off the court. Stomping his heel when he didn't like a ref's call or yanking up his tie over his head like a noose were just a few of his classic escapades. He did what he could to get attention. However, the players were always polite. They had to be. The adage of *do as I say and not as I do* was Coach's motto. He may have had good teams, but it wasn't fun.

The sport was the school's prize. The sun rose and fell on the blue and gold hardwood and more appropriately on the old English letter A. It was emblazoned on the center circle or the axis of civilization as alumni were prone to believe. Basketball was so sacred an event, even freshmen who were trying out were immune from hazing, I mean *orientation* until Coach chose the junior varsity and varsity teams. Then they were thrust back into the system.

Our students, the townies, and alumni, as well as St. Agnes' students, our sister school, jammed into our small gym for weekend games. The shellacked wooden planks that made up the permanent stands encircled the floor with a dreaded student section to one side corner. We were proud of being dreaded. The latest Catholic Regional Championship banner always decorated the wall directly behind the students. The banner partially covered a portion of a permanent banner that displayed our school sportsmanship code. The coaches were to go over this list of do's and don'ts, but I can't remember this ever happening. The Robes, as they did with God, put their blind faith in the coaching staff. The monks had their minds and hearts in other places. They were noticeably elsewhere and seldom did we see them at a game or a pep rally.

The 1973 championship banner hung in a school in Richmond. Our latest banner was claimed nearly two years earlier in March of 1971. It had now been the second consecutive disappointment for the school. We were not used to this, and Coach Kidder took the defeat as if it were a true disgrace. Scary, but his life was basketball and nothing else.

Last season, a missed last-second shot at the buzzer left the supporters in shock followed by anger, and depression. Not quite the seven stages of grief, but nonetheless sobering for some. In all, thirteen banners draped the cinder block wall and Coach Kidder emphasized that he could not and would not sleep an entire night until we pulled off another championship victory. We no longer had to utter the word thirteen. He was most superstitious in that regard.

No one talked much about the final game of three in the tournament. All that I heard from them was that we lost at the buzzer. I thought, perhaps, whoever missed the shot had graduated because no one uttered his name or even talked about that moment of no return. I wasn't going to bring it up, as Coach Kidder tolerated no discussion about losses or embarrassments to him or the team.

This was his way. It was as if the team was in collective denial. Sure, they knew they lost. Coach knew that two years would pass before he could find redemption in himself and maybe, more important, from the alumni. However, the subject was a powder keg. We were afraid of him. I avoided questions. I didn't care about last March—it was a game to me.

My love for the game and the need to fit in was probably the reason I endured the week of torture. Too, I fantasized about being on such a team with its camaraderie and earning the admiration of friends and family, that kind of thing. The allure of sports was front and center of my teenage brain. What was odd about that first day as well as every day after, more than anything else, was the fact that Aiden never showed up for tryouts. Aiden rarely talked about the basketball team and the honors he won over the years, but Vandy told me that he was the leading scorer on the team and his teammates voted him Most

117

Valuable Player last year. Aiden's absence stirred no conversation, and I put it out of my mind.

*****

The only thing I thought about was successfully getting through The Holiday, especially the first day. It all started when he blew that damn whistle.

"All right boys, gather around."

We quieted down within a second and ran over to the huge letter A that was at center court and we sat in a semi-circle around the coach.

"Good, good," he said, "you can follow instruction."

He folded his arms across his chest and proudly looked up into the rafters. He slowly brought his attention down to our level. Sweaty arms against arms, we were in his stew as I felt the heat coming from the boys next to me.

"Boys, look above you and at the walls. You see very little cinder block showing."

Of course, we looked around and he continued.

"See those banners? How many championships have we won?"

As most of the boys looked to the banners and began counting, Brody raised his hand immediately.

"Yes Brody?"

"Thirteen, Coach."

Coach Kidder smiled and nodded at Brody and said, "Thirteen—that is absolutely correct. Fourteen will give us the record. *I want fourteen.* The last two seasons we've fallen short. SHORT, SHORT, SHORT. That's not going to happen this year—I won't let it!" he spouted.

Stunned, I looked from side to side and saw that the other boys seemed shocked as well.

"Give me five laps around the floor. You heard me, get going," he hollered.

Brody was the first to jump up and led us in our laps. Coach Kidder stood motionless, arms still hugging his midsection, looking to the rafters, and admiring the banners. When we completed our run, we sat

118

at one end of the court. Still standing on the huge letter A, Coach Kidder roared at us.

"We have traditions here. Today is the first day we can hold tryouts. Yes, November 2nd—The Holiday. One tradition is that you help me coach."

I thought this whole little scene was bizarre.

"Yes, you heard me. Today you won't see a basketball, but you will help me decide who is on our championship team. I hope you are ready to run your butts off for a few hours."

He was right—we ran for two-plus hours. Suicides, sideway slides, fast breaks, relays, and other combinations of stretching, groin-pulling running. When I thought practice was ending, Coach Kidder announced to us that he was going to put us through a game scenario. This, I thought, sounded promising. It was nothing like I thought. It was more running, in fact, it was as if we just began our run for the day. He proved his point—it was a mental game and a physical game. Luis set the time on the scoreboard with two minutes and as Coach blew his whistle, the clock started. We had only seconds to haul ass ninety-two feet down and ninety-two feet back. It didn't matter if our group accomplished this in the predetermined time, but what mattered was that the second and third groups couldn't lag either. We *all* had to accomplish the run in the allotted two minutes.

As the rubber of our soles pounded the floor, Coach knew exactly what was happening as everything seemed to be recorded in his subconscious. Knowing the outcome would be torturous for all of us, we cheered on the slowest most out-of-shape kid to get his butt down the court as fast as he could. It was painful to see some of the kids nearly crawling at the end. There were many more two-minute runs to follow for a total of the eight-minute quarter.

The second quarter began like the first, but we were all a bit slower. We strategically placed the slow runners first, but little helped. It felt like it was four hundred and twenty-two degrees in the gym, and we were about to combust. When the time came for the make-believe halftime, we got a five-minute water break. I was seriously thinking about walking out, but Vandy reigned me in with a pep talk while we were waiting in the line for water. He gave me some bubble gum and with a pat on the backside assured me I'd get my second wind. He reminded me that life could become difficult for me if I walked. Waiting for my chance for a sip of water, I looked away and saw the backs of boys leaving. Heads downward turned, exhausted, and I knew they all wanted to cry but held back their emotions. The boys splintered off and I knew I did not want to be a part of their retreat. Startled by the whistle I gulped a swig of tepid water, rinsed out my mouth and we were at it again.

By the fourth quarter, I knew that it was almost over. My legs were like rubber. The bubble gum that kept my mouth from tasting like the Mojave Desert was now like a tumbleweed that I spit out behind the bleachers. I saw some kids barfing back there, and I asked myself if it was seriously worth it. Luis sat at the scorer's table calmly and coolly grinning with his grimy fingers on the clock buttons sipping on a Mountain Dew soda. I sensed his enjoyment.

The screech of the scoreboard horn sounded. It was over. So I thought, but Coach had a different idea. He proclaimed that because of our terrible performance and that he saw a few boys sneaking water, we were now in our first overtime. First! How many more!

This grueling mockery went on for two, five-minute overtimes that I do not now recall. I was on autopilot. By the time it was over, some of us to include me, stumbled and doubled over as some stormed the water fountain. The worst part was over. It was only over for the next twenty hours. For now, I thought, all was good.

FOURTEEN

Although I wanted to put it out of my head, the worst part of that first day of practice had nothing to do with the agonizing and exhausting drills. When you just think that things can't get worse, think again.

Six or seven of us laid flat on our backs in a pool of our sweat at one end of the court. We did nothing but catch our breath and calmed our hearts. Still breathing hard, Vandy began to mumble something.

"That was the worst yet. Four years of this crap. I guess it's worth it."

"Well, it's our last year and it's our chance to win number fourteen for Coach," Brody huffed.

"Why not for ourselves? The students? I mean it's our team. We're the ones out there playing. Let's win it for us," I said.

"Don't let Coach hear you say that. That's just what Aiden always said, and he and Coach always had it out," Brody said.

"Huh, that's the stupidest thing I've ever heard. The team is for us, the students, and the school—not for the coach."

"Hey Eli," Vandy said, "Brody's right. Coach Kidder thinks that we win it for him, then the school, then the alumni, and then the students—in that order. He doesn't come out and say it, but that's what he teaches. He's subtle but effective."

"I'm glad that Aiden didn't show. More time for me to play...he's not as good as people say. Don't need his type on the team anyway. That's why I ditched him as a roommate—I hate his *type*." Brody said.

I held back my emotions and my tongue. Brody got up and lurched to the locker room leaving his nasty puddle dangerously close to me. I turned to Vandy for some answers.

"What did he mean by that? *His type?* And is that why Aiden's not here?" I wanted to know.

"Well, it's kind of a long story. That's for another day. I've got to get a shower and head back. Got a massive exam tomorrow," Vandy said as he sat up.

I knew for sure Brody and Aiden were not exactly friends. Like a slow drip, Brody seemed to relish revealing his opinions about Aiden to me little by little. I didn't know what to think. Brody was the ultimate suck-up and was stuck on himself. I did my best to avoid him whenever I could, but if we were to become teammates that would be hard to do.

The gym was emptying, but Vandy sensed my anxiety and hung back with me. There were a few other boys who lagged as well; it felt like a vote of solidarity. As we finally headed out of the gym and down the concrete steps to a cool, damp, and dimly lit hallway, I welcomed the change of temperature. Some boys, with wet combed heads, passed us going the opposite direction. Entering the locker room there were still about a dozen boys showering or dressing. Brody was still screwing around and decided to wind his towel into a rat-tail and began snapping it at some bare butts whom he singled out. You can find a *Brody* on every team, I thought. Cocky and pompous described his modus operandi. He was the type who would spend his time torturing insects or little animals as he hid behind an angelic face.

We showered in a large room with nozzles around the perimeter. As in all gyms worldwide, showers and toilets share plumbing, so Brody made sure that he rhythmically flushed all the commodes before entering the steamy room. He held some kind of power over most of the boys as no one ever stood up to him. I didn't do anything either and was just like everyone else. It eats at me to this day.

A bunch of the boys began talking about their expectations for the next day's practice. I just listened in. It was then that we heard someone singing off-key in the other room.

"Shush...be quiet you guys," Brody commanded. "Is that who I think it is?" he asked with a jack-o-lantern grin.

It was Luis picking up dirty drenched towels, disgusting socks, and nasty jockstraps. Some of the boys just chuckled at his solo performance. I didn't, however—the guy sounded happy as he dealt with our scum. Brody and his buddy, Mark, secretly whispered to each other and they ended with simultaneous nods. They had cooked up something. Brody then came over to us and asked if we wanted to have a little fun.

"Dude, not interested," Vandy spoke up.

I shook my head. Vandy and I walked out of the shower to dry off. We headed to our lockers and began to dress. Only a moment later we heard a barbaric war cry as three or four jerks ran out of the laundry room and jumped on Luis. Shocked wasn't the word for it as no one had any idea what they were going to do next. Vandy and I looked at each other in horror as the mob tied Luis' hands with a dirty jockstrap and put one over his face. Brody punched him in the gut. As if that wasn't enough, they dragged him to the shower room and face down dropped him in a puddle of grimy water. The whole hideous scene was no more than twenty seconds long.

We heard Luis sobbing. Brody, Mark, and the others, half-dressed, grabbed their belongings and as fast as they could, ran out hooting and yelling nonsense. Vandy and I rushed to Luis, pulled the jockstraps off his hands and head, lifted him, and carried him to a bench. He cried into my shoulder. Unsure of what to do, I patted his back trying to calm him as Vandy sat on his other side. A few minutes later, Luis pulled away from me keeping his head down and wiped his tears with his wet shirt. He got to his feet and tried to say something, but nothing came out. The moment was awkward and tense, and all I could hear was the drip of the shower. He stood and looked at both of us and he attempted to smile but his eyes were hauntingly dark and sad.

"Are you going to be okay?" I asked.

"Yeah. Yeah, I'm, ah…good. Really," Luis' voice cracked, and he turned and walked out of the room.

An empty and cold sensation engulfed me. The hollow feeling, somehow, seemed to deepen. I began to feel guilty because I did nothing while all this was going on. NOTHING. Hell, I didn't try to prevent this assault from happening and didn't even respond immediately. I felt sick. Vandy and I watched the whole injustice play out in front of us. *I did nothing.*

"Hell, Vandy, what should we do? We've got to do something."

"Don't even think about it—Brody and the others, well except me, are his first string. Besides, Luis said he was okay. Let's just leave it alone."

Coach had wrapped his whole pitiful life around his starters. Maybe Vandy was right. Jeopardizing *his* next championship seemed suicidal. Besides, Luis *did* say he was okay. Yeah—he said he was okay. Nothing good could come from this no matter what. Even if Luis was *okay*, there was no easing of the sharp pang that ripped inside of me. I was a coward—no better than Luis' aggressors.

As we left the gym, it was getting dark, and with it came a cold and occasional whip of a November wind. As I pulled the hood of my sweatshirt over my head, Vandy and I talked about everything but the last hour.

FIFTEEN

Haunting images of Luis laying helpless on the rank tile floor, and the crazed laughter coming from his assailants, plagued my consciousness that night. Tossing and turning in my bed, I conjured up repulsive thoughts that replayed in my mind of the exploit hours earlier. It was much more than a high school prank.

So much ricocheted in my brain that I could not process it all. I forced myself to think about a daffodil in the sunlight, a bowl of chocolate chip ice cream, and even my upcoming history test—anything, but every attempt to steer me away managed to lead me back to that moment.

Pranks are funny and innocent, but this revolting action was cruel—it was criminal. I couldn't rid the sinister smirks that ensnared Brody's face from my mind. What was abundantly more troubling was the fact that he was a rabid animal at best. There's no way to describe his behavior as he had no reason to do this—no reason. Like a shark's puny eye, his was lifeless and icy. His sinking black pupil surrounded by a striking pool of steel blue was most revealing. There, I saw venom. If he possessed kindness of any measure, he hid it from all. He was contaminated and any good in him had shrunk a hundred times to a wrinkled, pocked seed with little hope of germination. I could not help the way I felt. This was just who he was.

He was very charming and likable on the surface. Brody was popular. Everyone wanted to be with him and to be in his clique. Good-looking, physically fit, and intelligent, he seemed to have many qualities others wanted. Despite how he appeared, he was a tad too pretty by my standards. Something about him that I could not isolate was just not right. His hair was a little too blond, his eyes tweaked a bit too much in their corners, and his smile an iota too flawless.

Seeing him in the Commons shooting pool surrounded by other boys was typical. They all hoped, somehow, his *coolness* would rub off onto them. Just being around him was something others thought would nourish some part of their pathetic lives in a warped way. Brody spent much of his time impressing the hordes of his sexual prowess and his conquests whether they were real or not. He would give them tips on how to score and have their way with girls. He was hedonistic.

The most frightening part was that I stood paralyzed during the attack. I knew what was right and wrong. *Damn it!* Watching in fright, unfortunately, and avoiding the mayhem looped in my thoughts. I realized, though, they would never have lured me into participation, and acknowledging this to myself kept me sane. At least I wanted to believe they could never have lulled me into such an act.

Somehow, after many attempts, I managed to compartmentalize that moment so I could carry on. Focusing on basketball tryouts was my answer. Those first days of tryouts were grueling. It was much more than agonizing aches and pulled muscles—the fatigue of practice seeped into my mind. Getting up each morning was difficult. It wasn't just basketball, after all, I still had classes and homework. Practice, study hall, exams, and other responsibilities zapped my energy. I was never in my room just to chill. This was my therapy.

In a *compartment* or not, I stayed pissed at Brody, Mark, and the other first-stringers—minus Vandy. I tried not to let my feelings show. No way did they need to know what was going through my head. Ignoring and avoiding them before, during, or after practice was nearly impossible, but that was my aim.

When each practice was over there was a mandatory study hall in the library for those participating in tryouts, so once I got back to the room, I was too tired to do anything. Aiden would already be asleep. He never stayed up late anyway. By about the third day of tryouts, I started to think more about our new situation. I sensed he was putting some distance between us and didn't know why. I think he faked being asleep those nights. Why? When we had a moment here and there, he would tell me that things would have to wait, or he'd say he was too busy to stop and talk. A moment later, he'd be gone. It made me feel empty. I didn't like it but didn't know what to do about it.

*****

I remember we had a penance service in church around that time. We had to be there, but we didn't have to actually go into the confessional and confess our sins if we didn't want to. Even though there would be this translucent screen between the priest and me, I wasn't convinced this confab would be anonymous. That made me nervous to the point of sensing sweat drops under my shirt running down my sides from my underarms. I listened to those sweat drops. Like others, I sat and prayed, or at least, looked prayerful. Besides, God knew what I had been up to, so I figured I'd cut out the middleman and say the five *Hail Mary's* and five *Our Father's* and *promise to do better* since this was the usual penance given by the priest.

Going a bit further though, I prayed as if I had never prayed before. Prayer was always a chore for me—never understood prayer. What was it all about? If any being was omnipresent, wouldn't they know my prayers, hopes, and aspirations. Not so sure if I believed in the power of prayer, but I said I was sorry a thousand times for what I didn't do for Luis. Putting it all out of my head, I sat there. How many times can I say I'm sorry?

Why would God truly listen to me any more than the boy next to me? This question rolled over and over in my mind every time I thought about praying. If we both prayed for opposing events, both morally good, to whom does God listen? Multiply that by millions of people in hundreds of countries by people of EVERY religion and a lot of prayers are happening. Like asking for forgiveness—or asking for an A on a test—or asking that children are safe and have food; obviously, only a few people out of billions get their prayers answered. So, who gets the goods? Maybe we should limit our prayers to asking for kindness, or better yet, just for world peace. If we all did that and only that, think what the outcome could be. But it's a free-for-all and it's more like melted ice cubes in a flat Coke.

My prayers were mostly trivial compared with what was going on in the country or the world. Hell, tyrants, and villains were slaughtering children across the world. Why would God have any interest at all in listening to me unless it was about them? The eloquence of my thoughts and any altruistic or pure thought, which I cooked up, still

127

seemed so empty to me. I just kept thinking of all the people saying prayers at that exact moment all over the planet. I was convinced that on God's priority list of answering prayers, mine must be down at around the ten-trillionth marker. I thought, however, I better do it anyway.

One thing I do remember about how I prayed, then, was that I made it a habit of not asking God for too many specifics. The Robes always drilled into us never to make a covenant with God because he does not make deals. This was not the way to go, but now and again, containing myself was difficult. God had to be used to it. Everyone since the beginning of time has asked for self-serving stuff. I'm pretty sure about that. Can't cite any data right now, but I'm pretty sure. Not sure if I should have done it, but I prayed for a spot on the team. That prayer I made, out of design, was a short one. Droning on, I thought would be a bad way to handle it. Short and sweet, I believed, should be perfect. That day I asked God for a spot on the team, not to start, but a place on the squad. In a day, Luis would post the list of the first cuts on Coach Kidder's office door, so I wanted to pull out all the stops. I didn't think it could hurt, that is, to pray.

After I said amen, I looked around the church. In this building full of boys, I knew that in their hearts and minds they all had a desire or a wish of some kind, some grand and some small. I knew many were selfless in their thoughts, and if I had to place a bet, they were the ones that God listened to. I thought of my self-serving prayer and where it stood on God's list just among the other boys, and it brought me down a peg or two. Here I was asking for inclusion on a basketball team with Brody—this depraved kid, and I could only imagine Luis' prayers. He sat a few pews ahead of me with his head bent down and his hands together. Seeing beyond his facade and beneath his exterior, I felt for him. Not only because he was a victim of a heinous act, but now I looked at Luis differently. I now saw Luis as someone more like me, or I was more like him. We were all packaged differently and getting beyond the package was what most of us couldn't do. I paused at that moment and asked God to scratch my last prayer and replaced it with one for Luis.

As I looked around, I saw that most of the other boys were pensive, calm, but some, asleep. Brody and Mark were together as usual. They had their own sort of alliance. Brody had the skill of inciting a mob that would be a blind following at best—even in church. Mark, I was sure, was so happy to be in his presence and do anything for him. Obviously, they were whispering in the direction of Luis' ear. Squinting, I tried to read their lips but just couldn't decipher what it was they were mouthing. Luis paid absolutely no attention to the two and scooched further down the pew. *Good for him.*

The more I thought about Brody, the more I loathed him even in church. I knew hate was wrong but just couldn't change my feelings. I didn't like it and it tore me up. I never thought this way about anyone before, and that's the bombshell for me. Perhaps, that was the most troubling self-revelation I uncovered so far in my life—I could hate. Brody would be out of my life one day, but he was the one who exposed a filthy part of me—to me. Conveniently, I blocked this from my mind because I knew he was pretty but dangerous. After all, he could be a teammate of mine very soon.

Aiden entered church late by a side door and slinked in undetected and sat next to me. When I glanced over at him, it hit me like a baseball bat that over the last week, we've spoken maybe three full sentences to each other. I didn't like the fact we had not done much of anything lately. The more I thought about it, the more I knew we would be doing less and less if I made the team. It was hard enough that I had to spend time keeping up my grades but throwing basketball in the mix was creating a monster out of my life—a monster I was inviting to hang out with. Gosh, it was another yin and the yang that was always in my face.

I knew then, my life at St. Gus' would be even more different. True, it was going to be exciting. I would travel with the team while being a part of something so important. Reclaiming the championship was going to make us all heroes. Fantasizing about the final game, being the one who takes the shot at the buzzer for the championship looped in my mind. Aiden would understand. Sure, he would. He was on the team for three years and knew what it was all about. He would be right there cheering me on. I just knew that.

I knew too, I would have no time until March for anything other than my studies and basketball. Then Aiden and I would resume our journeys that I had come to love. Then we would take the time to explore and to talk just like before. We would have a little over two months before exams and graduation in early June. I turned to Aiden and whispered.

"So where have you been? It's like you sleep in the room, but I never see you anymore. Next cuts are tomorrow so the final team will be announced in two days."

"I've been around—I'm sure you've heard why I didn't show…so you going to make it?"

"I think so…yeah, I think so."

"Hey, remember, don't believe everything you hear."

Aiden noticed Coach Kidder and pointed him out to me.

"Look at him over there. I guess he's praying for a victory…so, are you going to confess some sins today? It's good for the soul," Aiden continued.

Maybe he knew what happened to Luis and that I did nothing. Or was I just being paranoid? I then refocused on the comment about why he didn't try out. Right after the penance service, I meant to ask him but before I knew it, he was gone. I was still too nervous to ask him, so it was fine by me.

I went to the library.

SIXTEEN

After our last classes on Monday, we raced to see if Coach included our names on the team list. By the time I got there, I was already behind about thirty boys, and too far back to see anyone's name. Tense, dejected boys with drooping shoulders and heads down walked past me in the opposite direction. They were silent and probably couldn't say much even if they wanted to. Others erupted with bubbling smiles and cries of delirium. Ping-ponging emotions ran rampant in the room as I pressed forward to see the list. It didn't take long for me to edge to the front as boys peeled away in a flash in record time once they knew their fate. Now to where I could see the names on the list, I scanned it up and down while my eyes jumped from name to name. There were about twenty names in all, and it was in no order. Then I saw it. I made the first cut. Excited, my smile ignored my attempt to contain my emotions and hijacked my face.

"You've got ten minutes to get your asses dressed to play and out on the court," shouted Luis.

In the locker room, emotions ran the gamut as some boys were gleefully preparing for another day of brutal drills, while others hurriedly cleaned out their lockers in a sullen hush. As an arrow leaves a bow, these boys were gone, but exhilaration now filled their space.

In less than five minutes, I was on the court. With the second and last cut coming within the next day, getting in as much practice as possible would be the smart thing to do. Coach Kidder was already on the floor with his arms folded tightly across his chest, his bottom lip stuck out and quivered as if it had a life of its own. *I better make all my shots today*, ran through my head, *and don't try anything stupid*. As the court filled with boys hustling for loose balls, Coach hollered out to me, so

131

I high-tailed over to him. Watching the others practice, he never took his eyes off them as he spoke to me.

"Eli, you're looking really good out here. I'm impressed. Most boys don't even attempt to make the team as seniors if they're new to the school, but I think you've got a good chance. Yes, a real good chance of getting some good playing time."

"Thanks Coach," was all I wanted to say. There was no way he could misinterpret that.

"A player I used to count on last year is now a disappointment—AWOL. And I could care less. I've got to make some decisions. You need to work hard, and you'll be just fine. So, if I were you, I'd listen and do as I say," he said pivoting his head and zeroing his eyes into mine. His stare dug in—how uncomfortable.

"Yes sir, you can count on me," I said thinking immediately that I should have left off, *you can count on me*—too peppy.

As he was orating, Brody wandered by and was within earshot. This was not good. I was the only one who needed to hear Coach's appraisal of me. I wanted Coach to wrap things up, but there was no end in sight.

"See, I run a simple but effective offense. No need to jazz it up—it works—that is if YOU practice it over and over again. Repetition is key—no need to think it out so I don't want you to think it out, so don't! If you know what I mean. I'm not looking for better ideas but looking for players who listen and work hard. I need good foot soldiers. Do you know what I mean?"

"Ah, ah yes, yes sir."

Looping in my head, I just kept saying, *speed it up, man*. I glanced at Brody, and he was drinking it all in.

"Well, I can tell you," Coach said, "all the others have been through the drill. They know what's coming. Our offense is quite simple but very effective if executed properly. See, Eli, that's key. Effective execution of what you know. First, you must know it or learn what it's all about, then you've got to practice it and then when the time is right, you've got to execute it. That's the way it is in life. We're all cogs if you know what I mean. Don't stand out but fit in and you will be successful. Repetition is crucial."

"Yes *sir.*"

"Now you go back with the others and practice a bit more before we begin. Oh, and take Brody with you." If nothing else, Coach could see the warning signs, so to speak.

Brody didn't like the fact he was called out but slapped on a big grin for Coach's sake and ran back with me to the other side of the court. Brody buttonholed me and gave me his own pep talk.

"So, Eli, you got your first little one-on-one with Coach. I wouldn't give it another thought. He tells everyone what he told you. He really likes when we take the initiative and a few risks when we play. That's what he's looking for in his players. He likes the excitement."

I saw right through him, shook my head, and began to walk in a different direction. I would not allow myself to be his fool. He grabbed my shoulder and he got into my face. He took another, firmer, tact.

"Hey, he's going to cut someone, Eli. He's not going to carry extra players and you don't think it's going to be one of us who have been here through it all—newbie! You know? Look around. He's not going to cut the fellas who've been here victory after victory and championship after championship. Besides, he's asked a couple of sophomores to work out with us, you know, to learn the ropes. They are the future. I wouldn't bank on wearing the blue and gold just yet, bucko," he said jabbing his index finger into my chest.

"Oh really, championship after championship? Really? Weren't you on JV when we won the *last* championship? Brody, you're a real piece of crap. Just stay out of my way."

As other boys dribbled balls and launched their shots to the hoop, Brody continued his harassment. Others heard what he said and although they did not speak up in support, their silence signified a quiet brotherhood. Vandy too said nothing, but I figured he had a different target on his back as he was one of the few black students. Not to take anything from him, but at his height and obvious ability and talent, no one fooled around with him. Vandy being such a good-hearted person never participated in demeaning acts but never did much to stop them. He was neutral most of the time—like Switzerland. I never looked to him to come to my rescue. I didn't need anyone to do that anyway. I just needed to suck it up.

I hated Brody before at a troubling distance but one that I could handle. Now his toxins were working their way into my pores, and I didn't like it. Was it worth it? I mean, I could see that it wasn't just Brody but also his entourage that could make my life miserable.

Coach blew his whistle and practice began. We started with running like usual, but it wasn't long before we moved to precision drills that were parts of actual plays. Coach divided us into smaller groups to work on specific skills depending upon our positions. He paired up Brody and me several times because we both played the second guard position, or as I like to think of it—shooting guard. Hard to believe, he was a good sport most of the time even when I got the best of him in some drills. Wishful thinking led me to believe that if he could see me as a decent ballplayer and a teammate contributing to the team, then he may loosen up and the others would follow.

In the last half of the practice, we scrimmaged. The gold team was the veteran team, while the blue team was the rest of us. The game was nothing out of the ordinary. Neither team outperformed the other. We were all sloppy with passes and hitting our spots with our plays. At certain times, though, it was like magic. Maybe at the time I didn't think like this, but basketball when done right, was something other than a game. For reasons for which I don't know why, ten players, a couple of coaches, and a thousand spectators, all at once could believe the most important part of life that very moment was *that* basketball game.

The plays we learn, the perfect passes, and the beauty of movement, if there was any, meant nothing if your ball did not go through the hoop more times than that of your opponent. The most important spot of the game was not on the court, but it was ten feet above at an invisible point in which the ball can go nowhere but through and down. That spot was it. That spot always made the difference.

The second half was the opposite of the first. It was as if the championship of the free world was on the line. No more smiles. No more Mr. Nice Guy. It was intense and it was warfare. Out of the gold's arsenal came clandestine shoving and pushing which Coach rarely acknowledged. I was sure he knew what was going on, but ignorance was always bliss, especially when it came to the stars of the team. I looked at Brody as I guarded him coming down the court. He had that look in his eyes that I had seen a week earlier during the locker room assault, and I didn't like it. I knew I was in for trouble, but I had my own agenda and Brody was just one of the ten of us.

On the dribble, he attempted a move I had seen him do many times before. I reached in and got my fingertips on the ball and was able to swat it away. With my quickness, I beat him to the loose ball and sped down court for a simple lay-up. A few minutes later, my team had the ball, and someone took a shot. I went up for a rebound, felt a jab in my gut, and I dropped like a bag of rocks to the floor. Coach didn't call the foul, but I was the last one down the court as I held my side. Brody gave me a jagged smile, and at which moment he, again, reaffirmed my dread for him. His smile showed his imperfections coming through. I knew what he was thinking. The heat continued beyond the boiling point.

Growing embittered as the bout wore on, I endured shoves to my back and points of elbows to my ribs all from my newly confirmed nemesis. This was not my doing, but my retaliation would be on my own terms. With intensity escalating, my heart hammered, and adrenalin rushed the more the ball hit that invisible magic spot when I shot. I had blinders on which helped me focus on the objective of depositing the ball successfully through the hoop. This only fed Brody's grotesque nature. Time after time, I physically paid for my successes with shoves and elbows.

It wasn't basketball. It was more of a cockfight that heaved from the fervor of the court. No longer did I care about earning respect from my potential teammate, but I wanted to squash him where it counted. He, too, took no victims as he drained a few baskets. Too bad he was such a jerk. With ten seconds remaining and down by a point, I controlled the ball. Seconds passed and time was running out. I made my move to the basket and found daylight. As I launched what would be the game-winner, Brody pummeled me hard, and I hit the hardwood with an echoing thud. Coach called the foul and, this time, he scolded Brody. Vandy reached out grabbed my hand and pulled me to my feet.

I took my time as I walked to the charity stripe. As I did, Brody went out of his way and approached me with a silly grin and patted me on my butt. He paused and with what appeared as a handshake to make peace, Brody pulled me in and whispered, "I hope you have the balls to win the game unlike your wussy roommate last March."

I said nothing because my free throws would speak for me. We won the scrimmage, and I sealed my fate—both as an obvious new member of the team and as someone who needed to watch his back. Brody would surely create new strife for me on this team.

After practice, Coach told us he would post his final team the next day. Vandy and I stayed on the court as the others went to the locker room. I wanted to be alone, but I appreciated the fact Vandy read the tea leaves and decided to hang back.

"Is it true, Vandy? I mean was it Aiden who missed the game-winner?"

"It's true. We all like Aiden, well except Brody and a few of his tight groupies, so we don't bring it up."

"I thought so…just didn't want to ask. Is that the reason he's not here? Did he bail out because he let the team down?"

Vandy paused and looked away, "I don't know Eli. Aiden keeps some things to himself. He told me he had other things to do with his final year and basketball wasn't a priority anymore. It lost meaning to him. I think he doesn't like that some things come down to winning and losing. Don't get me wrong, Aiden likes to win like the next guy, but he sees much more than the final score."

"Yeah, I think you're right," I mumbled.

"He was the reason we won most of our games last year. Some see him as a quitter, but they just don't know him. He's anything but a loser. You know that." Vandy said with a nod.

"Hmmm, I don't know Vandy. He talks a big game. Not showing up makes him look weak—it makes him look like a loser and a quitter. How can I believe him now when he spouts off like he's an authority on stuff?"

Vandy glared at me. "Where's your heart, man. Besides, if he were out here, someone would have to go. Coach keeps the same number every year. Only four graduated last year and he always keeps four sophomores no matter what. If you do the math, you'd realize that your spot was his—or Brody's. You guys all play the same position."

"Vandy, if I make the team, it's because of me and not because Aiden didn't try out."

"You're probably right Eli. Maybe it's Brody who is the lucky one after all."

SEVENTEEN

Some things, like it or not, just have a way of gnawing at you. I didn't know if I was seething because of Brody's evil ways or the discovery of Aiden's legacy. Maybe it was the nasty mixture of everything down to the way I felt about myself. Taking things to heart has always been a big problem for me. My semester so far should have been a meaningless episode in my life. What was sure, however, was a grinding and raw sensitivity that rooted itself at the seat of my belly. The day after I sank those free throws, I felt like something was grinding inside of me. Despondent, I couldn't get these thoughts out of my head as they all had a knack for contaminating my best attempt to focus elsewhere.

I FELT ALONE.

The zeal and excitement that comes with the drive of competition came to me with little warning. Primal reactions kicked in. Aiden, it seemed, couldn't hack it, and he outright abandoned the team. He didn't even clue me in. In all this, I did not know where I stood. Trying to make sense out of suspicions knotted my state of mind. I did not know how to understand my feelings about any of these experiences. This disturbed me, and I didn't like it. My feelings came from a part of me that I didn't know existed—a place I've never been and wouldn't know how to get there if asked.

Wishing I had never met Brody, my hatred for him festered even though the problems in my head were mine. In all honesty, he had very little to do with them. His petty goading, however, unleashed my flood of emotions. No one should be able to do that—no one. I despised him for managing to help me to dismantle my safety valve that I thought only I controlled.

Why didn't Aiden tell me about this before? I was pissed that Brody leached out, very methodically, his tainted views about Aiden to me. He used my friend's misfortune to attempt to create mine. But it backfired on Brody. I was victorious and proved to him, to me, and everyone else that I'm a player. I earned it and the respect that was due me—every ounce of it. My victory that day, however, shined a light on Aiden. Maybe dimmed now, this glaring light will be back, and I fully know that many more battles were charging my way. Was a game worth all this? Was anything worth this?

So, feeling this way, basketball was over for me. I decided not to return. Maybe I, too, was a quitter. Maybe I couldn't hack playing on *this* team. It was my decision, and it was based on my gut feeling—my intuition—for a change. Because I usually calculated my every move, this decision of mine made no sense to me. I mapped things out, but not this time. I listed my pros and cons to diminish risk, but this time was different. This was my decision and only mine. It came from a place I rarely call upon, but the greatest thing about my decision is that I didn't even agonize over it. Yeah, I agonized over what led up to it, but not the decision. My heavy lift was over, and I was gratified by what I decided.

Deep inside I knew I wanted to spend more time with Aiden.
Deep inside I knew I didn't want to spend most of the time with those people.
Deep inside I knew Aiden had his reason.
Deep inside I knew I was beginning to own up to myself.
Deep inside I knew I was changing.

I needed to do things differently and realized it was going to take a long time for me to understand what was really going through my head. No, it was all about what I was feeling.

Wondering why I didn't show up to check out the final list for the team, Vandy stopped by the room that night. He told me that my name was on the official list and made the final cut. Maybe a bit overconfident, but I expected it due to my performance on the last day of practice as well as everything else I did. At a place where they revere aggression, my display was admirable and was ultimately rewarded. Hearing the news from Vandy didn't move me one way or another.

Nothing came from within. Happiness, satisfaction, or pleasure didn't register anywhere in me. In that natural state of mind, I was sure my decision was the right one.

Vandy clued me in that a hungry lion was tame compared to Coach Kidder's reaction to my absence from the next practice just hours after the posting. Not showing up for the first day of practice and telling no one was perhaps a mistake but was Coach's anger the normal emotion for my action? Hell, I could have been dead for all he knew. In a way, I was. In another way, I was more alive than ever before, but it would take time for that to kick in.

*****

The next day was overcast. Alone, I stood in front of the heavy wooden doors of the gym. I inhaled the cold air, held it for a moment, and then slowly exhaled all I took in and then some. The cold air I sucked in had turned warm.

With my shoulder, I pushed open the doors and walked in. It wasn't much warmer in the cavernous building, but at least there was no wind kicking up and slicing into me. What little there was, only natural light filtered through the smudged windows and deep, long shadows invaded the court. No one was in sight. It was thirty minutes before the start of practice. I was alone.

Picking up the lone ball that sat at one end of the court, I dribbled it as I walked down the blue sidelines. Each bounce echoed and seemed so much louder today. I got to the team bench and sat. Looking up at the numerous banners, I began to daydream. Hearing the squeak of Chuck Taylors' on the hardwood, I looked to the scoreboard, and it showed a tied game with one second remaining. The cheers were loud and looking around the bleachers, were hundreds of screaming fans. I saw myself on the free-throw line and...

"What the *hell* are you doing in here?"

Jolted away from my daydream, I heard Coach Kidder's bark. I jumped up nearly out of my shoes, dropped the ball, and faced his direction. Saying nothing, I watched the ball bounce a few times and roll toward him. He began walking my way from the other side of the court. Approaching half-court, he stopped in his tracks and picked up

139

the ball. He looked up to the rafters inspecting the championship banners. I decided to meet him at half court and took my time with each step until I stood squarely on the letter A. At an arm's length in front of him, I was just far enough away that he couldn't land a punch with any kind of ease. He shifted his attention from gazing up to peering at me. This was the first time I realized he was an inch or so shorter than me. His eyes...they were green.

"Thank you," I said.

"Thank you! What are you thanking me for?"

"You chose me for your team. Thank you. I'm sorry, but I won't be playing on the team," I said keeping my eyes on him.

"You're damn right about that. You gave that up the very minute— the second—you didn't show. That was a very stupid mistake, sonny."

I was already among the multitude he called *sonny*.

"I know, and for that I'm sorry—should've let you know right away."

Coach Kidder said nothing but, again, we maintained this uneasy eye contact. Part of his face twitched here and there. His lips moved up and down in what I gathered was a nervous response. Then he spoke.

"I suspect you have your reasons, and I respect that. I'll leave it there. I don't need to know or want to know," he said. Just then, absolute quiet shrouded us. I nodded and he pursed his lips and looked away.

I turned and began to walk toward the door. Then I heard something that I will never forget.

"You're a good man, Eli."

*****

When I returned to the room, I still gave Aiden the cold shoulder. Planning to bury my feelings, I couldn't stop, and it just happened. My reaction emerged from somewhere as it stunned me. *I wanted to hang out with him—damn it! The big reason I quit!* He probably knew from Vandy, but I never told him I quit. Just didn't feel like talking to him. But as truth had it, my cold exterior was the reaction to a smoldering boil inside and it was getting worse. Even when I knew I was being a jerk,

I became more of one. Not proud, at all, of how I acted. Not knowing what to say to him, what little that slipped from my lips was anything but what I intended to convey. My reaction was to dodge him as before, so I left the room. I came back late and went to bed. Perhaps I thought he owed me an explanation and if not an explanation, it seemed that he owed me the truth. He owed me something—that was for sure. Or did he? It was just too much all at once. Things between us weren't right. I didn't like the feeling.

After taking my last midterm the next day, I was the first to finish and left the building. I walked throughout the campus and saw no one. The gusts of wind were blades thrust at me as I wandered around the grounds. Overhead the sky was a shade of bitterness and blended with the hues of the gray boulders of the buildings at St. Gus. These stones were like mood rings mirroring a pathos from inside me. The only glint of color that day came from the few obstinate orange and fiery red leaves that fixed themselves to bony branches or swirled singularly and flitted around me. Despite the dates on the calendar, fall gave way to winter over the last week, and, to me, its stirring entangled my soul.

In succumbing to impending heartless weather, the scent of nature was gripping. The fleeting smell of the mishmash of leaves intimated a tang of death—or like a foul incense that bothered me. It was a sacrifice of nature as the sorrowful and sweet bouquet of life rang out and replaced with the callowness of the impending season. Leaves, controlled by an invisible force, chased each other in a circle that was a blur of their individuality and were now dirty little cyclones going nowhere. There is sweetness and bitterness in nature in every season. Why winter seems to get a bum rap I will never know. Because without its cold and gray lining, we would never appreciate the warmth of the summer sun. I just need to keep remembering that.

Headed nowhere, my head down to shield my cracking lips from the breath of winter, I kicked pebbles from the path. I meandered. Startled, I felt a point digging into my shoulder. Looking behind me was Father Meinrad jabbing his slender finger my way. He was carrying two large boxes. With caution, I commandeered one to relieve his burden as we exchanged the basics of a greeting. He motioned with a smile and a nod signaling me to help him on the rest of his journey to his office. Of course, I was gracious and accommodating.

I followed him into his office and closed the door with my heel. It was quiet. Buffered from outside and amazingly cushioned from all that was inside the rest of the building, I was in a sanctum of sorts. With unsuspecting intensity, I contrasted the scents of outside. Like an emerging animal from a dark den to the glare of a stark blanket of snow, it was two worlds. The mixture was of tobacco, coffee, and smoldering embers in a fireplace. It all cavorted with the faintness of harp music emanating from invisible speakers.

After we put the boxes by his desk, Father asked me if I wanted to sit for a while. I nodded my head and sat. He offered me a cup of coffee that he made about an hour earlier. Oddly, as I guardedly sipped from a Disneyland souvenir mug, I pleasantly discovered the coffee was fresh.

"Father, this is straight up the best coffee. How come we don't get this at The Hurl, ah, ah Hurley Hall?"

"Eli, you're lucky to get coffee at all. Every other year or so, we discuss whether or not we are harming our youth by offering coffee as part of your meals. As you must imagine, we have so many important issues at stake to discuss," he said with his quirky laugh.

"Your fire is going out, Father. It needs to be stoked."

"*My* fire is still quite hot," he said with a chuckle. "But if you mean the one in the fireplace, yes, please take care of it. While you're at it, tell me about you and Brody and the basketball team."

In front of the hearth, I squatted with my back to Father and pulled open the screen. As I placed a split knotty log on the blistering cinders, I agonized over what my response would be. Punctuating the calm, Father cleared his throat as he sat back in an overstuffed leather chair that let out a puff of air that forced me to smile.

"Sounds like..."

"I know...I know." Father said with a quirky laugh.

Out of the corner of my eye, I saw that he reached for his pipe and matches and went to reignite his smoke as he tried to rekindle our conversation. I took a deep breath and the aromas of Columbian beans roasting, hard oak charring, and Edgeworth tobacco glowing all mixed and swirled together in a friendly and alluring concoction.

"So, Eli, what's going on? Come sit down."

"I quit the team and I'm not sure why. Don't get me wrong, it was a good decision, I just can't pinpoint the exact reason why. Something about that team I just didn't like. I kept telling myself that it was going to be great and not to worry," I said poking the logs in the fireplace.

"Enough with the fire. What do you mean Eli?"

"Father, it all started to look like crap. Oh, sorry, Father. What I really mean is that Aiden bailed on the team and didn't even try out. On top of that, he was the one that choked last year and couldn't deal with it, so he quit the team. Aiden showed his true colors to me, and I'm all mixed up."

"I see."

"I didn't know why and didn't ask either, but Brody told me all this on the last day of tryouts. He showed me what Aiden is truly all about, and, I guess, it was hard to swallow. And it hurts because I like Aiden and it's all very confusing to me. It didn't seem like going for this team was worth all this shit…, sorry. I mean, it didn't seem worth the effort."

"It's okay. If it looks that way to you then just say it. Shit!"

"Okay, shit. There, I said it . . . shit, shit! There I said it again."

"No, Eli, you proclaimed it." With that, we laughed. I whipped the fireplace screen back into place and sat in an overstuffed chair facing Father. It let out a fart of its own and we both smiled. He brought us back on track and resumed the conversation.

"Maybe Brody showed you what Brody is all about." He paused and took a few puffs of his pipe. "But it's true. Aiden missed what would have been the winning basket at the buzzer. A lot of pressure for a young man, don't you think, Eli?"

"Yes, Father, it is. But I can't help how I feel. I just can't believe he quit. It doesn't seem to be his style. He's so self-assured. He's so confident. He's so…"

"Oh, I wouldn't view this as a kink in his armor. That's not why he's sitting out this year. First of all, did Brody tell you that Aiden scored twenty-two points, was seven for nine from the line, and had five rebounds and five assists that night?"

"Well, no. He, he told me ah . . ."

"Did my boy Brody tell you that with five seconds left *he* caught what would have been an assist from Aiden and *he* missed a lay-up? Some would say an *easy* lay-up."

"No, I didn't know any of this."

"And did Brody, or any of the others, tell you that Aiden's last-second shot was a twenty-five-footer on an inbound pass with one second left on the clock?"

I shook my head again and couldn't believe it. Here I wanted to be a lawyer and I didn't get any of the facts. I believed the one person whom I truly detested. *What was I thinking?*

"Eli, I believe some of his teammates, who cannot think past their noses, blame Aiden as the reason they lost the game that bitter day. They are not willing to see that they all had an opportunity to make a difference. They all wanted someone else to step up. None of them came to play. They could have all joined me in the stands and contributed as much."

"Hmmm. Now that I know most of those guys, I can see what you're saying."

"As you know Eli, it never comes down to the play of one teammate. When it came down to making that difference, they depended too heavily on Aiden. And it wasn't just his teammates. It was the coach, it was the cheering section, the alumni, and the good Fathers. Well, Aiden is a boy; he is as human as they come. They were looking for a superhero to cure what ailed them, to save them, to cloak the school in another meaningless championship banner. How many of those damn things do we need?" he asked soberly.

Father hesitated as if he were waiting for me to answer. But I assumed it was rhetorical. Even in his pain, he remained calm and pleasant as always. Eye contact lost, we gazed into the popping fire for a moment. At first, I thought he was ready to leave it at that, but he had more on his mind.

"The point of winning and losing obscured the adventure. The adventure of growing, learning, and playing. Of enjoying what they were all doing. Goals are good and are needed, but when all else is lost or abandoned along the way, what good are goals?"

I sat in silence. Never had I heard Father so passionately share his thoughts. Suspended on each thought, I realized how stupid I was.

144

Father told me Aiden didn't leave the gym a loser that night. They had talked and he knew he did his best every day he played. He gave it his all. That, Father reminded me, was all that anyone could ask of his fellow man. The coach and his teammates wanted and expected more. Father continued with his message to me.

"Brody has done much to taunt and tease Aiden since then—and before, actually. He has humiliated him and some of the boys now believe Brody's words. He said other things that have nothing to do with that night that has been hurtful. I liken it to brainwashing. Sorry to say, Eli, but he caught you in his net."

"He has a way about himself. Even though I knew I shouldn't listen to him, I still did," I said.

"Sure, he's charismatic, and when he talks, he sounds like he knows what he's saying, but unfortunately, he speaks from a shallow spirit and a hardened core. I truly don't know why, but Brody fascinates me. I love him too."

"What? Oh yeah, you have to love everyone."

"No, in fact, I don't, but I find it easier to go in that direction with people than the other way. Instead of using my energy hating, I use it to love. Love always wins—always, Eli. It's a far stronger force in the universe than hate. Always remember that, my boy."

I nodded and it made me think. Father continued. "He's so convincing and smart, but he's daunting at best. Maybe it is how he grew up. The two are a regular Cain and Abel."

"I know it didn't turn out well for Abel, but do you think they can become friends?"

"No. As difficult as it is to say, there is no reason for their friendship. Perhaps we do not need to be friends with everyone that comes our way. However, we must learn from all who do come our way, or we will forever possess the smallest of small hearts. See, it's not about accumulating friends, it is about loving ourselves so that we may love all others. Yes, if we are fortunate, we will attract a few *real* friends along the way."

During our conversation, I found out both Aiden and Brody had similar backgrounds. Both were from the Valley, although different towns, and Brody didn't know his folks either. They both lost their parents before they knew them. Brody's response to his upbringing was, I thought, completely the opposite of Aiden's. I never thought about those who endured hardships growing up, but I was sheltered with no reason to know at that time. That kind of awareness comes as time moves on and as we see life through the eyes of others.

I sat in awe. It was difficult to believe Father was telling me this tale. It was all true, at least how I now saw it. Though we were talking in confidence, the more I thought about it the more I detected something more in his voice. What, I just didn't know.

"Eli, in my many years at St. Augustine's, I have worked with hundreds of boys, but Brody is the first one of which I have not made sense. If anyone has failed, it has been me. I have let him slip away. Don't get me wrong, I'm still on his case so to speak. I will not give up hope, and I love him as I love you. He will find the good in his heart one day... I hope."

Father became mellow now editing out his emotions as he spoke. His love for the boys of St. Augustine's was robust and so alive. His actions showed this, but his words underscored his compassion. He wanted us all to experience the joys of life but to understand the sorrows allowing them to help us grow. Now, I could tell why Aiden sought to learn so much from this man. Father had a gift to guide whether I wanted him to or not.

"Eli, I don't want Brody to be the catalyst to drive the good from others. Also, please don't judge Brody. Just avoid him, at least right now. Although you will not be on the team, he still sees you as some kind of threat."

"Huh? A threat! Father, I don't know what you're talking about."

"My son, you and Vandy were there to give a fallen schoolmate comfort and compassion."

His statement surprised me. "Father, are you talking about what happened to Luis?"

Father nodded. "Yes, I am. Frankly, it is not you who needs to seek amends, but I wasn't about to let you fester in the excrement of another's vile act. I want you to know that Luis is grateful."

"Thanks Father."

"Good is only good because we have evil—unfortunately. My son, be aware of evil and its ways. See it, but don't let it sway you. Find solutions in the goodness of your heart."

"We helped Luis, but we stopped short."

"You, Eli, have much to learn, and I want you to be open to learning your entire life. You have learned from this horrific experience and if you are ever confronted with something like this again, you will respond differently—I know it. You helped Luis. It is as simple as that."

"You learned all this straight from Luis? Luis told you?"

"Yes…he will be fine. But Brody, I'm not so sure. I don't know how long he can go terrorizing others," Father said stroking his chin. "I don't like thinking this way, but the universe has its ways."

"Hmmm. Do you mean God?"

"God is our way of understanding, so I see God and the universe as inseparable."

"Gosh, I'm blown away with this conversation."

"My dear Eli, the more we are willing to stretch ourselves, the more we may be—in your words—blown away."

I'm sure you're right. But Father, what about Aiden? I mean he must have been pretty fed up to decide to quit."

"Aiden learned that life is full. He committed much time to play basketball and by every measure left it a winner. I admire his courage to admit he was ready to close a chapter and start a new one. Many people hang on much too long. I, also, admire your ability to make your decision for your unique reasons. A game, a contest, may be fun and exciting but that is all it is. Its moment ends soon enough."

"You're right. I am beginning to see that."

"It stirs our passion; it gives us a glimpse of euphoria, but when that moment ends, as I said, it is over. We must lead a life in which our happiness doesn't emerge from only brief moments, but from the thread that passes through all these moments. I call this thread, joy, Eli. It is far more gratifying than the highs and excitement of momentary happiness. Believe me, it's the *thread* that gives us the joy."

"Yeah, I was totally driven by that excitement," I added.

"Yes Eli, competition can bring out our best and our worst. Like good and evil, games would be nothing if losing were not a part of the experience. No one would attend the World Series if both teams were winners. We as humans cannot yet create games that are truly analogous to the essence of what we truly are—humans. Humans are not there yet. I mean we create games around a singular dimension of what it is to be human, like competition. We are so much more. But *competition* has captured the masses since the beginning of time. If only we emulated how children play."

"Father, you really think about stuff," I said nodding. We both smiled.

I don't know why it hit me at that very moment, but Aiden must have presumed because of my cold and distant demeanor, I sided with Brody. In fact, and unwittingly, I guess he was right.

"Father, I'm beginning to figure out some things. It's like I willingly joined this sparring match with Brody and, for the time being, I thought I came out ahead. I bulldozed headfirst into the worst part of competition and that was for all the wrong reasons. Worst of all, I believed the creep and didn't listen to myself. I've got to listen to my gut."

"Yes, my boy I think you are correct."

"He poisoned my thoughts, but the scary part is that I allowed him to do so. I sent him an invitation and he accepted. To be honest, most of all, I figured out that I want to spend time with Aiden. Is that normal?"

"What? Why of course that is normal. *Know thyself* as Plato once said. "What do you mean?"

"When one truly knows who they are and knows the good they possess, they do not need to apologize. Eli, you need not ask if you are normal or what you are doing is normal. After all, who defined *normal?* Man in power—man has his fingerprints on everything. Sometimes he tries to convince us that *his* definitions are *His* definitions."

"Hmmm. Lot's going on in my head right now."

"Give it time. You know you have someone to talk to."

"Yes, thanks Father."

"So, coming back to the mundane, what about your love for basketball?" Father asked.

"I think intramurals for the dorm will be enough for me now."

"I understand, though, you *did* win the scrimmage for the blue team. Will intramurals truly be enough?"

"No, Father, I won it for me and for all the wrong reasons. I'm fine… there's something more out there that I should be doing. I made the team so that's good enough for me. I left on my own terms—so that's even better. I'm fine with where I am."

"My boy, you're going to be okay."

"I think you might be right."

"Eli, be kind to yourself. You are a good man."

*****

Later during the day when I got back to the room, Aiden was there lying on his bed tossing a football toward a tiny dot on the ceiling. Saying nothing, I walked over to him. He continued throwing the ball just barely grazing the dot each time. He stayed focused on his rhythm and did not acknowledge me whatsoever. So, I held out my arm to intercept the ball. As I did, I mistimed the speed of the descending ball, and lost my balance. To avoid landing on him, I leaped over him careening to the floor. It was a total wipe-out, and I looked stupid. Covering the floor like spilled milk, all that Aiden could see from his vantage point was my outstretched arm clutching the ball and holding it high.

"Touchdown!" Aiden shouted.

We laughed until tears streamed down our faces.

EIGHTEEN

One biting December Saturday afternoon before the Christmas break, Aiden and I faced the frigid temperatures to trek to the *old lady*'s house. The sun made its presence known through gleaming billowy clouds that encircled its glare. Yet, like a block of ice, nature was locked in its own frozen existence. The trunks of the trees and their spindly arms stood motionless like cracks against a somber sky. The hush by itself was, perhaps, a harbinger of what was to come.

Before too long we found ourselves sitting in the parlor around a stingy fire that we made by using a few left-over charred logs and random sticks and twigs we found near the front of the house. Neither of us wanted to spend any extra time searching for kindling to burn. Sounds odd, but we chose to be lazy over being warm. Although our meager fire kept most of its heat to itself, we could just about tell we were out of the cold. Our backsides, however, depended only upon the warmth our bodies produced as we sat in old mildew stinking, but formal, wingback chairs.

We went there to take a break from the pressures of midterm lunacy. Presumably, I would be a part of it, if not a major contributor to the fervor if I were in the library studying with the rest of our classmates. The library was steamy, sultry, and smelly due to the sheer body count of everyone virtually on top of each other. It was oppressive. This alone pushed some of the kids closer to their breaking points. The stressors of knowing their grades could make or break them and hinder them from acceptance to their first choice of college were unnerving for many. Worse yet, the thought that their dad would take away their wheels over holiday or summer breaks hung heavy in the balance as well. Reacting was the only way to act as teenagers. Yes, it was rough here, but I had little concern for those who pissed away their semester and tried to cram the day before an exam. That just doesn't work.

Enticed by Aiden, I gave up my last-minute studies—it was more of a final review anyway. I was ready. Prepared as I would ever be, now was a time to relax and mellow out. This was the first time I had ever thought this way before exams, and it was an *awesome* feeling. Aiden, nevertheless, was prepared as he got the grades without cracking a book most times. There was a time this would have singed my ego, but I liked Aiden too much for that to get in the way. My self-worth seemed to be growing right in front of me. It wasn't any of my business, but if he were a studier, who knows what he could possibly do with his life.

Without warning, my mind went another way, and I began to vacillate. Next thing that came to mind was the thought I made a mistake and should be in the library breathing the putrid air, elbow to elbow, with the likes of Luis, Vandy, Brody, and the rest of them. Little steps…little steps, I kept saying in my head.

Anyway, here we were. It was difficult to believe this house stood abandoned. Alone, it survived like a monument built on holy ground. The place was like something one sees their entire life and never takes the time to read the bronze plaque at its foot. The students showed very little interest in this place, and the Robes knew of its presence but for most, it was too difficult to make the trip, especially this time of year. Likewise, because of the oppressive heat and humidity of the summer, you wouldn't find any of the Robes nearby. The way here was not long, but the path overflowed with serpentine and exposed roots and stones that presented obstacles for low flying feet. Although others found their way here on occasion, we never crossed paths with anyone else. Funny, but we never saw others coming or going, but we knew we were not the only visitors.

The place was a forgotten haven decaying from the inside out. For me, it was special. The artistry, the imported Italian marble, the South American influences carved in the molding, and the mantels were all very intriguing. Everything told a story. Looking back, I would find that others would see this place as unique for completely different reasons. I never let on to anyone that I liked this kind of thing. Aiden, somehow, could pull it off but not me. They didn't need to know all about me. Besides, I didn't need to subject myself to, what I was sure, unneeded heartache from their reaction.

Other boys, we were certain, saw the house as a place where they could smoke pot or have sex without fear of getting caught. We just knew the potheads hung out here even though we never found any hard evidence. Curious, we snooped around on occasion. The Robes were unaware of any of this, we were sure. As far as sex, St. Agnes was not too far away through the woods so I'm sure that was a possibility. At night, though, this place was creepy for anyone to visit for any reason. That was my guess anyway. Changing times would invade this refuge, but for now, it was definitely a throwback to simpler days. Simple times have a way of turning one-eighty degrees without much warning, but maybe that's the way it's supposed to be.

Aiden rekindled the fire and threw on a scorched log from a previous fire. As time stretched on, it seemed to produce more heat. Mesmerized by the glow of the flame, I sat back with a book in hand. Aiden wrote, nonstop, in his journal. Opening the book, I thumbed through the pages but instantly decided I was bored.

"So, what are you writing about?" He didn't answer. "You writing about our canoe trip?" Nothing. "Are you really Brody in disguise?" Silence. "Oh, Brody *is* your evil twin? I see..."

"Huh? Did you say something?" he asked me.

"Nothing—go back to your writing." I laughed and Aiden scribbled away.

Sitting there and looking around without anything to do, I spotted a low wooden table in the corner of the room. It was fat and round and looked more like a tree stump than a table. It gave me an idea. I decided it would make for a perfect ottoman so I could kick up my feet and make myself comfortable. Bulky as it was, pushing it across the room to where we were sitting was no easy task. No getting around it, the scratching sound it made as I pushed the heavy chunk of furniture from one side to another was painful on the ears. Aiden glared at me.

"What? This thing is heavier than it looks," I volunteered.

Giving me a forced smile and a nod, he went back to his writing. I propped up my feet, dusted myself off, and it took me a minute to get comfy in my new setup. All the while, Aiden glanced over at me a few times. I didn't say a word, but it wasn't long before I was sitting back and mesmerized by the flicker of the blaze. It seemed as if I heard music as my eyes were unwittingly pulled to the blue and yellow staccato flames. The crackle and the rhythm of the flames led me to daydream. The moment was the only moment that mattered. I just liked hanging with Aiden.

Piercing my imaginary bubble, Aiden blurted out, "This is like *the spot* in a way."

"In what way? I mean, Aiden, it seems like it is the opposite of *the spot*. We go there when it's warm and it's a totally natural place. It's outside, we're inside."

"It has nothing to do with any of that. It's all about the moment. You know what I mean?"

"Yeah...the moment. I was just thinking about that."

"Yeah, you know what I'm talking about. So often when we are there, at *the spot*, it seems as if all is just right, you know, the feeling needs nothing else to sustain itself. Nothing that man can offer anyhow. Human words would do it an injustice. Hell, they would disembowel it."

"Huh? Yuck."

He continued on his tangent, "Gosh, I think there aren't enough words to describe everything, but maybe we'll get there one day. I mean, we have far to go before we can pull out all our feelings and convey them to others."

"Then again, maybe we shouldn't." I wasn't exactly sure what I meant by saying that, but it rolled forth from my lips without a thought behind it.

"You may be right. There are many ways we can communicate. You remember, we talked about that the first time I brought you down there. You know, to *the spot*."

"Yeah, you're right. I remember. What did you call it? Was it something like a moment of *phenomenal* or was it *astonishing*, insight?" I said with a trace of sarcasm. He ignored my attitude and he continued unscathed.

"It's in moments like these when humans have drawn the self-portrait, scribbled a sonnet or poem. Or they've written the lyric that evades consciousness, most times, but has been at the tip of his—or her—tongue but could never go beyond their lips."

I looked at him and said, "Aiden, you never cease to amaze me. Where the hell do all these random thoughts come from?"

"Can't answer that or I'd have to kill ya."

"Oh really? So, it's top-secret Mr. Bond?"

"No—to be honest, I just think that random thoughts are where big things begin. The more random the better—no rules. Shape and form come *way* later. In fact, if you find yourself getting to that point right away, it's not a good sign. It's kind of like brainstorming but, if you think about it, when people brainstorm, they add a lot of rules and desperately try to get away from anything that's random in a hurry. Yep, throw out a bunch of stuff and see what sticks and connect the dots. It takes a shape all its own and, there you go..."

"There you go?"

"Yeah, *there you go*—a unique thought."

"*There you go*," I kept the banter going.

*****

Aiden spoke like no other teenager I knew. It was all so long ago so what I remember and how it plays out in my mind is through my filter. That doesn't matter, as his teenage self was remarkable through anyone's lens. In everyone's life we come across, if we are fortunate, a peer who seems to be out of step and out of place with his contemporaries. A person who affected more thought, not only because he arranged words in an order you never heard before but also because the words came with more than sounds. They came with conviction. The words came with something more. Aiden was that person in my life.

Aiden seemed to finish what he was saying, but just then, he resumed at a more deliberate pace. He took his thoughts down another road.

"But sameness is death. It spawns an existence of incest. What stays the same disintegrates and dies. Most of our buddies don't recognize this. Hell, they don't even leave campus. They'll graduate from here, go to college and go back home. They'll see the same people, do the

155

same kind of jobs and be, well, the same. One day they will wake up and realize they are a carbon copy of their parents—good and bad."

I never knew what to expect from Aiden, and I think he liked that. It was who he was. He was as soulful as he was winsome. The molecules that came together to flesh out his form were from every corner of every original point in the universe. Weird, but it seemed conceivable. He didn't try to prove his theorems or reasons, and he didn't have to. He just didn't have to. Detached in a way, from the commonplace, he was free while other times, he seemed so grounded and connected as he worked through life like the rest of us.

He had a charm not so different from Brody's charismatic ways. I mean, Brody turned his charm on and off at will, Aiden's was consistent. A delicate line separated the two in that regard. Aiden, though, was true to himself and to others. Because of this truth, so much was open to him. He respected life and by doing so, he naturally added to it whether he knew it or not. Aiden thrived on his differences but never did so to stand out. He was, though, seldom successful in his attempt to stay in the background.

*****

"I've been thinking for some time, Eli. Let me lay something on you."

"Cool, go ahead."

"Well, thank you. Here it goes. If man was conscious of his being, you know, was aware of himself, his surroundings, and his own intellect, he would be a self-controlling creature. He could chart his own destiny. He would know what steps to take and figure each out as he needed."

"Yeah, yeah, yeah, what are you getting to?" Aiden tried his philosophies out on me. I guess he knew I would not bring them back to haunt him.

"Then how can man master the aspects of himself that do the mastering? You know, controlling his own controls on himself."

"Oh, Zen Master, do tell me more..."

"You are too funny."

"No, Aiden, really. Keep it coming."

"Simply, he can't. Western man is all about free will—we have control, but do we? What do we *really* control in our lives? Not very much. Man can't control the powers of nature so why does he think he can control the powers of nature that come from inside each of us? *Billions of us."*

"Good point."

"We control only so much as free will and fate just don't exist. We fool ourselves—humans do—to think we are in control. But I think we find our truth when we get beyond our defense of free will, and fate, and realize we only experience the present."

"I follow what you're saying and see your point, believe it or not."

"You do? He asked with surprise.

"Yeah. If some guy walked up to me and put a gun to my back, I can only react to that situation. I had nothing to do with what led him to pull a gun on me in the first place. *And* I am not in control of my future, at least at that moment. It shows that we are all connected—must be. Even if you live on an island, the actions of man, even one man, will find ways to influence other lives."

"Humans are gullible and easily accept delusions fed to us by other humans and continue their lives without any thought. It's easy this way," Aiden added.

"So, what about fate?" I asked.

"Yeah—it's an illusion too."

"Oh?"

"Yeah. Fate, all by itself, is all about giving up and letting some power control you. I say our existence is a blend of the two—fate and free will."

"Blend?"

"It could be fate that some guy sticks a gun in your back, but at that moment, your free will, and his, are at play. It's all about the present moment. I could be wrong, but that's what I think." Aiden said.

"Sounds confusing. I mean, how do we know the things in our heads are real? How do you separate the delusions, fed to us by man, from the truth? What thoughts are ours and what comes from some other source—good or bad?" I said leaning forward and tossing a twig into the fire.

"Good question Eli. I think it's always right in front of us every day. There's something about keeping a clear mind."

"It's hard to do when so much hits us all at once," I said.

"It's not easy. Yep, we're thinking alike—how scary," Aiden said as he stood and walked to the fire and stuck out his palms.

I continued, "How about this? Remember when we were out on the river, and we *thought* we had control of our destiny? You know, we *thought* we decided our every move. Well, we never had control. The river befriended us for a short time, and we befriended it as well. The river *allowed* for our passage. We used our oars in the opposite direction of the force of the currents to regain some semblance of control, but we never really had it. We *thought* we had control. The river faked us out."

"Yeah, the old fake-out. I like that," Aiden joined in.

"The river perseveres, and we are like a piece of cork bobbing on it. We are always at the mercy of the greater force. The calm of the current and the destruction of the rapid, we experience them both. Both beautiful, both are forces, and we go along for the ride. We ride as long as we can but know it will end. Ultimately we must know how we can go on from there."

"Wow, man. I didn't know you had it in you. Very impressive. No really, you just sent chills up my back and neck," Aiden said.

"Yeah, I have a few thoughts here and there too."

"Oh, I know it. I'm happy to hear it. Totally excellent."

"Aiden, I'm beginning to understand where you're coming from. I mean in a couple of different directions. The control thing, the force, the beauty, all this is the tip of an iceberg of what we're all about. Most of us don't see the big picture and don't care. What's important hides somewhere in us, and we don't, many times, want to search to find out more," I said as I joined him near the waning fire.

"Yeah, I think it's cool to think about this stuff. I mean, what are we on this planet to do anyway? To sell stuff? To add up numbers on a spreadsheet. To overpower the powerless? To make a boatload of money? To play political games and send kids to kill? If that's what it's all about, then this world is not for me," Aiden said turning his head and looked right into my eyes.

158

"Is that why you give me such grief over what I want to do with my life?"

"No, it's not. I see you doing so much more than what you're letting on. Uncover who you are! For Christ's sake, if you ask me, I want you to think about it all and discover what's best for Eli. But we all do what we gotta do."

"You sound like a grown-up but just not one that has ever been part of my life," I said smiling.

"Funny…you're calling me a grown-up."

"Wow, I think I did." We laughed and as he gazed into the dying flames, I looked at his profile and felt at ease.

"Hey, all I am saying is, don't let someone else decide for you—about anything. That goes for what you're going to do in life or who you truly are deep down. It's your ride, man, you just said it, and you only get one. That is one life, so make it an exploration, better yet, a quest. Yeah, a quest. Be the hero of your own journey. It's the only thing that is truly yours and even at that, we don't have full control. So be you!"

I got up from the hearth, dusted off my jeans, and sat back in my chair. "Well, I think I'm doing that." I paused a moment and rattled off a conflicting thought. "I want to reduce the risks, you know, since I only have one chance at the brass ring, I don't want to lose any time getting there. That's why getting good grades is important to me…and… and getting in the best law school. Once I graduate, I'll be twenty-six and I'll be ready to go and make a difference."

"You'll figure it out," Aiden said as he stood and walked back to his chair and sat.

"I do struggle with it. It's all I've ever thought of being. But sometimes I don't know where the original thought came from. Sometimes I do wonder if I'm going the right way. I'll admit it," I said as my thought ran out of gas, and I slumped in the chair.

"I hear you. But sometimes that greater force is from within and sometimes I think we must turn the opposite way to regain a semblance of control. You know—like the river. Then we accept ourselves. We know that, deep down, we are not in complete control. We become partners with the energy of the phenomenon and use it to help ourselves. This way we avoid conflict."

"Huh? You are going way deep," I said.

"I think of it as our own magic. The parts are not always identifiable. I don't think it's easy. Since it may not be so apparent, some of us will trudge through life and not even try to understand it. *Not even try, damn it.*"

"I'm not completely following you."

"I'm saying we may end up detaching ourselves from our true self because who we are doesn't suit others, and we deceive ourselves and act for others," Aiden said and leaned back in his chair, turned, and looked me straight in my eyes. "If there's something in you, like a dream or a passion or some other kind of feeling, one day it will manifest itself in a way that you will need to do something about it, or you will regret it. You will hate yourself if you don't. Sure, today you may not even recognize what it is, but not searching for it or acknowledging it when it shows up, is obscene."

"Aiden, let me lay something else on you. Would you also say that since they teach us to turn away from evil that when we do so we are making a wrong turn?"

"Hmmm. I'm not saying to turn to evil, but saying we need to free ourselves from the junk of other people and to know ourselves."

"You're saying to turn away from other's control."

"Yeah, that's what I'm saying. A Judo master swings with the attack. He goes with it and his aggressor pays the price. So, we must also use our inner conflict to move us to our peace. We shouldn't ignore, deny or even separate out our conflicts—we should use it."

"I like that Aiden."

"Of course, we shouldn't become or side with evil or evil ways, but we have to somehow use the power of evil to turn it on itself so that the destruction is elsewhere and not in us."

"What does all that mean though? I'll give it to you. You do seem to be someone who doesn't struggle with a lot of stuff that most of us do. You're comfortable in your own skin as they say."

"No, Eli, I *do* struggle. Like—why do people hate other people because they're different? That's a big one for me. I have so many questions inside of me, and I want answers. I feel different from other people and don't know why and get down on myself. Not sure if all the decisions I make are the right ones. I'm wrong half the time…yep, I have my weaknesses."

"Oh? Really? You hide it well." I said softly as I looked away from him.

Aiden looked to the ceiling and started chuckling to himself.

"What? Did I say something weird? What's going through your head Aiden?"

"When we got in trouble a couple of months ago and spent the day with soap up our noses. That was totally my doing."

"Yeah, but…," I tried to interject.

"And, you know I'm not so courageous. I haven't nailed the landing. That's been a goal of mine and, in fact, I tried to get you to show me the way. I don't know where I'll be a year from now. Hell, I work on stuff every day because I know, deep inside lie my answers."

"Soooo, that's where you find the magic—right?"

"Exactly—well, that's what I think. Maybe we shouldn't ask more questions but the right ones and maybe the right ones in the right order. I don't know. See I'm not so articulate with these thoughts all the time. And you, my friend, *are* the courageous one."

I didn't know what to say to that, so I smiled. We sat there longer saying very little until the fire was long dead and replaced with cold darkness. During this year, my mind wandered more than ever, but I liked it. As we sat there, Aiden lit a cigarette. I closed my eyes remembering what Father Meinrad told me at some point that year.

"…our worldly experiences pass like the glittering images and reflections of birds flying in unison over a lake. The likenesses are mere suggestions of our life. The muted and mixed shades of what we remember and the ghosts of what we cannot recall are all there and before us. The right turns, the wrong choices, the luck and fate, the good and bad times all become specs of our lives.

"Inner freedom is not a revolt against society and its standards, and it is not a turning away from our spirituality. Nor is it a justification of whom we are as we should never have to defend our being. An inner freedom is, however, the sum of all those hints and traces of our lives all woven together that forms one soul. The more we discover about ourselves, the more we are uncertain who we are. This uncertainty is good. For it is in the letting go of ourselves that we may fathom what the images of our lives truly mean. Mystical? No, it is rather ordinary as we must never allow the *ordinary* questions to end."

The last thing I remember from talking with Aiden that fall afternoon was that it prompted a gentle turn inward instead of my typical defensive reaction. Life was more than black and white and not always what it seemed to be. Aiden was so vulnerable but so freeing.

That moment is now a part of me.

NINETEEN

A iden was right. I didn't want to go home on the weekends as I once thought. The semester flew by, but Christmas break changed that, and I finally made it home. Like most of my friends, it was good to get away from the confines of St. Augustine's but by New Year's Day, I was bored and restless.

Today, however, was Christmas Eve. I loved this time of year and always wanted it to be better than the last. Visible in a sense, the appetizing aroma of turkey nearly done, stuffing and all that goes with it crept up our winding staircase. Our townhouse was full of pleasing scents, but this one was especially alluring as I had not had a home-cooked meal in what seemed to be eons.

Turning at will around Dad's room, like a spring garden, the aromas drifted down the hall through my bedroom door and into my steamy bathroom where I stood. The scent was lifted on the treble clef of the Christmas music sailing up from downstairs. It mixed with my rock music that was almost inaudible coming from my stereo. I wanted a foot in each domain.

*****

Our house was always full of freshly cut flowers, mostly wild. This was a way that my father remembered her. Mom loved flowers and wanted them around her. Bringing a bouquet home was just something Dad did, like stopping at a red traffic light. Flowers were part of the decor. Even without the flowers, this old home was full of exotic fragrances. I don't know exactly why but it was. The antique furniture, the herbs hanging in the kitchen, and the musty alcoves blended and agreed. All of this created a pleasing ambiance and one that I have only experienced here at home.

My father was a man of cosmopolitan and urbane tastes and wants. He fancied, if not pretended to enjoy, a cultured lifestyle. Not to be mistaken, he was not a blue blood. Because he attended premieres of shows, sipped Chardonnay at an artist's opening, or attended a ballet, it was all part of his plan.

He enjoyed such trappings. It only helped his personal cause to socialize in this way as an ambassador of our country. He seemed sincere and genuine in everything he did. He was who he was; to truly know him, however, was difficult. Perhaps this, too, was part of his plan. His life had order. Any aspect that he could influence or direct, he did. After all, it was his prerogative, so he thought. This was part of his success, so he told me more than enough times for any seventeen-year-old who would want to know.

One point that rendered Dad powerless was when Mom was in the picture, especially when it came to the family. It wasn't because Dad relegated Mom to the things of the home as that just wasn't ever going to happen. She was just a person who was hard to sway. Never obstinate, never boastful, and always kind, she innately and unobtrusively commanded a warm presence. An odd mix of words, but this is how she was. Dad could go only so far with her and then he would retreat. However, he never seemed to mind. They were good in this way. They took the best of each other and doing so was natural for them.

Since Mom's passing a couple of years earlier, Dad began a new Christmas Eve tradition for the two of us. We, or rather he, would have a scotch in his study, exchange a gift, have a late but formal dinner, and attend Midnight Mass. The downside of this new tradition was that Christmas morning now resembled any other day. A few short years ago, Mom would have had nothing to do with my father's newly ill-contrived custom. Christmas Eve was for preparation. That's what *eve* meant; she would remind us. On Christmas day, she would be the first to awake with the Yuletide joy of all of Santa's elves. She would turn on Christmas albums and this rousing was the signal for Dad and me. It was time to come downstairs to see what Santa had brought us. Dad always put on a good show, but he was uncomfortable with

Mom's homespun ways. Perhaps it was a payoff for all the formal dinners she had to attend hanging on his arm showing all her teeth whether she wanted to or not.

Mom and I never had the Santa talk. It was our secret. Saint Nick could do all sorts of things in our minds, and we didn't want to mess that up. He left us with mysterious packages the evening before and we were thankful that he did. No questions asked—but lots of half-smiles to one another. It was our way of keeping the enchantment alive in our kooky kind of way. Our eyes would always connect as we laughed on Christmas morning. Dad could hardly get a grip on our shared sense of humor.

Of course, we would be in our pajamas all day and our beautiful Victorian Georgetown townhouse would be full of tacky decorations. They were mostly old dime store figurines and plastic holly she kept from her childhood. Mom knew they were not pretty, well mostly, and knew they didn't lend well with the sophistication of our home, but that was my mother. She made things work. She was masterful in her ways and creative with everything she touched. Her sense of humor was like no other.

I would be lying if I said I didn't miss her. My heart was heavy, or it seemed I had a huge hole in it without her. Either way, it was difficult and continues to be so to this day.

*****

I had just showered. Scrunched over the antique porcelain basin, I rubbed the mirror smearing the condensation. Although blurry, now I could see my face. This time I had really done it. With very little to shave, I somehow butchered my face with a brand-new razor while showering. Plucking bits of toilet paper off the roll, I began to dot my face and under my chin to soak up the consequences of my botched work. From a distance, I heard Hilda our live-in housekeeper and cook, call out something from the bottom stair. I turned down my stereo to hear my orders. She hollered to me that Dad expected me to be ready, with coat and tie, and downstairs in his study in thirty minutes. I acknowledged her announcement and then turned up the volume to hear the Stones. I continued to dab tissue pieces on my face.

My bathroom was so hot, very unlike what we had in the dorm. I hoisted up the window and looked down to the street. Already, dusk had yielded to the approaching pitch of the night. The immense sky poked fun at the faint beams of light glowing from streetlamps. The dusky sky was like the pink tips of an iris, and the air had that smell of a looming snowfall. They didn't mention a white Christmas on the noonday news, so I didn't give it a second thought. The cold air hit my tortured face and gave me a welcomed tingle. Startling me, I heard a loud clang. It was a curious alley cat disturbing the aluminum trashcans in search of his holiday dinner. Responding was a barking dog, which was as ferocious as a yapping poodle. In a moment, it was again quiet. It reminded me of my first meal at St. Augustine's. I just had to smile.

Somehow, I was lost in all that I sensed. The sights of the street, the crisp air, and the scents of Christmas all randomly coming together stirred a part of me. I became wistful and forlorn. It was the kind of feeling I get without warning. Maybe it comes when I try to trample over my feelings when they attempt to tell me something. It has to do with the feeling of being incomplete. Yeah, knowing I still had lots to learn and many experiences ahead of me, I felt twisted. Not ready to be a grown-up, but it was coming, and it would be here soon. The faster it was coming, the more questions about how I felt about my life kept bubbling to the surface. It was as if something inside of me was scratching to get out. Sometimes I wanted it out and other times, I wanted it to stay buried.

I attended a good school, was top of my class, and probably going to one of the best colleges. I had a loving dad, good friends, and material things; all the stuff any seventeen-year-old would want to have. I wanted for nothing. It struck me at that moment how much stuff I *did* have. Shouldn't I feel complete? Visions for my future and a plan for my life were in my mind's eye but I was beginning to realize I also had an eye to my soul.

What made it worse, this empty feeling was undeserved in my mind. My parents never beat me. I never had one of those uncles who sexually abused me. My skeletons weren't so scary. Juggling in my mind all that was mine, I felt a sting of guilt piercing me when any trace of desolation came to mind. I've been so sheltered and thought most people were like me—wrong. It amazed me how so many people are so selfish and so self-righteous all the time…and people hate just to hate—why? Guilty feelings pressed heavily on my chest as I thought of our violent world and the souls trapped in an unforgiving and harrowing life. A life I could only imagine and doing a poor job trying.

So privileged, I mused, and therefore I had no right to feel despondent. This realization only made me feel worse. Apart from the last few years, I grew up in the suburbs. I knew nothing of the awful goings-on in the world except for watching Sixty Minutes or the evening news with Walter Cronkite. The abuses and atrocities that make up the lives of so many children strangle the blood flow of the goodness of man.

Yet closer to home, I question, what does Luis have? Beaten as a kid and treated with indignity by his peers. His poor mom was dead. Here I was, feeling empty. I suddenly felt ashamed. It's like the way I felt about prayer. Could God honestly care about my paltry prayers? I'm on the top of the totem pole of life. How in God's right mind could He even consider listening to me? My needs wants and desires are feeble in comparison. What would complete me was asking too much even if I knew what that was. No, I just had to figure it out.

I, then, thought of Aiden.

It was Christmas Eve, and he was in the sticks fifty miles from St. Gus' with distant relatives who he barely knew. He couldn't be having a very good time. I missed him. The thought of Luis rushed back to mind. He had nothing to look forward to, being a nerdy average guy. He's back in Philly at one of the parishioner's homes. He went to a different home almost every year. Confused, I figured I should think about all this later. I flossed, brushed my teeth, and combed my hair. I had an order to things and was about finished. In no time, I got dressed and went downstairs.

To enter the study, I would first have to walk through the living room where our tree stood—always. Passing it, I paused and realized that I had nothing to do with it this year. In fact, neither did Dad. It was beautiful thanks to Hilda and her daughter, Constance, who was visiting this year. This year all the decorating was done before I got home, so I couldn't have helped anyhow. That's how I decided to look at the situation.

Flames were ablaze in the fireplace due to expensive gas logs. This fire was for show and not for warmth—very unlike the fires Aiden and I would make at the *old lady's* house. But this world was the same every time I looked at it. Fresh holly and poinsettias were at every corner of the eye. Everything was quite picturesque like a Hallmark greeting card.

Entering the study, I found myself alone. At the end of the room was another fireplace with more roaring flames that were all dancing in unison. The track lighting and lamps threw off a dim glow making for a certain ambiance that Dad perfected. Like a B-rated 1950s movie, I expected a black and white Cary Grant, in a tux and holding a silver cigarette case, to enter through another door. That'd be cool, I thought. The Vienna Boys' Choir, or the saints themselves, seemed to be singing to me through concealed speakers. Dad had a wonderful ear for music, but this setting bordered on heavy theatrics. A good thing the volume was set low. Despite the theatrics, the room was warm and comfortable. The truth is, I liked it.

The walls were blue and the molding that framed the room was thick and rich in form and decoration. The shelves were teeming with tome after tome. Notably thick, leather-bound books bulged in all directions and stretched from one end to another on each shelf. I walked over to my father's desk. All items chosen to adorn its surface were precise and in perfect order. Used every day, his desk and all on it still looked as if it were a museum exhibit. The decorative quill appeared recently plucked from the behind of some bird and looked freshly combed. The paperweights were from celebrated establishments both earned and purchased. He liked what he liked— no doubt. The wall was full of certificates and awards. Funny thing, before I had not noticed he had so many. Like the books, I had not grasped earlier the breadth and depth of his interests. Perhaps much more substance than I gave him credit. He was a lawyer's lawyer. No wonder President Nixon approved his position. This was my father.

He kept an eight by ten photograph of himself and Mom on the corner of his desk. I was happy to see that. The picture was a good one of them both taken shortly before her death. My father, a tall angular man seemed the opposite of Mother. She was petite with an easy smile. Piercing blue eyes with flowing chestnut hair, she was beautiful. Dad was rather good-looking, too. His blondish wispy hair as a young man, now a bit mousey but attractive, was combed back giving him a straightedge of a hairline. His sandy thin brows accented his vivid and striking hazel eyes. Together they were a graceful and charming couple. Alone, though, they looked like any two people. They had a good marriage. They loved and complemented each other.

On a wall next to Dad's desk, I came across three small oil paintings that I had not seen in years. The subject of one was a baby in a highchair. I remember Mom saying that she caught me just right for this painting. She was proud of her accomplishment. The others hanging next to it were equally striking and, they lured me in for closer inspection. I remember seeing them hung somewhere a decade earlier, but they meant nothing to me at the time.

Another of the paintings was of a teenager, but it couldn't have been me for I was a mere child when she created that one. This boy was rather like Tom Sawyer sitting by a stream with his hands wrapped around his knees. Tousled hair and longing in his eyes, he appeared to be daydreaming watching endless circles emanating from a supposed drop of a pebble. It resembled me as a young adolescent. She looked into the future; I would like to think.

The third painting was of a young man painting a nude with a perplexed but charming look on his face. It had the flair of a Norman Rockwell in manner but definitely not a Norman Rockwell subject. Oh, it didn't show much, but it was clearly a nude. Original works of art, all three, but I never looked at them too closely years ago. Today was different. It occurred to me that she was pure and tender in what she saw and how she portrayed her expressions. Could she be telling me something? They were a part of her. Now, I wanted them to be a part of me.

Surprising me, Dad came from thin air and nudged my shoulder with a tumbler with its half-filled contents sloshing around. Couldn't believe he was offering it to me. Maybe he thought I was twenty-one all of a sudden, so I decided to play along. Giving me no choice in the matter, he assumed I would want the same drink that he adored. This was typical of Dad—it was scotch on the rocks.

The scotch was probably the best, but it tasted like gasoline to me. Acquired taste or not, I had to force myself to sip it without vomiting. I knew what he expected of me. Still, why didn't he ever sit with me, pour me a scotch, and help me to acquire *that* taste? I shouldn't have to *acquire* this kind of thing on my own. Hell, who in their right mind would drink this stuff if doing so didn't have significant meaning—like a rite of passage. He didn't want to go through the process, but he just wanted me already there. Ready-made. But, come to think about it, was this *that* time?

Dad, however, wanted the best for himself and me. That could mean that we drank the best scotch, ate the best turkey, and had the best position in society. He was looking out for me, as a father should. This translated to being the best he could be, but this was not, unfortunately, always enough. I had many people looking out for me. I needed to be the one to figure out what was best for me, but it didn't seem like I ever got the chance to do that. When I would, it was unclear. This was when I missed Mom the most.

We sat in huge leather chairs that faced each other. This reminded me of about a month earlier when I sat down with Father Meinrad in his office. This, however, was where the similarities went their separate ways. Father Meinrad listened. Well, that was his job, but even if he were a glassblower, he would have listened; that was who he was. Hell, Dad was an attorney, and they are supposed to be listeners too. Listening didn't happen much with him, though. He always seemed to be delivering his closing argument.

I don't think I listened to him that evening, either, as I forced down the first glass and extended my hand for a refill. He was happy to oblige my nonverbal request. While drinking in a hurry, I managed to keep good eye contact. I do remember that he told me that he had lunch the previous day with the dean of the Georgetown law school. I, of course, was to be impressed. I listened, and while doing so I must have *acquired* a taste for the stuff. I poured my own third glass and at that moment, the phone rang.

Abruptly turning to the phone with a finger or two in the air, he immediately ended our conversation. I am sure he ended ours for what, he anticipated, was to be a much more important one. To whomever he was speaking with, he tossed countless yeses and other insignificant remarks about. Before he could hang up, he told me that he would have to meet me at the church for Midnight Mass. Far better than a magician, he then vanished. Was I to sit in the other room and eat a turkey by myself? Leaving my final tumbler of scotch untouched on his desk, I went to the kitchen.

Happy to take me up on my invitation, Hilda and Constance said they would join me for dinner. No, they were downright giddy brimming with big smiles. As they scooped the stuffing and poured the gravy in the gravy boat, I browsed my father's wine selection and came up with something I thought we could all stomach. Managing the corkscrew was interesting, and I gave up to Constance's expertise. She apparently liked wine and had tasted her fair share in her twenty-four years. She approved my choice.

The three of us ate and drank for a couple of hours, and we laughed at everything that each of us said. It was amazing. I had never been so tipsy. Hilda excused herself from the table and began to clear the china. Constance and I talked more. Keeping the conversation pointed to her, we chatted about her brief time in college, her job, and her travels to Greece, Italy, and Spain with only a backpack and two male companions.

"So, you went with two guys...do tell?" I asked and immediately regretted my choice of words and inflection. I lay blame on the Chardonnay.

"Ummm. Eli, Eli, Eli you have much to learn. They were a couple. I thought you could read between the lines."

"Oh! They were...ah...they were...," I muttered.

"Gay."

"Yeah, that's what I was going to say. I just don't know anyone like that so it's not something I think about."

"Well, I think you do. You just don't know it."

"Huh? What do you mean?"

"I mean you *do* go to a school of all guys."

"Yeah, your right...so what else do you want to talk about?" I said desperately needing to move on.

After more stories, time was moving fast and like a dream, the evening was ending before I made sense of it. I struggled for something to say to prolong the interlude but could not. Constance excused herself from the table, and I sat there alone as Hilda came in and out of the kitchen in a chipper mood removing the dinner plates and leftovers. Hearing the crash of what I thought must have been a crystal wine glass hitting the kitchen floor, Hilda partially opened the door and wrapped her head around. She looked like she had just eaten a ghost pepper. I smiled, shrugged my shoulders and her pained expression evaporated from her face.

Sitting by myself and playing with a large spoon of mashed potatoes, my mind was in a fog. My eyes were beginning to close as I almost fell asleep in the cranberry sauce, which no one ate. Figuring it was time to call it a night, I managed to leave the dining room without tripping over my own feet and headed upstairs holding the banister with a death grip with each step. I made it to my bedroom. Dad would have to attend midnight Mass by himself; that was if he showed at all.

As usual, I jumped into bed and maneuvered the pillow and the comforter to the exact position that would send me to my slumber. The room was on the verge of spinning, so I kept still and stared at a blurred crack on the ceiling. It could have been a moment or an hour, I don't know which, but I heard the creak of my bedroom door. I saw a shape in the doorway. The light of the hallway created a silhouette of a woman. I thought I was dreaming so I lay there in a daze.

She floated toward me and while coming closer, the door closed behind her. It was now dark except for a faint light seeping in from around the door. Moonlight grew more brilliant in the darkness. In silence, she laid down on my bed. I pulled the comforter up and she rolled underneath. Without touching, I felt the warmth of her body next to mine. Like in a trance, I knew what to do. I reached for her and her for me. As we held each other, I felt my mind let go. Her skin was like silk, my hands moved along her curves, and my mind painted a portrait of her. I envisioned her laughing at dinner with her long dark hair streaming back and forth as we sat at my father's table.

We hugged and kissed. As we kissed, I felt nothing but the tenderness of her being. Our moment together was special, and I will say nothing more. She glided out of bed as if she was walking on air. As she closed the door behind her, all I could see was the soft light outlining its edges. The moonlight grew brighter as I drifted to sleep.

I woke the next morning due to an unexpected chill in the house. Drawing back the curtains, I saw a faint trace of snow on the sidewalk and yards. How much do they pay those weathermen anyway? Mom would have been thrilled, however. On my way down the hall, I noticed that Hilda had already made up my dad's bed, and he was nowhere in sight. I walked downstairs right past the tree and into the kitchen. Hilda told me that Dad had important business that had taken him away. Funny, but I didn't even ask her if she sensed he was angry at me. I bet he didn't show either.

Over orange juice, I asked Hilda about Constance. She told me that she was already on her way back home. Hilda explained that she had to be at work for an early shift. Today it would be Hilda and me. That was fine. Sitting back and balancing in my chair with my hands clasped behind my throbbing head, I grinned. I thought of my father taking that fateful phone call last night and the turn of events last evening. Many thoughts rumbled through my head. Some things were becoming clear, but I knew I would remember her and that moment for a lifetime.

TWENTY

"What a jammed-packed semester, Eli," Gabe said while using a twig for a toothpick. "I mean, lots went on— Lordy."

"Yeah, you're right. I don't know how I kept my grades up when I think about it."

"By what you've been telling me, it doesn't take a highly intelligent person to know what was important to you…I mean, you didn't tell me much about taking tests and term papers. Oh, I know you did all that, but it's not the kind of thing we look back on. Now is it?"

Hmmm, Gabe you're right. It isn't the kind of stuff we end up telling our grandkids about. Thanks for using my words—well, Aiden's words against me," I said with a quiet laugh. He followed with a big wink.

Gabe can cook. *Gabe's five favorite flavors* were a big hit with me. I eased up, though on the Irish coffee. For some reason, I went back for a few extra cups of regular coffee even though it was stronger than dirt. Kicking back, Gabe sat on the ground up against a big log with his ankles crossed. He had one hand on top of the other resting them on his lap. He just looked comfortable. On the other hand, I changed where I sat several times, I ended up on a very scratchy nylon fold-out chair until I decided to join him, cross-legged, on the ground.

"Got some dessert if you want it," Gabe offered.

"Oh yeah, what is it?"

"Got some beef jerky in my pack."

"Huh? Gabe, that's not what anyone would call dessert."

"You're right, it ain't. I was just trying to be polite."

I smiled at his attempt at humor. It hit me at that flash of a moment that over the past few hours, I had really become fond of the old warrior. He was the real deal. He was true inside and out. How lucky I felt running into him.

"Eli, tell me more. How did the ball team do?"

*****

1974

January was cold. I don't remember it so much. But I do remember February. In some class along the way, I heard that somewhere in time a sage described February as the month of atonement. This portrayal was precise this year in particular. With no inkling to me, Old Man Winter exhaled his last frosty cough in a gasp at the same time our mediocre basketball team's breath tapered off. This all happened during the Commonwealth Catholic Tournament at St. Peter's High School in Alexandria.

The *SAINTS* of St. Augustine's School was so disappointing that only the die-hard boosters found their way to the splintered pine bleachers for home games during the regular season. By mid-January, our lonely team played many visiting games with a mere twenty or thirty of the faithful huddled together. They sat surrounded by the crazed fans of our winning opponents. The loyalty of some was admirable, but like most of the others, Aiden and I were fair-weather fans. I cannot say I was proud of this distinction, but it was *only* high school basketball. I distanced myself for my own reasons. Perhaps Aiden did too.

*****

Aiden was his own sort of athlete, and he saw the world of sports and human athleticism in unconventional ways. I picked up bits and pieces of his way of thinking over the year but, oddly when I think about it, we never took time and talked about it like we did so many other subjects. I deduced, years later that Aiden paralleled the boast of fans and the hoopla shrouding sporting events as a kind of pagan ritual without substance that our ancient relatives were known to attach to things. Truth and ultimate meaning are afterthoughts in today's world. This fragment of lore I remembered reading in his journal the weekends during and after the annual tournament. He was different from most people in that he wanted me to read *selected* passages of his journal. I felt I should wash my hands or light a candle when he whipped out his diary.

By the middle of winter, I was accustomed to Aiden's Zen-like philosophies so when I read his words then, nothing registered to me as out of the ordinary like it did when we first met. It wasn't just his philosophies, but it was his attitude and his behaviors that were very Zen to my way of thinking. He was open to everything and was mindful of each moment. At the time, I didn't know anything about Zen or any other philosophies that seemed to be out of the ordinary or mainstream.

He would ask me to read this or that and after doing so, he would ask me what I thought. He would listen and nod at me and that was about it. I only wowed him that one time back in December at the *old lady*'s house—but I was okay with that. In the winter when he was cooped up, he vented or expressed himself through his writing. Someone had to validate his thoughts, I assumed, and that someone was me.

Looking back, he submerged so much in his words. I remember one such notion about man and evolution. Not evolution in the Darwinian way, but in the *Aidenian* way. Digging into the recesses of my recollections, it had something to do with the essence of humanity as being the same with our spirituality. Just who he was writing to, I may never know.

Since Aiden dealt with his own sports experience in his own way, I remember three journal entries that stood out that he asked me to read.

The first entry was on **January 15, 1974,** and went like this:

> ...the vanquisher of the modern contest can never seem to replicate that very first feeling of that very first win. No other victory can be as sweet as the first. Modern athletes

develop an overwhelming thirst that they cannot quench like a ravenous instinct to hoard more when the gut is full.

The time of gratification becomes shorter and shorter, and the victory loses the purity in which it originated. Winning becomes winning for winning sake—or money—just win, win, win! It is meaningless. Man says a loss means weakness. As we have a winner, we have a loser, and never may we think that man can win without clearly repressing, distressing, or oppressing his opponents. Then, he starts over.

Those that tried and lost, in my way of thinking, gain so much more than the athlete who only knows how to win and bemoans their eventual and inevitable losses.

I have found meaning with the second passage that he wrote on **January 22, 1974, …**

The athlete trains the body, mind, and spirit. Standing unfettered, a sport is neutral. Man is responsible for tainting those waters. Yet the true player competes with no one other than himself.

Simply, the true athlete finds his own victory in every contest, and with each, the meaning of his achievement only increases. He builds each win, each victory, squarely on the previous competition win or loss. A loss of a game is still a victory if the athlete finds something new about himself.

The Babe chased no man as he slugged each ball. Wilt Chamberlain had no peer. They played for themselves— that's what I believe. They made their mark and tested the limits. No one could call them losers though Ruth had more strikeouts than home runs, and it took Chamberlain many losses in his playoff career to come up with two national championships. They, however, found something within them worth more than the crowd's cheers and jeers.

Man always wants to win, but truly to do so, the mix of circumstances on any given day may never be the same. So, our response makes the difference between good and great, excellent, and extraordinary, and natural and supernatural. It's for the athlete to see this.

Other than felt banners sagging off a wall and drunk alumni slobbering on themselves as they revel in memories, which at best are more fantasy than truth, winning is not everything. It is a mere moment...and the moment ends.

This last entry is my favorite one, and dated **February 3, 1974...**

Most of what makes up a great athlete is finding his superpower. This was found by those few who know how to entwine the hemp of their own vital experiences with the precision of each contest to form something new— something original, I suppose, like a masterpiece. Something that, when joined, is strong enough to pull him through any contest or adversity. When arranged together it would be beautiful, but we might not always know how it all comes together and why it does so. It just is.

Even if we all possessed this superpower, there is still only one winner by the current standard, but I think differently. Every brushstroke, some painter takes, every word a poet chooses, and all the arranged notes a composer decides upon works the same way. To achieve greatness, each element must have its own beauty and its own reason. We can tell when it comes together and when it melds. It is in this blending that beauty bears. We may not know why, but we recognize good and beauty. We see it, hear it, smell it, taste it, touch it, or feel it. This makes all the difference in our obscure lives.

*****

A glimmer of hope for the multitude of fans faintly shone itself in the twilight of that short month. The tournament was inclusive of all state Catholic schools so all member schools could compete for a championship even with a flat record. Each school prayed for three victories that weekend as if God would favor the prayers of one Catholic school over another. With a record of fourteen and fourteen, the two wins on Thursday and Friday of the tournament opened the door for us to the championship game. It appeared that we had momentum. Everyone talked as if they *knew* a championship was a certainty.

The Robes rented two Greyhound buses and the entire school, it seemed, migrated north. I could not believe the drastic turn of events. Enthusiasm was mounting. I overheard conversations of visiting Trustees saying that Saint Augustine's was back to its old form. I admit that I was beginning to feel the excitement too. Aiden was happy for Vandy. Vandy put in the time, and more, during his four years at St. Gus'. Without a doubt, Vandy carried this team on his shoulders.

From the opening tip-off, it was abundantly clear we were not coming home with the banner. Like one last tired and cold gasp of life, any excitement real or perceived all but died. We lost by a dozen points, but we were never in it. Vandy was awarded a trophy as the tournament committee selected him for the all-tournament team. Many college scouts were in the stands looking for recruits so Vandy was at the right spot and did all he could. I noticed that Father Meinrad generously congratulated him. It was like a foggy dream watching all this from where I sat. At the same time, I didn't care about the team but hated to see us lose. No regrets, but I felt emotions that I couldn't pinpoint. Yep, no regrets.

During the awards ceremony that immediately followed the game, Coach Kidder stood motionless with his hands clutched behind his back. His piercing eyes stared off to some unknown point. He was passive at best as his tight expression was only highlighted by an obvious eye twitch. Suffice it to say, he found no joy in Vandy's recognition as his posture of preoccupation and emptiness was as noticeable as if he were clad in a vivid pink dress.

During the post-game ceremony, Aiden snuck outside to have a smoke. Undetected, I slinked out of the crowded gym and joined him as the others stayed captive for the rest of the ceremony. A ferocious wind whipped our ears and as it changed course our hair flitted like the flames of a fire—without heat. We sat on a rickety bench as I stiffly dug my hands into my coat pockets. Aiden did not want to talk much so we sat there and waited a few more minutes until we thought the rest of the boys would dart from the gym to fill the buses.

180

My sense was that he wanted to be in that gym. He wanted to be in the gym all season, I was sure. Regret on his part, perhaps, and I felt for him. This was the first time I empathized in that way with Aiden. Perhaps I was wrong, and he saw this event as yet another milestone in this part of our life as the year seemed to be rushing at top speeds to what might be a nebulous end. Whatever he was holding onto, I thought it was best not to ask—at least not now. Maybe something else was on his mind. Thinking about it more, I decided it was not good to guess as to what might be swimming in his head. We, however, sat there and looked at each other from time to time with a closed mouth, one-sided smile. He opened his mouth only slightly as I thought he was going to say something, but he then gave me a tight grin and shook his head as to say *never mind*. That was it. It was a minuscule moment, but it dissipated to what would distort it to a blur of something else as our classmates erupted from the building.

The trip home was quiet the first hour, but by the second and last hour, it was as if we had just come from Disneyland. Easy come, easy go, I guessed. This, I thought, was the end of basketball and Coach Kidder, at least for me. I didn't care so much—thought I would. Pangs of disappointment and second-guessing went in and out of my head as they did earlier, but my decision of opting out was one of my better ones looking back.

TWENTY-ONE

A week after our demoralizing defeat, I was walking from the library to the Commons. In the lobby, I saw two St. Agnes girls stapling posters to the bulletin board announcing the Winter Thaw Mixer. I paid them little attention until I heard a shriek.

"OUCH!" One girl cried out as a staple nicked her finger while positioning the poster. Stopping, I turned to her. Not knowing I was behind her, she turned around almost bumping into me. Our eyes connected at once. I looked away and then back at her.

"You, okay?" I asked.

"Oh yeah, I'm fine. It's all part of the job," she said adding a forced smile.

"Let me see it," and without thinking I took her hand and examined her pinky finger.

"I think you're gonna be okay."

"You've got really warm hands."

"Okay—do you want me to leave you guys alone?" her friend interrupted, and we all laughed.

"Sorry, sorry," I said, "hey—so what's this all about?" I asked as I read the poster. "My name is Eli, by the way."

"I'm Kali and this is Jenn."

"I'm Eli...oh yeah, I just said that."

Kali giggled and then spoke up, "It's kind of corny, but we hold this dance every year. It's next Sunday afternoon. Are you coming?"

"Oh, ah yeah. I wouldn't miss it."

"You're new, aren't you? I haven't seen you before," Kali asked.

"I don't feel new. I transferred to St. Gus' last August."

"Well, maybe we can meet up at the dance and hang out some."

"Yeah, that would be excellent," I said with some excitement but immediately toned it down. "Let's do that. Yep, I'll look for you there."

"Okay, well we've gotta run and put up the rest of these posters."

*****

The fog never lifted the day of the dance, and the air was fat with drizzle. The thaw and the undoing of the year had already started so it was an appropriate backdrop for a Winter Thaw Mixer. Looking out my dorm window, all I saw was a gray and haunting image of puffy fog camouflaging the mountain peaks that normally pierced the sky. No rain, but the mist embraced the landscape and seeped into every seam that connected the root to the earth, the moss to the tree, or the needle to the pine. The moisture of the day gave the gray stones of the buildings a sheen, and the crowned narrow roads a gleam of temporal polish. We had to get through days like this to know others would be better.

"So, you with me Eli?" Aiden asked.

"Yeah, I'm DEFINITELY going to this party."

"You sound a little *too* excited about *some* dance."

"Well, maybe. I met this girl who I'm hoping to hang out with."

"Oh, I see," Aiden said rolling his eyes. "I'm hoping to hang out with a few myself," he said and gave me a wink.

Aiden and I decided not to take the bus but to walk through the woods to their campus. He knew all the shortcuts. As we trudged along, I second-guessed our decision.

"Now tell me again why we decided to hoof it to this party in the mist and mud when we could have taken the warm and dry bus like the other kids?" I asked.

"Damn good question—damn good question."

"Well?"

"Quit your bellyaching. Don't you want the freedom to come and go as you please? Geez. If we took the bus, we'd have to follow the rules. Suppose we want to do our own thing? Anyway, I think I left my journal at the *old lady's* house. On the way back, I want to check it out. It's at the halfway mark the way I go. You know, as the crow flies."

We got to St. Agnes School a short time after the bus arrived. The paths through the woods were obviously more direct. We entered the gym through a structure that looked like a glacier. It was a wonder what

184

a little paper-mâché, tempera paints, and plastic wrap could do. As we walked through the ice tunnel it became warmer, and the ice gave way to a tropical motif. They went all out for this one. The girls would never see anything like this when we hosted a dance. It was quite elaborate and stunning.

"Where's Kali? You didn't make her up did you...?" Aiden smirked.

"What are you talking about? She's around here somewhere."

Minutes into the party, I separated from Aiden and hung out with Vandy and Luis. Aiden was at a table holding court with three gorgeous girls.

"Hey guys, who's that girl over there? The one wearing those polar bear ears?" Luis asked wearing a big grin.

"Where?" Vandy asked looking from side to side.

"Right there." Luis stuck out his face and pointed with his nose.

"Hey! There she is. That's Kali," I said. "She really looks cute in those ears," I said with my chin in the air.

"What? How do you know her?" Vandy's eyes narrowed and scrunched up his forehead.

"I know her—you know. I just know her," I said with a little nod and a long wink.

"Oh—okay," Vandy said with his own wink.

Luis started talking to himself, "Kali...Kali. Why does that name sound familiar?"

"Familiar? Only in your dreams," Vandy said with a fake laugh.

"No—wait a minute. I don't know if I would mess with her," Luis added.

"Why? What do you mean?" I half-heartedly asked.

"Yeah, come to think of it, Luis is right," said Vandy. "Kali used to date Brody."

"WHAT? Brody?" I blurted out taking a step back.

"Yeah, the one and the same," said Luis.

"Ah, but you guys said *used to date* Brody," I said and then cleared my throat.

Vandy pointed to his head and said, "Get a grip, Eli—think."

"I'm not worried about what was. I'm thinking about right now. I don't even see the jerk here. I don't think he came," I said chopping the air as I spoke.

I walked over to her and passed Aiden on my way. I patted him on the shoulder, and he looked up and gave me a faint nod, and quickly turned to one of the girls sitting next to him. I approached Kali.

"Hey, Kali."

"Hi. When I didn't see you get off the bus with the others, I thought you weren't coming."

"Well...I'm here."

"Yeah, you're here...so, do you want to dance?" Kali asked.

As we began to dance, I heard Luis shout out, "Way to go Eli." I tried not to pay attention, but Kali smiled ear to ear. But Luis' outburst caught a nun's attention who walked straight over to him. Out of the corner of my eye, I saw Aiden and Brody passing each other—Aiden headed out of the gym with a girl on his arm.

I yanked my attention back to Kali. Her almond-shaped eyes studied mine. We danced a slow dance and did so with a natural presence as if this were our one-hundredth dance. Her long warm brunette hair was soft to my touch. The scent of her neck was faint but alluring. I could only guess about the softness of her lips and the delicate touch of her skin. I liked her. Other than Constance, I had never actually been this close to a girl. My armpits seemed to gush, and my hands were clammy. Good thing I was wearing a sweater that hid my bodily reactions. This must happen when you like someone, I thought. I wanted nothing else but to like her. I made myself think of nothing else—not the music, not my friends, and not Aiden.

A nun cut our time short as she walked by and gave us the *look*. It was one of those looks only a nun could give. Kind of a neon sign that says, *the confessional will stay open late tonight for anyone thinking impure thoughts.* She probably thought all boys were the same. One impure thought after another. Or impure thoughts having impure thoughts. Well, she was probably right. Maybe she was, but I knew right from wrong. I had a conscience.

Kali and I walked over to a table in the back of the room and talked. "So, I'm going to come out and just say it—but I really like you," I told her.

"You're pretty nice too. I've met all kinds of Auggie boys, but none has been as nice as you. I mean you're a little shy and gentle and..."

"How's your finger?" I interrupted as I didn't know where she was going with her description of me, and I was beginning to feel uncomfortable.

She smiled and then reached out and put her hand on top of mine.

"What are you doing next weekend? I'd like to show you some cool spots between here and St Gus'. I mean, Aiden, you'd like him, and I have been all over this place and there are some great places to explore."

"That sounds like lots of fun. I love to hike. Maybe I can pull together a picnic."

"Yeah—very cool," I said as my mouth felt dry. "Hey how about I get us some punch?"

"See, that's what I mean, you're a nice guy."

"Well, you know… what can I say?" I said to my own astonishment. Why…why…why did I say that?

I excused myself from her and we smiled. Exchanging faint finger waves, I walked out of the gym knowing I'd find Aiden sitting in the courtyard surrounded by people. Instead, I found him sitting with a girl on a bench. From about ten feet away I signaled him to get up and walk over so we could talk. I knew Kali was waiting for me to get back with some punch, so this had to be quick.

"Hey, Aiden, I've been looking all over for you."

He wouldn't look at me and he motioned with his hand for me to go away. I stood there until he looked up.

"Huh—what? Can't you see we're talking here?"

"Aiden, I just need a minute. C'mon, just give me a minute and I'll be outta here."

He looked at the girl and said, "I'll be right back—save my seat." With reluctance, he got up and we walked about ten feet away. He folded his arms and just stood there.

"Aiden you need to meet her," I said with a rush of unexpected enthusiasm.

"Later. You can see I'm having fun too. I saw her—and you—on the dance floor getting sweaty. Obviously, you guys like each other to anyone who has eyes. She seems cool—so if you'll excuse me, I've got…

"Luis told me that she dated Brody."

"Yeah, I heard something like that but it's all over, I mean they met at a dance like this and went out once or twice. I'm sure she saw right through him and broke it off. So that's it. Go back and spend some time with her—which you should since you are totally blown away by her."

"Yeah, you're right."

"Look at you, your time is running out and you're turning back into a pumpkin. So, if we are all finished here, I have a certain co-ed that is waiting for me over on that bench."

He smiled and suddenly, I felt content. I turned and jogged back into the dance. I looked around for Kali but couldn't find her. I saw Vandy and Luis over in one corner eating chips and drinking punch, so I took a beeline over to them.

"Where's Kali? I don't see her anywhere."

Like a switch, Vandy's face turned from a smile to a frown. "Eli, you're not going to like it, but she came over here with us and we started talking. Dude, she is really into you."

"So, what happened? Where'd she go?"

Luis said, "I told her that you're nothing like Brody, and as soon as I said that he came out of nowhere."

"*He* as in Brody?" I asked feeling my heart pound.

"Yeah, he was standing right behind her—son of a bitch," said Luis.

Vandy spoke up, "Brody gave Luis a real hard time, and just then a new song started. Kali interrupted the two and asked if Luis wanted to dance. As she reached for his hand, Brody grabbed it and pulled her to the dance floor. She seemed kind of nervous about it and kept looking at us. She acted like she had no choice. It was kind of weird that way."

All the blood in my body rushed to my heart and it thumped until I thought it would burst from my chest.

"I can't believe it. She's so sweet. She's beautiful. Doesn't she know who he is? God, I'm such a fool. I should never have left her, not even for a second," I said as my body stiffened like a brick wall.

"Cool down, Eli. It wasn't her," said Luis.

"And don't be an idiot—you really don't know her and you're talking about not leaving her for a second. You need to cool out," Vandy interjected.

"Ah shit!" Not listening to them, I could not think of another way to describe my outrage. I knew the guy and wanted desperately to tell her all about him. I felt defenseless.

"Eli, don't look now but they are over there at the end of the gym," Vandy said.

With Brody's long arm against the wall, Kali was like a penned-up animal. I didn't know what to do and stormed out of the building. A new pall of mist just rolled in. Only a few people were still outside, but Aiden was talking with the same girl under a canopy. Noticing that I was fuming, he said something to her and walked over to me.

"What the hell is going on Eli?" Aiden asked and put his hand on my shoulder.

"It's Brody and Kali—they're together. I don't know what to do," I said looking at my feet.

"What do you want to do about it?"

"I don't know Aiden... I'd like to kick his butt," I looked up and gave him a slight smile.

"You're not really the butt-kicking type, no offense. Anyway, even if you were, Brody doesn't put on the gloves, he puts on the brass knuckles," Aiden said and shook his head.

"I just don't know what to do."

Like a spark, a gleam overtook Aiden's eyes. "I'll tell you what, I know what we need to do. Let's get out of here. I mean, there's nothing about this that looks good. You need to clear your head and not pick a fight—right now and in there. Call her later and see what's what. I mean she can walk away from the guy, so maybe you need to talk to her first."

Feeling down, I agreed with Aiden. We headed out the same way we arrived earlier that afternoon and walked. The mist was getting thicker in the air and the path in the woods seemed muddier than before. It was slippery as Aiden led the way.

"Aiden, where the heck are you going?" I asked but didn't really care.

"You'll see."

"What? I don't want to take the scenic route...I just want to get back and take a hot shower. I want to forget about today. I don't know what I was thinking," I said rubbing my temples.

"Hold on. You're overreacting. I didn't realize you were so dramatic," Aiden announced as if he were telling an audience.

189

"What? Dramatic? Me?" I was stunned. "What?"

"Forget it."

"What? I can't believe you think I'm dramatic. Can't believe this is happening to me. Show me the way to get to the dorm. I've had enough. Which way do we go? Shouldn't we be going that way?" I said with absolutely no idea as I pointed randomly.

"Hold on. There are many ways to get to where you need to go. With the way things are going today, I happen to know the right way. This is the best path for today. Just trust me."

"Yeah, yeah, yeah, I hear you."

We entered a familiar clearing. There, of course, was *the spot*.

"I knew you were leading us here."

"Gee whiz, you *are* a frickin' genius."

Aiden walked over to a huge slab of stone at the edge of the river and sat down paying no attention to me. I decided to follow suit. At this point, we were soaking wet so sitting on a wet slab of rock didn't really matter. It was quiet except for the gentle flow of the river. In the calm of the moment, Aiden reached down and picked up a rock. He looked it over and tossed it up and down a few times in his hand. With little fanfare, but with a grunt, he flung it high and into the water. Predictably, ripples emanated from the disturbance and as the wrinkles widened, they unfolded downstream.

"It may sound cliché, but those ripples always remind me that nothing ever acts alone. That every action radiates out. Yes, predictable, but we need some predictability—like comfort food."

Saying nothing, I picked up a rock and threw it high and toward the river. The rock hit a tree limb taking the force out of my throw. SPLAT. It plummeted to a large boulder not far from us. Aiden turned to me and erupted into laughter that was so contagious that I had to join in. Before our guffaw died out, Aiden grabbed me. Surprised, we began to wrestle plunging ourselves onto the muddy ground. We rolled and tumbled, and we couldn't stop laughing.

We laughed until there was no laughter left in our gut. We found ourselves on our backs looking to the sky. Out of breath, muck covered every follicle we had. Every inch of our bodies was gilded with grime, and we stunk of river mud. We laid there looking upward at nothing, but the thousands of sprites disguised as trifling winter spray.

"Hey, Aiden?" I asked as I looked at the gray clouds.

"Yep?"

"I did it."

"You did what?" Aiden turned his head to me and I to him.

"You know when I was home for Christmas. I did it." I couldn't help but to smile.

Aiden cleared his throat and asked, "You mean you had sex?"

"Well, we didn't go all the way."

"Eli, that's what *I did it* means. So you *almost* did it?" Aiden turned his head and looked back to the foggy sky.

"Yeah, you can say that. I *almost did it.*" I said keeping my smile in place.

Aiden sat up, looked my way, and paused. He seemed let down for a split second and then matched my smile with one of his own.

"Happy for you. One step at a time Eli—one step at a time. Just think about it, you didn't need my help. Proud of you." Sitting up, he looked to the horizon. The croak of a toad disturbed what otherwise was an unusually quiet moment. "Let's get out of here," he said matter-of-factly.

Funny, but this is where we left it. I thought he'd ask me all kinds of questions. Maybe he didn't like to be outshined.

*****

Encased in gunk we took a familiar path that would lead us next to the *old lady's* house. Aiden wanted to grab his journal that he thought he left there.

"I just hope it's there. Don't know where it could be if it's not there," Aiden ruminated.

"Surprised you misplaced it. It's not like you."

As we walked, I noticed something on the path that I couldn't quite make out. I ran ahead, bent down, and picked up a pair of costume polar bear ears. Confused, I studied them, and it took me only a moment to make heads or tails out of what I found. Aiden picked up the pace and as he reached me and saw what was in my hand, we glanced at each other. Simultaneously we took off and ran as fast as we could to the *old lady's* house.

Sprinting up the walkway, we were on the doorstep in seconds. Aiden tried the door, but someone locked it. We scrambled to a window and looked inside. We could see only the fireplace as furniture obscured our vision of who was in the room. I found another window and what I saw horrified me as it confirmed our suspicion. It was Brody and Kali. They were on the floor, and he gripped her hands as she put up a struggle. Jerking my head in every direction, I looked for something to break the window. A branch, a rock—something, but I could not find anything I thought would work. Just then, right next to me, I heard a crash. Aiden found a wooden barrel in the yard and heaved it through the window. We rushed in like guerilla soldiers. Grabbing Brody off Kali by his feet, I drug him, face down across the filthy and rough wooden floor as he twisted and squirmed. Kali bolted up and ran out of the house.

Surprising us both, Brody, cornered with nowhere to go, got up and headed for the staircase. Aiden lunged at him missing him by an inch. As Brody, in pain, humiliated and angry ascended the stairs, he grabbed part of the banister that was broken off and lying to one side. He began to wield it like a club. Aiden, only a few feet away dodged Brody's frantic swings, but Brody landed a blow squarely on Aiden's left wrist.

"OW! You bastard!"

"You, okay?" I shouted to Aiden.

"Yeah, I'm okay. Go find Kali. She needs your help," he said rubbing his wrist keeping one eye on Brody.

Backward, Brody stepped upward trying to escape Aiden's pursuit. I remembered Aiden told me that he fell because of a loose plank— Brody was inching closer to that same spot. I started to the door to find Kali, but before I could get there, I heard Aiden holler to him. Aiden saw that he was about to step on that very same spot that almost killed him. He shouted, again, shaking the rafters.

"Brody! Here—grab my hand!" Aiden extended his good hand to help.

Instead of reaching for Aiden's hand for help, Brody landed a strike on every inch of his wrist with his primitive weapon. In the same motion, Brody's own force and weight catapulted him down to the exact spot that I yanked him off Kali only moments ago. Lifeless, he laid there in a daze. Knowing Aiden seized the coward, I ran from the house to find Kali.

"Kali...Kali...KALI!"

I called her name and thought she would head toward St. Agnes. After about a quarter of a mile, I heard a faint cry. Following the sound, I found her not far away. She was delirious and lost. Sitting on a fallen tree to one side of the path, her hands covered her face as she was sobbing. I held her until the day's sky turned a shade of violet and the black of night was moving closer by the minute. When she was ready, I walked with her back to her dorm. No one saw us except for Jenn when we made it to their room. Without too many questions, she helped her.

Continually looking over my shoulder, I snuck out of her room to the hall phone. Luckily it was in an old phone booth so I could slouch down. I called Father Meinrad and he came and picked me up at the front gate. I was glad it was a dark night. When I arrived at my dorm, it was midnight. The room was dark, and Aiden was lying in bed in the glow of a small bedside lamp. I couldn't see his hands. Before I could say or do anything, he blurted out to me.

"So how is she?"

"Not great, but I think she'll be okay. She's going get some help."

"Good...good. So glad she's okay," he said. Exhausted, we just looked at each other and nodded in the stillness of the night.

Under the sheet, Aiden began to move his arms. He pulled both his hands up and out from under the sheet into the meager light. I was in shock.

"God! Are they broken?"

"No, I'm lucky. They are definitely a couple of shades of black and blue...I won't be painting—or anything else for a while."

I pulled up a desk chair and sat next to him. I was wiped out for sure, but we needed to talk.

"What happened to Brody?"

"I actually tried to help the guy."

"Yeah, I saw that you reached out to him."

Tearing up, Aiden said, "I saw that he was going to fall but he decided to take another whack at me instead—well, you were there. You saw what he did."

"Yeah, I wanted to help but where I was, I didn't know what to do."

"I just couldn't believe it. Even when someone tries to help, he does that. His eyes…man his eyes told a story in that split second. It scared me… and he fell. Man, he fell hard."

"What kind of shape is he in?" I asked.

"His leg is broken but he'll be okay. I carried him over my shoulder for a while and then he used me as a crutch the rest of the way."

"Wow, how could you do that with your hands the way they were? Why would you even want to attempt to help him after all that?"

"Brody's a scumbag but what would that make me if I left him? We're all brothers. We're all a piece of scum sometime in our lives." Looking up and at me. "We'll that is, except you, Eli." He said with a wink.

"Yeah, right—thanks, I guess?"

"What was I supposed to do? You wouldn't have left him either. Remember, I know you like the back of my black and blue hand."

I looked down at my hand and wiggled my fingers. As I did, I felt a sinking feeling in the pit of my stomach.

"As I said, this is a setback for me, but I have the rest of my life to paint that masterpiece or write the great American novel. What's a month?"

"I know why you did it, but you're wrong. I probably would have left him to die," I told Aiden.

"Now that you put it in those terms, I thought about it, but that would have destroyed more than just him. He's not going to be back this year. I'm sure of that. We will never see him again anyway."

"Yeah, I'm insisting that Kali call the cops and press charges."

"Eli, Eli, you're still so idealistic. Even if she presses charges, some lawyer will get him off. I mean, she's going to be the one on trial. They will say she led him on. They were on a date. All that kind of stuff. But you are right, she *should* call the cops. Did he, ah, ah…rape…"

"No! No, she held him off."

"Yeah, I hope she's okay," said Aiden. "You should go see her next weekend."

"Good idea. We'll both go. She'll want to see you too. You know something?"

"What is it?"

"I cannot believe you, Aiden. Maybe if I didn't take your advice and take that walk with you to *the spot*, there would have been a totally different outcome—something even worse."

"Oh, okay. I can do lots of stuff, but I can't predict the future. We know Brody is an asshole, but we didn't know he was that big of one."

Aiden may not have been a fortuneteller, but there was something about him that was hard to nail down. Unequaled—I'll leave it at that.

TWENTY-TWO

S pring decided to come early. The Valley always held tight to whatever weather that flowed in, so it was a welcome change from the glacial gusts we endured from time to time. Even the buds on trees had already popped by early April. Wispy wildflowers clung to the fringes of the campus. The grass was fresh and yielded a pure natural shade of green only to bide time until the soles of our shoes, and the dull blade of a mower would sully its richness. Chirping sounds of birds and bugs whizzing by caught my attention. A daily train, one I paid little attention to until today, chugged in the distance. Breezes, like willowy fingers, touched each newly created leaf of every aged tree.

The air took a different direction as it approached my dorm window where it affirmed my senses. Oddly, I tasted the newness of the day with each whiff I drew. The wafting aromas of scrambled eggs and Smithfield bacon interrupted natural and bold fragrances from the woods that wove in and out of my space. Everything mixed and indiscriminately merged toying with my senses. If hope had a scent, I was inhaling it. This moment was it—a perfect start to any Saturday that I could remember.

Conceived in promise, the day would build to a crescendo. Like most Saturdays, Aiden and I would venture to *the spot* just to *be*. Somewhat anxious and distracted that morning, I sensed he wanted to tell me something. This was just a hunch—call it an intuitive feeling. Intuitive feelings, at one time, seemed so foreign to me. He said nothing to suggest this, but suffice it to say, he appeared different that morning. Before we left the dorm, he spent more time than usual scribbling in his journal and forcing a smile and conversation. It was strange since he once described my communication style in this way. I imagined he found a renewed freedom since his bandages came off only a week earlier, but I honestly could not tell. All I knew for certain was that the sun was warm, and we were hanging out. All was at its best.

Escaping the confines of the campus was our plan. Aftershocks of a week of midterms reverberated in me and, and if I did not escape, I would implode. That, I thought, might be too gory to bear for either of us. Easter was a week away and I knew a Georgetown acceptance letter would be in my mailbox the following week. They promised, after all. A rejection letter was out of the question, but I felt unsettled when thinking about my prospects. Big plans were ahead of me, and I knew what they were, or so I thought. Tucking these anxieties away for a day would do me some good.

Not knowing Aiden for a long time as most friendships go, it seemed, however, like I had known him forever—*forever*. I likened this *forever* feeling to a childhood memory. As a kid, Mom took me to a department store to try on new school pants. As I stood on top of the carpeted block, my little eyes peered into the three attached full-length mirrors. I saw myself countless times—many images and many angles. The arrangement of the mirrors allowed me to inspect myself in so many perspectives and sizes that I was not sure it could, honestly, be me. Each image became smaller and even fuzzier as I turned my head and squinted to see how far my reflection appeared. At that age, I wanted to see if I could find something different as I looked farther into those likenesses. As it was, I could find no definable point of origin or no end, and it was as if the images went on forever. That's how I saw our friendship.

Like those many years before looking into that glass and spying for clues, I looked at Aiden in so many perspectives. Sometimes he appeared clear and crisp and other times he was blurry. I could not determine a beginning—or end. I didn't see any of that, but what I *could* see intrigued me, and I liked what I felt. Knowing him was like uncovering a part of myself that has always been there—hidden perhaps in my own reflection, but if the truth is known, perhaps that part has always been there in clear sight.

We started our journey that day, though, in an unfamiliar way. Mysteriously, we took another trail than the one I had grown accustomed to taking. Okay with it, he always took the lead. Where he and this trail would take us, I was without a clue and didn't even ask. Aiden as usual could meander off the straightest of paths as he soaked in his surroundings. To spur him along, though, I walked ahead at a fast pace. This was unusual for me, but I wanted to get to where we were going even though I didn't know where that was—yes, I know it sounds weird. My maneuvers, however, didn't move him any faster, but I thought it was worth a try. We didn't have to be anywhere at any given time, so it didn't matter anyway. As usual, I wanted to move beyond the moment.

Glancing back at him, he looked pensive or preoccupied. In retrospect, he may have been prayerful. No. Not prayerful come to think about it—that's just not Aiden. Truthfully, nothing now shocked me about my friend. We were so different, but today I sensed we were intersecting at some point. In nature, opposites attract. Never had I thought that way before, but Aiden always did. Those folks of like mind and similar backgrounds seemed to work best together, so I thought.

Come to think of it, we at St. Augustine's were much the same. We were mostly white Catholic schoolboys, with similar haircuts, and wore the same clothes when we didn't wear uniforms. Listened to the same music and we talked about the same things. Until recently, I thought we all had the same upbringing, but everyone who impacted my life that year, even Brody, was not the stereotypical St. Augustine student. On the surface, I *was* the stereotypical St. Gus' *man*. Could it be true?

I fit the stereotype: suburban boys who thought the world was just like them or aspiring to be just like them. We would all languish in the summer heat by a pool or at a beach, not working as we didn't have to or want to. When we did *work* it was inconsequential and changed nothing in our lives. The world would pass us by, and we would not care. Privileged as we were, we didn't even know it. Aiden wasn't any of that, but this described me and others who I knew. What I did know is that I have always felt different, and always had a desperate need to fit in—to be like *those* other boys. It gnawed at me from time to time. Aiden chipped away at me, and I was beginning to look at myself differently, like it or not. Pain precedes growth—the truth.

Where are those *other* friends now? I could care less to be honest— those same guys who I wanted to be, so to speak, in their shape and likeness. They were all probably doing what I was doing anyway. Trying to get into college to be a lawyer, or an engineer, or maybe a doctor or CPA…and so on. Of course, most of those I knew and including me, were all planning to make a lot of money one day. *Nothing wrong with that.* Oops, there I did it. My mind regressed, and I talked myself out of feeling a new way, or *my* way, only to push myself back to being like one of *the guys.* I never cease to amaze myself. Right then, I began to worry for the umpteenth time about my impending acceptance to Georgetown and ultimately to the law school. Surely, they would accept me. *Damn it!*

The route we were taking was not far from our usual path. It would come in and out of view from where we hiked. The familiar path was old and worn, but the path we now traveled was fresh and narrow. It had its fair share of fallen limbs and exposed roots that slowed us down now and again. At times the two paths would come only a few feet from each other but then branch off leaving the other out of sight. It seemed clear that the new path took us a different way down an embankment. But was it really a *new or different* way? Only moments later, as we crossed over the intersection of the two, did it dawn on me that they briefly connected. The original path, for this moment, now became the new path. For only a moment, it was the old way.

More evident than ever before, Aiden's subtle ways had influenced me. Why he chose this path, I do not know, but I was happy he did. Like those mirrors in the department store, my view of him—the deeper I looked—he was even fuzzier and more daunting than before. Either by design or by happenstance, he only revealed part of his persona. As I said before, there was no definable point of origin or no end when it came to Aiden.

*****

Taking a short rest, he straddled a fat fallen oak and I sat cross-legged on a boulder. The breeze picked up and it felt good.

"So, you should be hearing from Georgetown soon," Aiden said out of the blue.

"Yeah, I think they said after Easter I'd hear something."

"You think you're in?"

I turned to him and just gave him a look as if he asked me a stupid question. I could be an ass at times. I responded with a question of my own.

"Since you haven't applied anywhere, what are you going to do?"

"You should know me by now. The sky's the limit man. I don't know for sure but don't think I need to know right now—today. Maybe hike through Europe on five dollars a day... maybe join the Peace Corp and make five dollars a day. I could possibly move to Greenwich Village, work in an eatery, and try to get into art school and after the bills, live on five dollars a day. Some school might take me. Who knows for sure?"

"Other than we're both among the top three in the class, you know, we are absolutely nothing alike. We'll be headed in different directions soon," I said beginning to feel my throat tighten up, but I would never let him know.

"C'mon Eli. Do you think we are *that* much different from each other?"

"Well, it's pretty obvious. Just ask anyone."

"No. I'm not going to ask *anyone*. I'm asking you. I mean, don't you think our friendship, our bond means that at our very core we are similar? Whatever the word is for more than similar, I think that's what we are."

"Well yeah. I was talking about, you know, other stuff."

"Other stuff? Hmmm. You're probably right about going in different directions after we graduate. Yeah, it seems it's opposite directions for us, but you never know. Maybe I applied to colleges. You don't know everything about me. I might have applied to Georgetown or George Washington or one of the many colleges right around the corner from you."

Aiden took off without a hint and ran down another unfamiliar path. I followed but catching him wasn't easy as he exploded with his first step. He veered off the trail and through some brush until he emerged onto a meadow of tall grass with me right behind him. Like a deer, he just kept running. I caught up to him, again, but he sped up the pace—so I did too.

Again, I caught up with him. We were running side by side, an arm's length apart and looking at each other with every footfall. I saw his face framed in a blur of color. The swooshing sound of the wispy grass and the bluest of skies seemed to underscore a high that was intensifying with each stride. At the time, I didn't know what bliss meant, but it is now seared in my core. We were free, bold, and fearless as if we were the only two living beings in the universe.

Out of breath and sweat dripping, he kept going so I did too. Approaching the edge of the woods, he darted down a new path. I didn't know where we were going, but I had a suspicion. Coming to a clearing, we arrived at *the spot* from a different way. I caught up with him and he said nothing but shared a look of contentment. I followed him into the cave. Aiden headed to a part of the sanctum that was in the shadows and where only a few of the sun's rays managed to find. As I followed him deeper into his lair, it took a moment for my eyes to adjust. We finally collapsed on a few old bent-up aluminum lawn chairs.

"It felt good, Eli…that run."

"Yeah, I felt it."

He pulled out a couple of beers from a well-disguised cooler and tossed me one. We talked more and as we did, something a couple of feet beyond his shoulder came into focus. It was a new painting. I stretched my neck forward and squinted. Upon closer inspection, I saw that it was a portrait. I couldn't believe what I was seeing.

"Is that of me?"

"No shit, Sherlock. Of course, it is. Don't you know an artist doesn't like that kind of question?" He handed me the painting.

Knowing it was me, I couldn't put the right words together. This seemed the norm since arriving at St. Augustine's. It was full of brilliant colors, more detail than I even imagined I truly had. I was in awe. The care that he put into it was overwhelming in my mind. Hidden, but detectable, the background of the canvas was rich with the symbolism of our year. Among all things, I felt embarrassed. At the same time, I felt celebrated and honored—damn, I just felt good. Something inside me was touched. It was that string that connects your stomach to your heart and pulls involuntarily. They teach boys to downplay this string, and if we feel it, we were to deny it. Forgetting it as fast as it happens was the normal follow-through for us regular guys. I tried to keep my composure. Colors on a canvas, that's all it was. It probably wasn't his best work. What was I thinking? Hell, he did this with bandaged hands that had saved Kali.

Holy crap!

In a weird way, I could see him in this painting. Not knowing anything about art, maybe this was what an artist tries to achieve, and presumably, that was his legacy. It was heartening, and I sensed energy at my core. I sensed an introduction to something hidden in me but now I couldn't address it. I didn't want to think any more about it.

"Aiden, I don't know what to say."

"Well, do you like it?"

Knowing that I did, he obviously wanted me to say more. "I think it's great, I love it. I mean it's beyond words."

"Okay, okay, say no more. Uh-huh, I hear you. I wanted to do something for you. You know, in honor of your acceptance to Georgetown. I know you'll get in and do well. Hell, I need to be nice to you in case I need you to get me out of jail one day."

It hit me hard, his words. He had more faith in me than I ever had in myself. He wasn't just saying it, he knew I was getting in. I questioned myself, but Aiden answered as if he knew. The funny thing was he was probably right.

"Leave the painting here and let's head out by the river," Aiden said as he took the painting out of my hands and rested it against the lawn chair.

*****

The bright sun welcomed us as we passed through the cave's portal to the river. We sat on our usual slab of uneven rock. Leaning back, we both situated a hand behind our head to form a pillow of sorts, as our backs and butts fit naturally in and out of the cragginess of the boulders. Low and close to the water, we dangled our feet in an eddy that formed just for us. Cooling off, we laid there saying nothing only to hear the soft murmur of the flow of the water that nearly encircled us. As we felt an inviting breeze, we looked off to the mountains as they were clear and in full view. All was good.

Out of the corner of my eye, I saw Aiden scratch his head and when he brought his arm down to the surface of the boulder, his arm and hand brushed up against mine. As it did, his hand drifted and rested right on top of mine. He didn't move it. I didn't move mine. My heart raced, my skin tingled, and I was suddenly taking more breaths than usual. Without thinking, I turned my palm out to meet his and we wrapped our fingers together. A little scared, I didn't know what to expect, but I *knew* what I was feeling, and I liked it.

Lying still, I turned my head to give him a peek and all I saw was his profile. His eyes were closed. Just when I thought that I didn't want the moment to end, he gently squeezed my sticky hand for a few, long seconds. Still holding it, he sat up and let go of my hand one finger at a time. Slowly I brought my hand down and laid it on my stomach. With my other hand, I softly ran my fingers on my palm as if this would help the feeling to last.

Looking beyond the water, Aiden pulled up his legs and wrapped his arms around his knees. I swallowed hard. He glanced at me with a faint smile, and I gave him the biggest toothy grin I knew how. At that moment, our eyes joined, and our gaze was intense. Sitting up, I edged just a few inches closer to him. We sat for some time as we listened to the quiet, and in doing so, I heard a voice inside of me that I always kept silenced before that moment. This time I let it speak freely. The voice was clear, and it said to me that I am made of many parts and those many parts are good.

Aiden laid his arm across my shoulders, and I slowly placed my hand on his thigh. We sat hearing only the occasional flying insect whiz by and the rustle of the tall grasses as the warm breeze filtered through. A dragonfly landed on my hand. Like a gem, it was luminescent with rich blues and greens.

"They're a symbol of change—of growth. They mean new beginnings that bring hope and love," I said trusting my voice wouldn't crack.

"Eli, I like that…I really do. Always liked dragonflies and never knew why. I'm going to name that one, Eli."

A warm feeling coated me, and I choked up. The feeling was sudden, and I immediately sensed it deep inside.

"Eli, this is a perfect day. Just wish it could be like this all the time," he said as his eyes welled up.

At that moment, the dragonfly flew away and hovered over the still water in front of us. Wasn't sure if I should have said all that about the dragonfly, but glad I did. It was a first for me. After a moment of tossing a pebble or two in the water in our solitude, we began a conversation that whisked us off to another place that I just can't remember so well. It was just *talk*. I wasn't ready to just *talk*. I wanted to talk about how I was feeling—how he was feeling. I didn't know what to say or how to say it. I was hoping he would say something but in hindsight, he had already done so without so many words.

Perhaps, I did too.

*****

As we watched the sun move upward in the sky fixing itself directly above us, we could feel the heat of its rays become more intense on our bodies. It was like a healing sort of warmth. Buzzards circled us in high altitudes as we guessed at what was sifting in and out of their miniature brains. That was when the subject of flying came up.

"Look at those birds," I said. "I mean they can fly anywhere they want."

"They can see for miles without anything in their way. I wonder what it would be like to fly?" Aiden asked observing their movement.

"Yeah, we're kind of stuck on this rock," I said lightly patting the stone where we sat.

"Some birds are stuck to this rock like us, but some that can fly have a grace about them. You know, this kind of effortless glide like the condor that rarely flaps its wings. Those poor chickens and ostriches—I guess the master of the universe reserved the heavens for the few. The ones with star quality like the great eagle," Aiden said with a chuckle.

At that, Aiden sat up with a sense of urgency and looked at me.

"Today's the day. Yep, today."

"What are you babbling about?"

"I'm going to nail it. I'm going to dive from the top, and I'm going to stick the landing," Aiden insisted.

I didn't feel good about this decision and spoke up.

"I don't know Aiden. That's an extra fifteen feet—that's way up there. Besides, the river seems low today. It's yours for another day,

205

believe me, but I wouldn't do it today."

"I know this river inside and out. I know it! The deep part is right below the perch from where I'll be diving. God, Eli when are you going to stop worrying so much?"

Aiden jumped up and pulled off his tee-shirt. I sat up just watching him prepare. Aiden comically flexed his biceps and as I looked up at him, his head eclipsed the sun creating a kind of halo around him. That was *so Aiden*. I just shook my head and laughed. The sweat on his shoulders and chest glistened in the sun. In a way, it reminded me of the first day I met him.

I knew there was no stopping him. Wishing him luck was the only natural thing to do at the time. He started scaling the side of the cliff climbing like Tarzan. He pulled himself up by using tree branches and jagged, jutting rocks. For the most part, I was in the same position I had been in for the last hour or so just turning a bit to watch his ascent. Letting out a few grunts and groans along the way, he was quiet as he reached the summit. There he was standing much higher than what I expected. This was not right. I did not feel good about this at all.

Aiden shouted out that he was going to dive from a flat rock that was about a foot to one side. Echoes and all, the valley was his witness. He declared that it would be a much better surface to take the dive. As he stepped, a bowling ball size boulder cradling others, dislodged several other rocks. They plunged down the wall taking a few small tree limbs along the way; each splash stabbed my swelling fear. Aiden sprung back to his original position.

Somewhat fazed, Aiden was still determined. "Wow, Eli that was close."

"It sure as hell was. You almost killed me. Get down from there."

"Eli, it was just a close call. I'm already up here and I'm ready."

"Hey Aiden, come on down. There'll be another day for this. Maybe I'll do it with you then. So, what do you say? C'mon down."

Ignoring me. "It is really cool up here. You can see for miles and miles in every direction. I can see the campus—must be what eagles see."

Aiden stood as if he owned the cliff and was poised to dive. Just the way he carried himself sent a reassuring message to me. But my heart was already racing fast, and each pump of blood felt like it would spew itself out of my pores. I now pleaded for him to change his mind, but he would not budge. Just then, I knew there would be no dismount. As he bent his knees to begin his dive, his limestone perch gave way. In midair he desperately tried to regain his form as he descended in what felt like slow motion. My heart was nosediving along with his body. Suddenly, it appeared that he straightened out in time to hit the water with a perfect dive. My emotions went from a pang of fear to a gush of joy. I leaped with my hands stretched upwards.

"You did it! You stuck it...you stuck the landing. Man, that scared me, Aiden."

I was talking to no one as he had not yet surfaced. The next three seconds lasted an eternity. I thought it would be just *so Aiden*, like when we went canoeing, to play on my emotions and spring up behind me for shock value.

The ripples he made in the water disappeared. Panic seized my whole body. Erratically, I looked in all directions but didn't see him. I dove in and frantically reached everywhere and grabbed at everything in my way. I found his hand. Hugging his torso, we surfaced, and I pulled him to the shore. Cradling his head, I looked down at his face. He was conscious but blood poured from the back of his head and covered my hand. Aiden looked into my eyes and with a shaky voice, he spoke.

"Os...ost...ostrich?

"Eagle."

We smiled. A tear ran down my face and dripped into Aiden's eye, and as it did, he closed them both. I lowered my head to his and cried.

TWENTY-THREE

The day after the funeral it rained. Everything about the day was cold, and so was I right down to the tip of my nose. I sat, alone in my dark room. That's what I wanted. Kali called the hall phone and Luis and others tried all they could to get me to talk to her. I just couldn't. I hadn't heard from my father yet, and can't lie, I was happy about that.

Gazing out the window all I saw were sheets of water—gray and endless. Mesmerized by the steady downpour, I heard a faint knock on my door. It took me a moment to realize what I was hearing. I didn't want to see anyone, so I stayed still and continued to stare at the glassy blur outside of my window. Every so often, the deluge would pelt the pane sending shivers down my spine. There was another knock. This time it was louder. I told myself that whoever was knocking would eventually give up and just go away, but I was wrong. The screech of the hinges cut through me as the door opened. In the window in front of me, I saw Father Meinrad's reflection. Glancing back at him, I saw that he clutched an envelope. Without a second thought, I knew he held my future. It had to be the infamous acceptance letter. What else could it be?

Without uttering so much as one word, and with a sweeping motion, Father handed me the thick envelope. With a jerk and without looking at it, I stuffed it in a cubbyhole in my desk. With an inaudible word of thanks, I continued to sit at my desk with my back to him and scribbled on a piece of paper as if it were important. *Wasn't he going to leave?* Father stood there for a moment and then let out a sigh. Sensing a collision of thoughts, feelings, and emotions, he masked it all away and began talking.

"Well, aren't you going to open it?"

"I know what it says. I've been accepted," I said flipping the pencil between my index finger and thumb.

"Boy, aren't you the confident one?"

I slammed a book that lay open next to me and slid it off the desk. It slapped the floor. Making a fist, I pounded the surface of my desk and turned to him, and my red eyes ensnared his.

"What? Confidence—confidence? What are you talking about?"

I could stand it no longer. Jumping up and arching my back, I looked to the ceiling. Furiously, I ran my fingers through my hair wanting to pull out each strand, one by one. My aching eyes welled up and I had a stinging pain in my chest. One tear and then another rolled down my cheek.

"Son," he said as he reached out to me, "I'm here for you."

"No Father, no." I began to pace back and forth in my small room. I balled up my hands into fists. My body felt stiff as nails. Thinking about Aiden, as I had been since our last moment together, I felt littered with an endless sense of torment. Carved out and worthless, I did not know what was keeping me alive. No way I was going to discuss my feelings or my thoughts or anything…not now and maybe not ever. Father's mere presence and persistence were coming dangerously close to an area in me that was off-limits to everyone.

With each passing minute, my anxiety climbed. Disoriented and feverish, the light was waning, and the world shone through in sepia tones. Overwhelmed, fatigued, and scared, I lost it. I *really* lost it. With an eruption of all the emotions stuffed in various places throughout my body, I screamed, "You are wrong, old man! I have no confidence. I'm a worthless sack of shit. I'M NOTHING. Leave me alone."

Spewing random thoughts, I was no longer in control. My heart hurt. What was bubbling to mind and what was coming to my lips was now gibberish. Nothing made sense. My heart felt something, my mind thought something else, and my mouth stunned me as it spoke on its own.

My rigidness gave way as if my bones disappeared, but somehow, I remained standing—barely. Now frazzled and spent, I was a pile of mush. Father did not know what to make of my tirade and my sudden shift. He stood back and looked on. His eyes—his eyes bulged with pain. With my unsure footing, Father reached for me and pulled me to him. But finding a hideous strength, I pushed him away so hard he almost lost his balance. I hated myself even more. With a calm resolve, he again pulled me to him and held me tight; I stood lifeless and wept like a dying man with nothing but a life of regret—maybe that *was* my reality. A moment later, Father guided me to the edge of my bed, and we sat. We sat for minutes in silence only broken by my muted and intermittent sobs.

"Let it out son."

"Father, I let it happen, I'm the reason. I, I ..."

"Oh no. I know you are in pain, but please son, you cannot—should not think that way."

I pulled away, walked to the window, and stared at the lifeless smear of white and gray. Pulling up the window, I stuck my head out as the rain beat down on my face. I screamed until my throat tightened with a twisting pain. Wrenching myself back in my room, I yanked down the sash. Dripping, I turned to Father.

"I can't take it," I whispered. "I just can't take it."

"I know you are enduring horrific pain in a place deep in your heart. Your wound is beyond imagination, I know. Believe me, I know. It is only natural to mourn his death and to experience the anguish and grief of his passing. We all know life is unfair and this is a stark realization of just that. I have prayed not only for Aiden's soul but for yours as well. You have so much ahead of you."

"SHUT UP—SHUT UP!"

Although he was trying to say all the right things, he seemed rehearsed, distant, and too priestly. What he conveyed, in both words and actions, was not what I wanted nor needed. He didn't *know* how I *felt*. How could he know?

A sharp needle inside me came from somewhere and pressed at a point in my gut and a sick sensation shot upward. Rage, as I never felt before was smothering me. My anger only worsened, and my emotions exploded. I demanded Father to leave. Father still appeared calm, but his strained spirit was evident. Numb, he just sat there staring at me. I looked at him and now, his inaction, set me off even more.

Again, I screamed at the top of my lungs, "I am the reason!"

Still cool in manner but an ache entered every line of his face. His eyes welled up, but it did not register with me at the time. He was in agony too. I will never forget his face to the day I die. Father walked to the door and turned to me.

"My heart and my door will always be open to you Eli—today and forever."

He walked away and headed down the hall. As each clomp of his heel grew faint on the hardwood floor, so did the pain I was enduring. Don't know why. Sweaty, disgusted, and lifeless, I fell, face first, onto my bed. I was alone. That's what I needed. I kept my eyes closed but the tears forced their way out. My eyes burned and my body twitched as I laid there. Soon, the insanity that streamed through my head dissipated and I fell asleep.

*****

When I awoke, I was still dazed and confused. The colorless day had turned into a black night. It was late. Drenched in cold dejection, I didn't want to be here anymore. I wanted to get out—I needed to ease my pain. Feeling worthless to anyone, like a shadow I left my room. Seeing no one, I took one of the passageways Aiden showed me a month or so earlier that led down to one of the tunnels. It was dark and chilling. It smelled like dead rats. The pipes lining the ceiling glistened and the sound of *drip, drip, drip* rang in my ears.

Walking beneath the campus, I occasionally looked over my shoulder—but no one was nearby. That's what I wanted—to be alone. Knowing I was alone in the world echoed in my mind. Yeah, everyone needs some time alone, but this kind of alone is a lonely feeling. This was a sharp and desolate feeling that had become way too familiar. Without Aiden, my loneliness had become my closest companion— just like before I met him. Not quite like the others, I could never pinpoint why I was or, much less, what I should do about it. Never did I think I could sink this low.

Walking further through the tunnels, I felt the warm, thick air radiating from furnaces to one end. I kept walking. Surrounding me, the dark crusty walls, I thought, were never supposed to see the light of day. Someone designed this place to be a dark, steamy underworld that attracted vermin. *Drip, drip, drip.* I was in the right place. The sick smell of death was all around me. I kept walking. Truthfully, I know what brought me here. Ridding myself of what I had become and who I really was and have always been, turned over and over in my head. I wanted out.

My face streamed with sweat, but my lips were dry and cracking as I nervously dug my front teeth into my bottom lip. Glowing misshapen and undefinable images lurked to the sides of me and seemed to know me. They were inviting me. The hiss of the pipes made themselves known—they were alive as they spouted steam and played with my mind. *Drip, drip, drip.*

"I belong in this ugly place that Aiden called the catacombs."

Shocking lightning flashes in my head came from nowhere. Visions of rocks falling from under Aiden as he struggled suspended in air seemed so real—they *were* real. These images, overlapping each other all looped through my mind's eye.

"I'm the reason. I AM THE REASON! I hate myself—I'm a failure! I'm so ashamed and will always feel this way. I know it. I'm sick, I'm stupid, and I want out. Out!"

I looked up and saw pipe after pipe and I picked one. Unbuckling my belt, I pulled it from my pants. Holding it with both hands, I tugged at it. There was an old crate to one side, so I pulled it over and placed it directly under the pipe. Emotionless, I stepped up on top of it and now the corroded piece of iron was in reach. With my fingertips, I felt its rusty pockmarks. Then I tugged at it. Pieces flecked off and into my eyes. I deserved it. Throwing the belt over it, I fastened the buckle and twisted it into a figure eight. My heartbeat pounded in my ears and got louder with each thump. Louder and LOUDER, it thumped. I hated who I was. Millions of needles pricked me, and my overall detachment led to more confusion if that can even be possible. I could not feel my body and wasn't even sure I was there—right there. *Drip, drip, drip.*

My mouth tasted like sand as I continued to bite down on my lip. Looking down at my hands, they were trembling. I turned them to see my palms, and with the fingers of my left hand, I slowly caressed my right palm—like that day. With a tingle, for a split second, I felt warm, and the trembling went away. I saw Aiden's face, but without warning, a quivering smile overtook my leathered and bloody lips. After a second or two, my thoughts of destruction shot back into my head like it came from a sniper's rifle.

Just like that, I re-entered my disgusting reality. Drip, drip, drip.

I slipped my head into the loop I created and closed my eyes. I tried to go limp, but my body remained rigid. I jostled the crate I was standing on, but it didn't budge. Salty tears ran into my mouth as I attempted again, this time I did so with as much strength I could muster.

Frustrated, I heard a voice.

"Eli, Eli you're going to be okay. It's me Luis, and I'm with you brother. Come on down. Give me your hand, and I'll help you."

My eyes opened and there stood Luis holding the crate with one hand and reaching up to me with his other.

That's all I needed.

I slipped my head out of the belt, grabbed his hand, and collapsed to the wet concrete floor. Luis sat down beside me. I cried as he held me tight for what seemed like an hour.

"How did you know to come here?"

"Gosh, Eli, I don't know. I woke up and couldn't go back to sleep, and it seemed something just wasn't right. For some reason, my gut was telling me something. Something crazy was going through my head, and I couldn't make sense of it. I walked out of my room and my steps led me here. I can't really tell you. Maybe it's karma. You showed up for me. Now it's my turn."

"I'm so sorry…I'm so… so…"

"Sorry? Hey, Eli you are good. You hurt but you're gonna be okay. Aiden is still with you. He's here now. I just know it. He's right here," he said pointing to my chest.

*****

Weeks passed.

My mind was clear and ounce by ounce, I began to feel some self-worth build up. I felt better but still felt hollowed out. Eating little, but going through the motions each day, I simply existed. Merely living like an amoeba, I was shapeless and basic. Wanting to keep to myself, this self-imposed isolation just had to be better than giving up. I believed Luis. Aiden lives in my heart.

214

I asked Luis to keep everything between us if I promised him, and me, to talk to someone about what I was going through—and what I attempted to do. He stayed on top of me. So thankful for him, he checked with me several times a day. Another week passed and was almost to the point where I was ready to reach out to someone for help. I feared, though, that I had burned a bridge to the person who could help me the most.

As a type of cruel reminder of what I was looking to achieve, even doing the bare minimum, I did not risk losing my valedictory status. Who cared about that anyway? I SURE AS HELL DIDN'T anymore. Not sure when it would strike, but I was convinced that a wrecking ball was aimed right at me. If I didn't figure things out, this steel, lifeless ball would raze me leaving behind a hole—a deep, nasty, cold hole. Darkness loomed above all my waking moments and entered my dreams at night. This is who I was—at that moment.

Aiden should have known it, of all people. What went wrong? Rolling haphazardly in my head were so many careening thoughts. I had so much more to tell him. So many more moments were waiting for us, Aiden and me. Those perfect times we had were over and were never to come again.

Never.

TWENTY-FOUR

One Saturday about two weeks before graduation, I was sitting on an old stone bench on the quad. It must have been about seven in the morning. As usual, I could not sleep the night before. No one was up except the Robes as this was their time for morning prayers. Chants and praises to God in song sifted through the monstrous church walls to where I stood. In all honesty, I loved the music they brought into existence. It transported me to a different time or realm—that kind of thing. I of course would not have shared this sentiment with any of my teenage friends, well, except for one.

As I sat, the sounds of the breeze and the solitude were uplifting. I envied the Robes on this particular day. They were at peace with themselves. They were always at peace, or so it seemed. Putting up with the grief we gave them every day, they still lived the vow they had committed to earlier in their lives. They were mere men, and I never saw them as anything more than that, but today I saw them as something more. Men, yes, but I saw them as completely committed to their beliefs. I saw them as strong men although many were physically frail and riddled with diseases of old age. Sacrificing so much in a lifetime, but a sense of gratitude was evident especially now as I listened. That's who they were. I could not believe I did not see this before, but never took the time to care.

The morning chill was still hanging in the air. The day was going to be hot, but now, a coolness surrounded me. My mind was amazingly clear and open. Perhaps it was too early in the morning for the demons to be awake. I was experiencing my version of mindfulness and this recognition was soothing as I was learning to value such instances.

For an unknown reason, I thought of Mom, and she was trying to tell me something. I could not quite make out what she was saying but seeing her in my mind's eye was enough. My thinking prompted

Aiden's image coming from another compartment of my brain. My memory was no longer full of fatal moments as the edges of each recollection were beginning to soften. Instead, more joyful images were beginning to crowd out the painful ones. These new visions took me elsewhere and they were becoming real. Damn it, my thoughts were not *becoming* real they *were* real just as the cold stone bench I was sitting on or the rising sun before me—or the mountains and the river and all the paths we took.

My thoughts were real.

Was it time to move on? It *was* time. I think Mom and Aiden were telling me the time had come. That had to be it. Ironically, just at that very moment, a sense of loneliness whipped through me like an electric shock. But it was okay as I now realized I had to take steps. I needed to cut myself some much-needed slack... *and why wouldn't I be lonely right now? It's okay.* It was okay because this gap would take time to fill and ultimately, doing it alone was not the best answer. That's the difference. I still had a long way to go. It's funny how things change in a snap of time. I told myself it was okay—Luis told me that.

I covered my face with my hands seeing only reddish lines that separated each finger. Seeping in beyond my control, my anguish replaced any positive thoughts of only a moment earlier as despondency filled the space. The deceptions that I kept buried and would never say aloud gushed forth. He made me, after all, so nothing I could say would be shocking. *Nothing about me could be surprising to the one who created me. I AM good and He knows it.* I couldn't help this sudden shift of thinking, so I prayed. Gathering my thoughts, I just muttered what came to mind. My ramblings gave me comfort. Remembering nothing of what I said, the feeling that enveloped me was uplifting.

Pausing, at least for the moment, I removed my hands from my sweaty face and looked around at the purple and blue Allegheny Mountains. The billowy fog had already dissipated; what was before me was magnificent. With this beauty came fear. At my feet, I noticed a beetle that somehow had flipped over on his back. I knew what it was like for that little bug as it flailed its many legs. It must either harness an internal momentous motion to save itself or receive the help of a strong but friendly outside force so it may resume its life and fulfill its destiny. If one of these things does not happen, a hungry bird decides its fate. Reaching down and with one finger, the same finger I touched the rusted pocked pipe, I turned him right side up. Within a second, he took to flight, and my eyes followed him until he was out of sight.

I did not know why I began to feel this way, but as a warm embrace, I was ready to forgive the one person I never seemed to want to forgive. Yet reality had not changed, nothing would ever be the same. Nothing can change what has been done, but I can decide what my reality will look like today and tomorrow. To do that, I must be truthful with myself which is harder than one may think.

Just don't know—like a rickety carnival ride, I felt myself spinning back as I do so often. People probably think I'm a failure to a friend in need—and a coward. Boy, I'm a coward about a lot of things, I might add. Folding my arms, I cast my eyes downward to where the little beetle struggled moments earlier. Like him, I needed to be flipped right side up. Closing my eyes, I wanted to open them and wanted everything to be okay. I wanted to open them and be set free.

At that moment, I felt the tenderness of the touch of an open hand on my shoulder. As I turned my head, I saw Father Meinrad. As a surprise to both of us, I smiled. He was brave to come close to me after my reaction of a few weeks earlier. His touch immediately began to dissolve my indifference toward him as I had wrongly treated him. Making no excuses, I allowed my pain to control me, and at this moment he certainly risked more of my cruelty.

Father sat next to me and said nothing. I broke the silence, and as I began to talk our eyes met. Upon looking at him, one tear different from all my others escaped and rolled down my face. It was an old tear, bottled up from the last day I saw Aiden. I knew it would freely come one day. Unlike the others that came from grief, anger, and sadness, this tear came from my fear of what will be—of the unknown. I needed to let go, but I was frightened. When the first drop streamed down my cheek it was like an unexpected summer storm and with little warning, I let it out. This time, I did so without thunder.

"I try and try and try to think and feel differently and just when I think I am doing better, I feel like the crud under my shoe. Father, I try to convince myself it's not true, but I have so much hate in me. I am evil—I'm nothing. I tell myself that I am good, but how could I have let this happen? It's all my fault. I watched him climb, knew he was in danger, and did absolutely nothing. What kind of friend does that?

Father said nothing so I continued.

"He was incredible to me, I was a letdown to him, and I know that. The day I threw my duffle bag on the bed was the beginning of his end."

Father put his arm around my shoulder, and I felt his warmth. He said nothing.

"Can God forgive me? Is Aiden in a place that he can forgive me? Can souls do that kind of thing? Hell, I don't know what I'm talking about anymore. I'm worthless." I left it there.

"Eli, you are loved, and you are good. You did nothing wrong. Nothing at all. On the contrary, you did everything right."

"Huh?"

"You remain a beautiful and remarkable friend to another wonderful young man. I know this because I saw how you two treated one another; how you interacted. I know this too because he told me things. He shared with me many heart-rending and exciting stories of your days together. He told me that this year was the best year of his life. His best Eli! That's because of you."

"You really think so?"

"Absolutely. You may not know this, but we spoke often. It is I who spends time at the *old lady's* house. There, Aiden and I would talk. It was kind of our secret."

"I knew that you two were tight since my first day here."

"Eli, in all honesty, I am puzzled and bewildered with what you are telling me. What do you mean you are evil and what is it that you let happen?"

"You know. Only someone evil would let a friend risk his life on something as meaningless and trivial as a dive from some ridiculous height. I did nothing to stop him. Father, he was my friend and I—I—I—I loved him," I said swallowing hard and feeling shaky.

"I could tell Eli. Don't be ashamed about how you feel," he said hugging me. I grabbed him too, and I sensed safety and love. "And no need to say it in the past tense. Your love continues," he said gently pulling back from me to look into my eyes.

220

"Thanks Father…so it lives? It lives on?"

"Absolutely! Love transcends the physical world. That's why love is the most powerful force in the universe."

"But Father people who love others don't stand by and do nothing. Don't you see? I feel everything about me is evil. Hell, I gave him nothing. He did so much for me, and I gave him nothing in return. I didn't want it to happen, Father."

"I know, everyone knows, and God knows," Father Meinrad said. "Let me ask you something. Did you force him to climb the embankment, and did you push him from the platform?"

"Of course not!"

"Exactly. You didn't! We all have free will. No one would have expected or wanted this outcome. We cannot see the future. Don't tell me you can see into the future," he said with a wink.

"Well, no."

"But you can see the present—can't you?"

"Well, yeah."

"And by all accounts, the day was full of joy, of life, and beauty. Love was with you both. Your love vibrated through the universe."

"It was the happiest and saddest day of my life—and Aiden felt that way too. He told me. How can that be? I mean we shared so much," I said looking down at my palm.

"Eli, things change in a flash of a moment. I am so very sorry, dear boy, as we all hope a day of such joy would not be scarred with such sorrow. Relish that joyful moment forever. Together, it is your moment for eternity. How joyous!"

As I looked at Father, his eyes comforted me, and his presence was like a familiar and worn blanket.

"Even though our bodies are temporal, our souls live on. Sure, all of us want to live a long, healthy, and meaningful lives. That, I think, he accomplished. He celebrated a moment like others celebrated a year. Aiden lived longer than most. *He lived.* Don't you see Eli? He lived. All who met him knew his life was full of meaning. You know this and you both shared such meaning and such brilliance."

"I never thought of that before."

"Most people don't. Eli, you are good and so was Aiden."

"I'm beginning to believe it. I think."

"We all need to be affirmed and reaffirmed and, unfortunately, that comes around infrequently."

"Thanks, Father."

"You affirmed Aiden…and you must realize that it was only a matter of time and Aiden would take that dive or some other kind of risk. He tasted life from both ends. His senses were full. All six," Father said laughing.

"What? What do you mean by all six? We only have five."

"He had something else going for him. He had an innate sense of his surroundings and the people around him. He was highly intuitive. That is what I mean about a sixth sense."

"Yeah, there was something about him—something that I never felt from or about anyone else. I've kept that to myself. BUT we both knew, and I feel good about that. But like always, I keep certain things to myself."

"Be careful holding too much in, Eli. Open your eyes inward to the marvels of what is not new but is hidden. Don't hide what makes you, you."

I knew what he was saying and nodded but looked away as I felt some awkwardness. Although I felt safe with Father, the world appeared to me as anything BUT safe. It was quiet for a moment and then Father spoke up.

"I would like to tell you a story, Eli. A very special story that an old Buddhist monk told me when I was just a little older than you. Not many know this, but I spent three years in a different sort of monastery."

"A Buddhist monk? What? That's awesome Father." We both smiled, and he continued.

"A long time ago there were two friends, one who played the harp skillfully, and one who listened skillfully. When the one played a song about the mountains, the other would listen and say, 'I'm on top of that mountain.' And when the one played a song about the river, the other would say, 'Here, right before us, is the running river.'

One day the one who listened became ill and died. Out of love, the first friend cut the strings of his harp, and never

222

played again."

I said nothing. Catching my attention, a squirrel scampered by and scurried up a tree. As my eyes followed him on his climb, the mountains appeared in full view.

"I'm not sure if I follow you, Father. I'm not so sure that story is true for me."

"Don't you see? It is the cutting of harp strings that is a sign of the most intimate of all friendships—when someone would give up something so dear for the sake of another. That one celebrates what the other brings to the relationship and cherishes moments that only they two shared."

Again, we sat in silence as I tried to make sense of what he said. "So, I understand that, but according to the story, I should have been the one—who died."

"I beg to differ, Eli."

"Oh. How?"

"You, my dear boy, sell yourself short yet again. Both you and Aiden were skillful at playing the harp. Both you and Aiden were skillful at listening. You both imagined a joyful life and saw it come to bloom through the other's eyes—and heart. Don't think for one moment that he did not listen to you and take to heart what you shared with him. You drew upon and from each other. He heard what was in your heart and you, Eli, heard what was in his."

"I talk myself out of so much. Father, I needed to hear this from someone."

"I know but remember as wonderful the sound of the harp may be, it only lives, and forms love if that sound becomes a part of us. Yes, the joy first comes from the strummer, BUT the joy—true meaning—also comes from the listener who takes the beauty and imagines a reality that the music creates for both. The joy comes from shared moments and then, blossoms for an eternity."

"So, *we* cut the harp strings?"

"Yes, my dear boy. Your time together in the physical world, sadly, is over and it will not be repeated no matter what. But by keeping him in your heart your love, and his, lasts forever."

"I'm afraid of how I feel. I didn't plan it. I—I know he ah, ah *liked* me too, but it was—it was much more than that."

"I know, I know. You gave each other so much. He hungered for someone like you. He loved you, Eli."

I nodded a little, and my throat tightened, and it was hard to swallow. My eyes welled up but just couldn't get out any words.

"You complemented each other. The relationship you had was extraordinary. You gave him insights into a different world and he, too, gave you an understanding that will hold with you for the rest of your long life."

"I know you're right about that, Father."

"And I know you are afraid of how you feel but give yourself some time…be kind to yourself. In time, open up to someone you trust. I'm here, but don't limit yourself. Don't try to find all your answers at one time and from one person, my good boy."

"Father, he wasn't like the others, and neither am I."

"We humans tend to stereotype without even knowing it. We place people in boxes, and we make snap judgments so that we can escape learning, caring, and feeling for others. These boxes, we are convinced, justify our actions and from that, we begin to think of others in convenient ways."

"What do you mean? Convenient ways?"

"Our reaction to those we place in a box runs the gamut even allowing us to hate. Depending on how a person is *boxed*, we tend to think of them a certain way. That goes for us too—we must overcome the temptation to put *ourselves* in such societal boxes and poison ourselves to believe, *they* are right. They are *not* right!"

"Father, it seems that my life is nothing but these boxes. This year has been kind of confusing, but in a good way."

"Ah, you have hit the nail on the head, my boy. We only grow as we move through what is uncomfortable. I dare say you inspired one another. Your differences brought you together. Your attraction was unique to you both. If only those of us in the rest of the world connected like you two, we would indeed, live in a better place. A place you have already seen and tasted. Eli, you have been to a special place."

"But I miss him so much."

"I know you do, and it is okay to miss him. It will take time, but it will get better. As it should—give it time. Be good to yourself."

He smiled at me and when he did, I saw Aiden. I needed that.

"Eli, it takes courage to listen to your heart, and even more courage to act upon what your heart tells you," Father said as he gently tapped his chest and continued. "You need nothing more than that and that, my son, I hope you never forget."

"I was looking for someone or something to make it all better for me. You know, to fix everything right now."

"You'll find all that deep within and not from someone else, but we all need someone we can trust to help us pull the veil from what lays hidden. Time, Eli—give yourself some time." Father said.

"Cutting of harp strings—so it's like I'd do anything for him, and he'd do the same...hmmm."

"It is the dearest and most intimate love that one may possess—and give. It is one that most of us never experience at all."

We sat in the beauty of the solitude. In Father, I now saw what Aiden saw. We looked off to the mountains and although the river was not in sight, *it was right before us.*

TWENTY-FIVE

Another week passed and I recall that I awoke on Saturday and felt, well, unboxed. It was weird, as I didn't have a hangover, but the night before I polished off half of a fifth of rum that Aiden and I found in the woods. We had hidden it in our room for some *special* occasion. I had to do it. We promised each other that we would sling back the rest of the bottle before we graduated. It was more like a few shots—I've never felt right when I've exaggerated. That night I played the Aerosmith song—the one by Steven Tyler, *Dream On,* over and over—I do remember that.

Funny thing is that I wasn't in my bed when I woke up. When my eyes halfway opened, I laid still. It was quiet except for the stylus on his stereo. It was making that clicking, scratching noise when it keeps rubbing up against the paper center of an album. After a yawn and a stretch, I turned my head from side to side and learned I was laying on top of Aiden's *impeccably* made bed. I leaned up, rested back on my elbows, and scanned our room. Looking around at all the photos, posters, and everything else we plastered and tacked on the cracked walls, I couldn't help but to smile. Focusing on the article he taped up about The Gipsy Moth, and then thinking about our voyage in that ratty green canoe, made me beam brighter.

Remembering nothing of falling asleep the night before, I actually began to feel refreshed and invigorated. I dreamt of something. Just knew it but couldn't remember what. I'll never know but it gave me a feeling, or else it was from the rum, but it was as if something clicked in my head or opened some unknown passage to a part of my heart that was hidden.

Looking out the window, I saw streams of blended colors in the sky so different from any other morning. Vivid hues of pink, purple, and orange toyed with the horizon. The early morning was special to me. That was the time when Aiden dragged me from my solitude and slumber to swim, or to hike, or just run free. This was always the time to discover.

The gold sunlight was slowly taking over the sky. It was warm and bright. All I could see, think, or feel was acutely sharp and close enough to touch. All before me was so alluring. So much jumped at me as I was searching for something, but just not sure of what. There was something that I knew I must find. Uncluttered, my head was free of destructive thoughts. I kept thinking that today was going to be full of new experiences. Thinking of my talk with Father, I zipped from one magnificent thought to the next. Every new thought expanded my smile until my face hurt.

So fascinated with the brilliance and radiance the sun shed through my window, I decided to leave through it. Climbing out and landing on my feet, I walked. My gait grew faster. My stride lengthened and began to run. The sun winked at me through the dappled green leaves overhead, as each leaf captured a part of the sun's glow and only allowed for whispers of light to reach me below. The leaves were now a blur of greens as I only saw white rays warming all that was up ahead of me. I felt untethered to everything—my books, the school, people, and most of all, my future. It was the *now* that mattered. Only the present time counts. What came before *is* etched in stone but what lies *ahead* is still to be written. It is the *now* that matters as it is over in a flash and its meaning can be evasive—but it doesn't have to be that way. I'm in control.

My *now* leads me. I ran faster.

Many cardinals had been born since the day Aiden defined a new world to me. Each new birth comes with new hope for beauty. Now it was easy for me to distinguish between the different hues of each green leaf. The nuance of the woods filled my senses. The unceasing murmurs of the river bubbling over the stones in the distance, and the cooling breezes that wafted downward through the boughs of the crooked trees were now part of me. Cedars, which peppered the landscape, bore a sweetness that sailed into the air that was propelled by the squirrels hopping and tumbling in their branches. So much was in front of me that I would never see, but I felt a serenity to be among its presence. I didn't have to see it as it was in me, and I was in it. Obvious to me, I was not alone.

Out of breath, I doubled over at the foot of the cliff. Sweat ran down my face and dripped to the ground. I turned and saw the river. All I could hear was the gush and babble of water, as it was a song like none other. I realized that today was a carbon copy of that fateful day. Today, however, I celebrated all that was in front of me, and I reveled in all that was inside of me.

Still bent over with my hands on my knees, I crooked my neck and looked to the summit of the cliff. I brought myself to its base and began climbing. Grabbing the next stone or branch, I pulled myself upward. The occasional rock would slip, and like the shiny metal balls of a pinball machine, it would bounce erratically and plunk into the river.

Inside, I felt a burst of emotions emerging from somewhere resonating deep within. Never had I ever felt this way before. It was a cross between anguish and euphoria. Maybe I was on the ragged line that separates the two for it was two distinct and indescribable simultaneous sensations. Opposites begot a host of feelings, like the yin and yang, the Alpha and the Omega, love, and hate—Aiden and me.

I moved with fervor up the cliff. When I reached the top, I looked to the horizon seeing what Aiden had once seen. With outstretched arms, I closed my eyes and raised my face to the sun. I felt the newness of the day stream through my hair, on my face, and over my body. Kicking off my shoes and watching them drop to the bottom, I heard a muted thud that reminded me that life cannot be separated from risk. I pulled off my shirt. Nothing but the moment played in my mind as it was the only time that was real. I was going to do it and did not care. Or perhaps, I cared too much.

Then, I did it. I dove.

A million thoughts went through my head as I entered the surface of the water. I heard a hush and then bounded upward. A sense of completeness came over me, and I was euphoric. As my head surfaced, I thought I saw something—or someone. But it was nothing—I saw no one. Yet, what I felt was awesome. I felt a presence, it was sensational, but it was elusive. What I felt was real and was strong.

Unafraid and resolute by this mystical presence I played in the water. I smiled and my smile made me laugh. I swam to shore and pulled myself onto the slab of limestone that had once been the place for both of us to kickback. Laying on my back with my arms stretched out, I slowly caught my breath taking in the sweetness of the woods. I opened my palms to the sky.

Still mesmerized by all the beauty, the sun was bright, and I looked at the billowy clouds. They interrupted the azure sky with the shapes they formed. Coming out of the froth of clouds I saw something in the deep blueness of the heavens. It was an eagle with outstretched wings lifting itself on a current. Just then, I saw a second one join the first.

"Cutting of harp strings," I whispered.

I was at peace.

TWENTY-SIX

"**G**abe, that's my story, and that's why I'm back."

"Oh my. Oh my. Oh my! I'd be back too! That Aiden sounds like he was a special breed. You are too, Eli. I'm not telling you something you don't already know, now, am I?" asked Gabe as he jumped up and gave me hug.

"Yeah, I miss him. Some things don't get better with time. Oh, I grieved for him and got through it, but I think about him and what he'd do in certain situations… what we might have done along the way."

The back of my throat seemed to close, and I was choking up. I had to pause and compose myself. My heartbeat ticked a tad faster and my hands were sweaty, so I rubbed them together. Taking in a deep breath, I sucked in my pain and then exhaled affirming thoughts.

"Gabe, I appreciate you asking me to share my story with you. Thanks for being patient. I'm genuinely grateful to you—really. Not knowing it when we first met, I must admit that I really wanted—*needed* the company. Friends tell me I ramble, so I don't think I've ever talked to anyone about all of this. Maybe bits and pieces. Just don't think they would listen, so thanks."

"Oh, don't give it another thought. I appreciate that you trusted me enough to tell me these things. I truly valued this time with you, Eli. Gotta say you're courageous, and that I admire. Don't get me wrong, but you *do* have a gift of gab. That's a good thing too," he said, lightening the mood. He laughed and I followed.

"Well, I'd better get going," I announced.

"Ho. Hold on for a minute. You ain't gonna spill your guts and then leave me without getting my two cents, are ya?"

"Ah, ah, well I guess not. I just didn't think you'd have anything you wanted to tell me. Sorry."

"See, we only just got to know one another, so you don't know but ole Gabe always has something to say. Yes indeed."

"Well, okay. Yeah, please…"

"So, as far as I can tell, you have another stop to make."

"Another stop? What do you mean?"

"The way I figure, but I could be wrong, that you've got to go back to the cave—*the spot.*"

"Hmmm. I've never gone back there, well inside the cave, since, since…" I sputtered.

"Exactly—and that's part of your, *er*, problem…uh if you don't mind me saying? He switched and asked with a softer tone. "Maybe I shouldn't be so blunt, but you've got to go inside—*inside*. You said it yourself. Sometimes you need to reach in a place you'd rather not go. Do you know what I'm saying to you son?"

"Yes, I know what you're saying." I scratched my head and blurted out my first thought. "Are you related, somehow, to Aiden?" Gabe laughed so hard and so loud you would have thought I was a standup comedian.

"Could be, never know about these things. I've been here a good long time—by the way, I *knew* Father Meinrad."

"What? You *knew* Father Meinrad?"

"Oh, I'm sorry Eli. I assumed you knew he passed."

I shook my head and looked down, "I knew I should have kept in touch. If nothing else, I should have sent the school my address for the alumni newsletter. I could have written…or called…or visited."

"About a year ago. Eli, he was an old man. He had a good life and helped so many young men. He was a good, good man. SOOO, drop the guilt—life has a way of moving on whether we're ready to or not."

"You're right. He was a good man. He was like no other Catholic priest."

"You got that right. Wasn't always easy for him, but yeah he was one hell of a man."

I nodded. "I'm sure it wasn't easy. He knew so much."

"Well, enough of all this. You need to get rolling. You've got to get your bearings and head to campus—take a fresh look around. Best to

232

begin where you two always started—so take the path you told me about and head on down to *the spot*. Do you hear me? Get going. I've got some more fish to catch. You hear me?"

"Okay, okay. You're right."

"Yeah, I may be an old country boy, but I know what I'm telling you."

*****

I listened to Gabe and began my way back to the campus. My mind wandered as I journeyed toward St. Augustine's. This reunion, the twenty-fifth, Luis touted would be special. I don't know how he found my address.

I don't regret *my* decisions along the way. We aim to do what's best, but other's expectations of us have a way of luring us into a trap. Sometimes things take us in a different direction altogether. I own my paths—every one of them. Things have a way of changing as much happened in those years in between then and now but that's for some other day.

I began to think of Father Meinrad and regretted losing touch with him. I recalled he inspired my graduation speech. What Father shared with me after Aiden's death meant so much to me, but so did all our conversations that whole year. All a bit foggy now, he gave me so much and I probably didn't deserve it. That I know. Graduation day was the last time I would see Father. But my moment on the podium was a dual affair. No, it was more than the two of us. Aiden was there too. I can only take credit for being the transmitter of notions and thoughts that came from somewhere else.

*****

I walked to my old dorm and discovered much had stayed the same over the years. Big box fans in the windows, music blasting from inside, and boys, a few thousand since me, were doing what boys like to do—throwing Frisbees and playing basketball, and anything else that they wanted to do. Although some of the *boxes* that Father told me about still existed, the walls of this generation's boxes were fuzzier. I hope that when I come back for my fiftieth in 2024, all the boxes will

233

be gone.

The boys streamed in and out of the dorm. *So* young—babies in my eyes born only a short time ago. I stopped a few on the steps and struck up a conversation.

"Hey fellas, got a minute?" Two boys stopped and looked at me. "You guys seniors?"

"Yes sir, we're graduating in two weeks."

"Well, how have you liked it here?"

"It's been a real drag. You know this boarding school stuff is way nerdy, I'm embarrassed to say."

The second boy concurred as he wisped back several strands of blond hair that were invading the corner of his mouth.

"Yeah, man, there's like nothing to do here. The Robes have a problem with how loud we play our music, and we can't have cell phones in our, well, cells. They come down on us about the video games we play and force us to do other things. If you ask me, it's pretty lame. It's just like a prison. I'm ready to get outta here."

"Do you guys ever explore the woods or hike in the mountains? I mean, there is so much out there and down those paths."

"No way! Some dude died in there a long time ago, and you should hear the stuff we've been told about the *old lady's* house. We heard some crazy shit happens out there. Oh sorry, sir—didn't mean to say the *sh* word," the blond boy said.

"An old Robe once told me that if it's shit, well, call it shit. But in this case, that's not what it is…at least I don't think so." I drew in a breath and tried to approach the boys differently. "Boys, nothing crazy happens in there. The crazy shit happens everywhere else but in there."

They looked at me as if I were off my proverbial rocker, and I didn't mind it so much because I would have thought the same thing when I was their age. I concluded our conversation and bid them good luck.

"Later, dude. Have a good time partying," one boy said holding back laughter.

It did not take much to realize the place may have appeared unchanged but the layers below the surface were probably all very conflicting. Then again, it always was.

I walked ahead and took a detour through the monk's cemetery. Never had I visited Aiden's gravesite after the burial so I could not remember exactly where he was. Father Luis told me that they could bury no one here unless he was a monk, but they made exceptions. Aiden was one of those exceptions. The Shenandoah Valley was his home. The monks were his surrogate family. Luis also said that when they made exceptions, they buried those souls away from the monks' plots as well.

I looked for an area of headstones that were set apart and saw several in the far corner. I counted what looked like three plots. I took my time and walked toward the markings. Occasionally, I hesitated as stepped over some of the graves as I looked to see if any names were familiar. As I approached the three graves, I remembered what Luis said about exceptions, and thought this is where I would find Aiden. Looking down, I locked in on one and saw that it was Father Meinrad's grave.

"Why would he be set apart from his brothers? That's weird," I said under my breath. Then it hit me. I walked over to the other site close by, squatted down, and brushed some fallen leaves from the plaque that laid flat on the gravesite. It was Aiden. Surprised and confused I muttered to myself.

"Luis must be wrong. I mean Father is right here next to Aiden. Why is Aiden next to Father? I knew they were close, but Father died only last year. He would have *chosen* to be next to Aiden and not among the monks".

Then I looked to Father's other side, and it was Clementine Van Patten—the old lady. Very strange. She had been dead now for forty-three years. This was all too bizarre for me to comprehend. She was buried here first and then Aiden and then…Father.

"They buried Father next to her?" The hideous caw of a crow sitting on a branch nearby pierced the silence and jarred me from my thoughts. I decided to put everything out of my mind, at least for now.

It was at that moment I decided it was time to go to the cave—*the spot*. I began the hike. Like I did many years ago, I picked up my pace and jogged down the path. It was second nature to me, and I remembered every turn although the trail seemed narrow and overgrown but none of that mattered because I could follow this route blindfolded if I had to. With some age and a little more weight that had become a part of me over the last several years, I felt awkward but soon that feeling faded, and I saw myself as seventeen again. Wending around the turns of the path, I stumbled slightly slowing my passage. No stranger to it, I have had the occasional stumble in my life both self-imposed and unwilled, so this only brought me a smile.

I reached the river and looked up to the cliff. I felt the warm arms of the forest around me and was content. My attention turned to the entrance of the cave. A waft of cool air flowed out and met me as if it were calling to me. Before taking another step, I looked in all directions, and once again drank in my surroundings. The sharp, jagged cliffs drew my eyes further up to the blue sky. The beauty and the spirit that encompassed the landscape being constant, but each moment taken singularly, created something personal. Moments like these, we easily overlook. Fragrances were acute and colors were vivid as a kaleidoscope. Recollections filled the air and heightened all my senses. Absorbing it all, my mind wandered. Just as I took note of the dorm an hour earlier, I was tempted to think that time had stood still but knew this was dangerous thinking.

Drawn inward, I walked through the large oval opening. The sun's rays shone with great intensity into the portal. It was damp and the rock walls muffled the noises of the day as I went further into its marrow. The same slabs of rock where we once sat and talked unleashed a rush of memories. Grinning and with faint laughter, I reached down and picked up an empty green bottle of Rolling Rock. Everything was how we had left it. In some cases, though, time and water damaged some of the treasures collected years ago. Most of the cave's contents, however, were well preserved. Many paintings that Aiden had worked on were still resting on the ledge but were mildewed. Poking around, I stumbled on a large footlocker. It was out of place and neatly tucked to one side where Aiden liked to sit.

"Hmmm—don't remember this. Maybe it was Aiden's and I never noticed it before."

Pulling it out to capture more light I kneeled and opened the trunk. Once inside and directly on top of a blanket was the old photo that Luis took of Aiden and me as we served our *sentence* washing cars after that prophetic day when we skipped school. I touched Aiden's image and closed my eyes for a second or two. I placed it gently to one side and then ran my hands through my hair and smiled. Looking away, I took in the moment and, again, closed my eyes.

Pulling back another small blanket and there, in front of me, I saw the portrait. Mesmerized by it, I gazed at it as if it was the first time.

"How could I have left this behind?"

I touched it and felt the brush strokes running my finger in the tiny delicate grooves that Aiden had made with each stroke. Like the warmth and smell of a favorite sweatshirt, I sensed I was home again. I noticed, for the first time, how he signed the painting. Like a message or letter, the artist signed it, *Yours, Aiden* along with his fingerprint next to his name. This led me to believe I must have missed other images fused in his work. Examining it closely, the interwoven symbolism in the piece conjured up more hints of thoughts and emotions that were once dormant. I looked into my painted eyes as if I was looking into my soul—his soul. What I saw in the pupil of both eyes overwhelmed me. It was the images of two boys. So tiny it now stood out larger than life but was always there. Closing my eyes, I filled my lungs and then slowly let the air escape as a calmness entered my being.

"My God...just mind-blowing. Just so completely... wonderful!"

All other symbols, as I remembered, pertained to what he perceived were my interests at the time.

"Law school! Boy, was I naïve?" I chuckled.

I did not know the meaning of truth and no law school could or would ever teach me. The truth was that I lived my life for others and not me. I felt trapped but didn't know it as I was on autopilot. Who I thought I was and where I was headed only clouded who I truly was at that time. In reality, I never completely looked inside and figured it out—even to this day. Gabe was right. If I'm not willing to go inside, I will never know who I am. That takes courage, and that I am afraid I have always lacked.

I pulled out other items from the trunk. There I found his journal. With a paperclip, someone attached an envelope to its cover.

"*My name!* What? This letter's to me. Someone knew I would be here. How? Hmmm. Whoever wrote this letter must have collected everything in this trunk and put it in here. Who? Who could have done this? Wait, I know...I know..." I mumbled.

Taking a deep breath, I flipped the envelope over two or three times before opening it. My hands trembled and my fingers were failing me, but I managed to pull out the letter. At first, I noticed the date—it was just last year.

This very day and this very moment were now becoming much clearer to me. Few knew about *the spot*. Few knew about his journal and the painting…and the photograph. My eyes darted to the signature line to confirm my suspicions. My lips quivered in the corners and then my face was one gigantic smile.

> Dear Eli,
>
> Welcome dear boy! I knew you'd return. This trunk holds the symbols of two remarkable lives. They are all symbols of Aiden and you. After all, you and he both, cut the harp strings.
>
> This is my gift to you. Read his journal—yes, he would approve. I have come here every year on his birthday to meditate, to think, to feel. It has been my refuge and my refueling. My brother, Gabe, helps me today, as I am sure this is my last visit. No reason, and I mean it, to be sad. It's rather nice to know.
>
> My son, I hope you have found your truth—the truth that has always been with you. Look inside. Ask yourself and not others. Every part of you is good. Eli, you ARE good.
>
> Now, give your soul the lungs, heart, and mind to continue to live a remarkable life. Live your life full of compassion, intimacy, and love. I have left behind a blank canvas and journal. Test yourself, be free and let your soul guide you. Look inside and let your soul sing. Sing!
>
> May only goodness come your way and always be open to love again.
>
> Love to you always,
> Meinrad

I left the cave and basked in the warm rays of the sun. A light breeze filtered through the leaves of the trees. The river flowed in the way it did those many years ago and will continue to flow for many more. The sound was soothing. A dragonfly zipped by and then, hovered nearby. I named him Aiden. How I love the dragonfly.

It's a maze—life that is. Sometimes, for moments here and there, it appears otherwise with clean lines and crystal facets. Not often. Life is more than what I thought. And I knew this all along but wasn't willing to believe in myself—*to believe me.* Aiden showed me, but it was for me to act.

Love is a strange thing, and I yearn for it once more. I don't need to give it much thought, I just need to give it sunlight and space to grow—to run in a field of tall grass and be free.

The moments, the challenges, the beauty, the pain, and all of life's many contradictions, all merge into a singular path—like the rays of the sunlight, the rainbow of colors come together to form the brilliance we all possess. I knew a long time ago but refused to believe it, that a power much greater than man created me adding many parts and that *all* those many parts are good. I *am* good.

I will cherish all the paths I took and the many more that lay ahead as they have made me and will continue to make me, who I am.

Now, there's no turning back.

"Suddenly, quietly, you realize that - from this moment forth – you will no longer walk through this life alone. Like a new sun this awareness arises within you, freeing you from fear, opening your life. It is the beginning of love, and the end of all that came before."

Robert Frost

ABOUT THE AUTHOR

E.G. Kardos, a fiction writer, is the author of four books. Important to him, he bases his work on the beauty that surrounds all of us—both in nature and in each other. His view of spirituality, friendship, love, and connection to the universe inspired him to write CUTTING OF HARP STRINGS.

Never truly leaving school since kindergarten, he has worked in a prep school and two universities for his entire life. He and his wife have four children and live in Virginia.

Visit and connect with him at edwardgkardos.com, Facebook, Twitter, and other social media.

CPSIA information can be obtained
at www.ICGtesting.com
Printed in the USA
BVHW030056050122
625449BV00001B/49